Hospitality

To

Angels

Madeleine
Purslow

Chapter One

It was just after Christmas, that very first, bleak week of January, when everyone is desperately trying to get back to normal but feeling as forlorn as a bride folding away her dress after the wedding. It didn't seem so very long ago that they had all been looking forward to The Big Day, but now it was gone and the lovely decorations just looked like party guests who hadn't known when to leave. This particular January had begun badly, with a funeral in the village. It was also to be Elizabeth's last year living in Newton Prideaux, but of course she didn't know that then.

Kim's death had come as a huge shock to them. Most people hadn't even heard anything about it until Boxing Day. Typically Ellen had kept it as quiet as possible, "He wouldn't have wanted to spoil people's Christmases," she said. And so there they all were on that freezing afternoon, paying their final respects to Kim Kitteridge, all huddled together in the chill of St Martin's, waiting for the coffin to arrive.

Only a few months before, Elizabeth had been sitting where Ellen was sitting, right at the front of the church, chief mourner at her mother's funeral, but that had been an altogether different affair. It still filled her with guilt, guilt that she had felt so very little, that she hadn't really *suffered a loss.* All she had felt, was a sense of relief. The funeral had been the final duty that she had been required to perform.

For Kim the church was filled with genuine sorrow. In the damp chrysanthemum scented gloom the grief was almost palpable. He had been such a gentle man, well loved. Elizabeth looked across at Ellen's pale pinched face and thought that was how real sorrow felt. Next to Kim's widow sat their only daughter Belinda, or Bunny as she was known in the village. The one person who should have been a comfort to Ellen and ultimately it would have to be the other way around.

Bunny Kitteridge was approaching forty, but her mind she was still like a child's. Growing up, the other village children had always been told not to tease *poor Bunny, she couldn't help being backward.* The villagers said *she might improve as she gets older.* Looking at her dressed in her overly large black coat and with an ugly cloche hat pulled down to just above her eyebrows and gazing vacantly up at the church ceiling, Elizabeth knew Bunny would always be the same. Stolid and silent Bunny, she could have been anywhere.

As the service began and Reverend Donovan's mellifluous tones floated steadily up into the old stone bell tower, beseeching God to accept the soul of their beloved brother Kim, Elizabeth's mind wandered. A change in the village was never welcome and she couldn't help wondering if Ellen would even stay on without Kim. But what she did know, without any doubt, was that God would accept Kim Kitteridge into his Kingdom.

She remembered closing the door when everyone had left after her mother's funeral. That wonderful sense of independence. Her mother was gone. She had ruled Elizabeth's life for nearly forty years and now it was over. Because of her mother, Elizabeth had stayed in the village and watched as all her friends ventured out into the world to start their lives. But not her, she had been left behind.

Becoming aware of the congregation around her getting to their feet Elizabeth returned from her reverie and automatically rose. As the introduction to *All things Bright and Beautiful* wheezed into the cold air from the ancient church organ, her spirits lifted momentarily. She still had many things to be grateful for: her job at Pearson's, all her friends in the village, her faith in God. It was always good to count one's blessings and she hoped that Ellen and Bunny would find the same comfort she did, standing there with all her friends and neighbours. She really believed it then, before everything changed.

After Kim had been laid to rest in the dank green graveyard at the back of the little church, the mourners all filed silently into Ellen's cramped cottage. A few people had suggested that The Cock might have been a better venue, but Ellen was old school and old school said everyone was required to go back to the house. So they all crammed into Ellen's dark living room and tried not to look too uncomfortable.

On the dining table at the centre of the room was a buffet overflowing with sandwiches, cakes and snacks. It's odd, but when you have lived amongst people for so long, you begin to recognise their ways. At a glance, for example, Elizabeth knew the strawberry scones would be from Sophie from the 'new houses,' the over-elaborate quiche would be from Dina Watkins and the drinks would have been organised by Bryan and Roger, through their links with 'the trade.' She was glad that she knew these things, they were comforting and safe.

For a while people talked in respectful whispers, politely passing the time until they could leave but then Bryan spoke up, his distinctive Irish brogue cutting through the general burble of conversation. "Do you remember that time Kim was the umpire at the cricket?" he said. "Ah God, you wouldn't believe the patience of that man. There wasn't one of them in the team that was sober; it was a something to see that was. I'll never forget, as long as I live, the sight of your Kim, Ellen, trying to help Peter on with his pads. It was like watching a man putting up a deckchair in the wind."

Ellen managed a thin smile and the atmosphere in the room began to lift slightly. Many people didn't care for Bryan McConway, with his tall tales from his days in hospitality, but Elizabeth liked him. To her, he represented the outside world; places and people she would never know. She could have listened to Bryan for hours.

His great friend and ally, Roger Hayden the landlord of The Cock, joined him, reminiscing about various other visiting cricket teams and their antics, and she was glad to let herself be drawn along. It's always difficult to attend these things alone. Before of course, she had always had her mother as a companion. Now she had to go solo and very often ended up feeling like a spare part. Having someone holding the floor, so to speak, was always preferable to small talk.

To her surprise, she noticed how well Bunny seemed to be coping with it all. Normally she was a quiet sullen lump of a woman, but now Elizabeth could hear the monotone of her voice explaining how she had helped her mother to make sandwiches and had put all the cress on them for decoration. She seemed pleased with herself and Elizabeth couldn't help but wonder if she really understood what had happened to her father, if she realised that it wasn't just some strange sort of party.

She picked up one of Ellen's bone china cups neatly laid out on the oak sideboard and poured herself a tea. It was really just something to do. She knew she should try and mingle but socially she was awkward and she knew it. Bryan was now holding court over in the corner and she envied his ease with people; he actually seemed to be enjoying himself.

"Of course they were eventually apprehended, but they were half way to Gloucester by the time the police caught up with them…," he was saying. Could Elizabeth ever hope to mix like that? She looked over at Bunny, and it ran across her mind that they were very much alike in some ways, and she hated it.

Then without warning, Dina Watkins appeared at her side, "Elizabeth, how are you? This must be difficult for you, after your poor mother. One never forgets a funeral, does one? And you'll find when you get to my age you attend far too many."

Her sharpness always took Elizabeth by surprise and the way she phrased things left no room for argument or contradiction. Dina was married to the local G.P. and had acted as his receptionist come secretary for years. She was a tiny wasp of a woman and she was to be handled with extreme care.

"Dina, hello." Elizabeth's face flushed as she immediately realised that she had nothing more to add to this greeting. Her companion stood and looked expectantly over gold rimmed glasses at her.

After a short pause Dina stepped in, "Poor Kim," she said "such a nice man." When he had been alive she had often heard Dina say that Kim was much too meek and mild for her liking, 'a weak straw' she had said, but everyone has amnesia at funerals and Elizabeth held her tongue.

"Now," said Dina, abruptly. Having paid lip service to the deceased, she was quite ready to move on. "I was thinking about you," she said, watching Elizabeth keenly.

"Oh, yes?"

"Well, since your mother died you've been a bit of a hermit. So I was thinking I'd get you on my committee."

Newton Prideaux had a vociferous residents' committee and Elizabeth wasn't at all sure that she wanted to go anywhere near it, but Dina was full of enthusiasm.

"Yes, you must come out from your mother's shadow. Come and speak up for yourself, get involved. We meet on the first

Wednesday of the month. We're in the Village Hall at the moment but we are trying to get Mr Hayden to let us use his back room. It's warmer you see. Anyway, I'll let you know on that."

"Well, I am quite busy, really," she said, knowing it would do no good. "I help out at the church quite a bit and I have my cat…"

"Oh, you can spare us a bit of time, I'm sure. Now what else have you got planned? You must keep busy. I'll be saying the same to Ellen. I've seen bereavement a lot in my line of work, it's always best to stay occupied."

"As I said, I do have my cat to look after. He, er takes up a lot of my time."

"Well, I don't see how," said Dina. "I had a cat for years. I just fed him and let him get on with it. They are independent creatures in my experience."

"But Lawrence is a Siamese," said Elizabeth, only too aware how silly it sounded.

"Oh yes, you took that cat on, didn't you? A Siamese… Well I never did like them. They have pointed little sly faces. So, is that all? You are busy with your cat?"

Now beginning to feel a little humiliated Elizabeth searched desperately for another excuse, and then, one of those odd things happened.

"I am also busy planning a party for my fortieth birthday," she said. The truth was, she had been toying with the idea for a while but hadn't decided one way or the other. On her more confident days it seemed like a good idea, but she hadn't meant to say it out loud, not yet, not just like that to Dina Watkins. But she had, and thinking about it later she could only imagine that she said it to please Dina, and to make her think she was approaching normal.

Dina couldn't contain her astonishment. Her tiny shrew face crumpled with thought. "Forty? Yes, I suppose you must be, time flies doesn't it? Yes, you and Bunny; you would be about the same age. Well, I hope I shall be invited to this party of yours," she said.

"Yes, yes of course you will," she added, digging a bigger hole for herself.

"So, anyway, I'll expect to see you at our next meeting. Oh, and Elizabeth, I really wouldn't mention your party to anyone else here. It's not quite right is it? At a funeral, I mean."

As Elizabeth watched her tiny frame busily make its way across the room toward the buffet, she felt like a silly child who had just been chastised for showing off.

Embarrassed, she immediately began to wish that she could leave and was wondering how she could make a quick escape, when she noticed the first two people taking their leave of Ellen.

"So that's it then," said Bryan in a loud whisper. "Polite o'clock has arrived."

Elizabeth knew he was right. Once somebody leaves it's okay to follow on and very soon only the inveterate 'tidy uppers,' like Dina and Roz would be left, just as they had been after her mother's funeral.

She finished her tea as rapidly as she could and made her way to the door with Sophie and Rob, who had also decided to make a move. She had no idea what she should say to Ellen and so took the coward's way out and slipped quietly away.

Or at least she tried to. As she stepped into the porch a hand grabbed her arm. It was Ron Pickard.

"So, we'll be seeing you at the meeting then? Good, we could do with some fresh blood. What are those new people like at Yew Tree Cottage? Not being a nuisance with all the renovations?"

Elizabeth mumbled something about not having noticed and made her escape. As she said goodbye to Sophie and Rob, all she wanted to do was go home to Lawrence and hide in her cottage, like the oddity she knew she was.

Chapter Two

Elizabeth could never decide whether her mother had been horribly disappointed in life or whether it was just her nature, but whatever the reason her default setting had been to discourage. It was almost as though she had a dark crystal ball, through which she was able to see all the possible pitfalls and dangers ahead before they even happened.

All Ruth Menier had in life was Elizabeth and her Christian faith, and she clung to both with an almost frightening tenacity. As a very little girl Elizabeth had been unaware of her existence being slightly odd. She just accepted it, it was normal for her. But as she grew she realised other people had very different lives from her own.

She was Elizabeth and she was different. Just the fact that she always used her name in full alienated her. She was not friendly Lizzie, Liz or Beth; she was always Elizabeth, formal, set apart from her friends. It made her stiff somehow. But it was her mother's incontrovertible rule, her name was never to be shortened.

"You're not a sheep, Elizabeth," her mother would reason. "Why do you have to do it simply because others do?" This was a very convenient argument which she used over and over again, under the guise of teaching Elizabeth to think for herself. As a result Elizabeth had very few friends. Who wants a friend who is never allowed to go anywhere or do anything?

Ruth had come from a wealthy background. Her family had owned quite a lot of land in the county at one time and Elizabeth's father had left her well provided for when he carelessly died, leaving her and infant Elizabeth alone. The truth was, she could have afforded to do most things but she chose not to, and worst of all, she chose for her daughter too. No holidays, no trips to London, no dining out, no cinema, no theatre. All these things Elizabeth's peers took for granted, she didn't experience.

And so when all the teenage girls of the village started catching the bus into Crayton to visit the hairdressing salon, Elizabeth was told it was pure vanity to waste money on such things. They came back with fashionable 80's spikey short crops while Elizabeth kept her long straight mousey coloured hair.

And now at nearly forty, she still had the same waist length hairstyle. She had promised herself many times that she would cut it off. Maybe she could even donate it to a good cause, but two things always stopped her:

One, was that she had no idea at all about hairdressers, blow drying, heated rollers and all those other things people did with their hair these days; and two, somewhat shamefully, each time she lingered outside the hairdressers she could hear her mother's voice quoting forcefully from Corinthians, "If a woman has long hair it is her glory", and so Elizabeth went back to laboriously washing and drying it, and carefully pinning it up each day.

As a child it had been bad enough to find herself a bit adrift and an oddity, but as an adult her lack of experience made her feel positively peculiar. And that was why Bunny Kitteridge bothered her so much. They were alike: retarded, held back, odd little people who were not quite in step with the rest of the world. The only difference was Elizabeth realised it.

There was one fabulous thing however, that Ruth did do for her daughter. She insisted that she learned to drive. For some reason, unlike anything else Elizabeth had ever wanted to do, this was deemed essential. "Everyone drives today, Elizabeth, you don't want to be left behind," and for the first time she had felt like an adult.

As it turned out she wasn't a natural driver and struggled, week after week, stalling and jumping her way around the lanes of Oxfordshire. But eventually she had passed her test. She was elated and waited for her mother's praise, but it didn't come. Instead she was advised to be careful going round those tiny lanes, so many accidents happened when people went too fast. Even then her mother hadn't been able to bring herself to say well done. A timely word of caution was all she had received.

Whenever mother and daughter went out together in the car, Ruth always sat in the back like a member of the Royal family, occasionally remarking on things in the village that displeased her. However, she never once criticised her daughter's driving, though neither did she praise it. It was like an unspoken rule between them.

Elizabeth drove, and her mother refrained from comment.

When Elizabeth's mother died, she was horrified to find that she didn't know how she should feel. She was free but she didn't know what to do about it. To the outside world of course, she had had to appear sorrowful, but horribly she felt strangely happy and excited, as though her life was about to begin.

She prayed and prayed looking for some sort of guidance. She knew she shouldn't feel like she did, but God knew what was inside her, he knew all she felt was relief. Honour thy father and thy mother, it was God's commandment. Could she honour her mother, but not love her? Had she been such a bad daughter?

All she knew for certain was that she had tried. While her mother had been alive, she had done her best to please her. Now she had to close her mind to these thoughts. Her mother was with her God now, and she had a life to get on with. It seemed a little late to be starting life, but it was what God had given her, and so she had to wait for his guidance. It would come, she was sure of that, all she had to do was to listen and be ready.

In the meantime, she began to make small changes but it's so difficult when you had always been told what to do. Making decisions was an entirely alien concept and she wrestled with it. She desperately wanted to do something with her life, but at nearly forty it almost felt too late to be doing anything too drastic.

And so she started small. It seemed ridiculous at times, but the first thing she did was the buy different brands at the supermarket. Her mother had always been so particular about things like that: the tea must be Twinings, the marmalade, Frank Coopers. Now Elizabeth tried different things. Sometimes she liked them and sometimes she didn't, but the important thing was that she had chosen them.

Financial affairs were difficult. They were an utter mystery to her, and getting things changed over into her name was tedious, but once she had discovered the joys of the direct debit, it all became a lot easier. At thirty nine, she had a thrill that probably no one would envy, the sight of bills dropping through the letter box with her name on them.

Little by little she made the cottage her own, moving furniture, buying little bits and pieces. It was her home now and she didn't intend to leave it. Putting her mother's winged back chair into the garage was without doubt the most difficult thing to do, both physically and mentally. As she manoeuvred it through the kitchen she had slipped and caught her fingers between it and the fridge. They were black for days, a constant reminder of her betrayal.

But by far, the biggest change in her life and the most joyous, as it turned out, was her decision to get a cat. She had always loved nature and animals but her mother had absolutely forbidden anything of the sort in the house. They were full of germs and infections, she had said.

After her mother's death, Elizabeth reasoned that she had seen many cats about the village and to her knowledge none of their owners had dropped down dead from deadly feline infections and so she decided to risk it.

Looking back it still seemed miraculous that she had found a pet at all, he was now so much a part of her life and it was hard to believe six months ago they had never even met.

She remembered at first she had been hoping that someone in the village would have a cat with kittens, but when nothing happened she started to search the local Bicester Advertiser in earnest. Each time she turned to the small ads she offered up a prayer but for weeks there was nothing. She learnt later that this wasn't the right time of year for kittens but she continued to look.

Finally there was a lead. Not a kitten, but a discreet little advert that intrigued her. It had been placed by the local Lorelei Cattery. She knew the place, as she had driven past it many times and occasionally glimpsed the tops of wire pens set behind the cottage. It said:

Loving home needed for young male Siamese. Please contact Lorelei cattery for further details. No time wasters please.

A Siamese? It wasn't something Elizabeth had considered. She would have been happy with any sort of cat. But a Siamese, now that was interesting. Weren't they slightly haughty and a bit wicked, like in Lady And The Tramp......we are Siamese if you please?

There would be no harm in ringing the number. The truth was she had got herself so excited about having a cat, and since there were no kittens to be found, this might just be the answer. After all, if it was a little bit older it wouldn't need to be housetrained and it wouldn't be as much trouble as a kitten.

Perhaps this was the sign she had been waiting for? Perhaps this was the cat for her?

Chapter Three

Working at Pearson's, Elizabeth had been forced to deal with phone calls. At first she had jumped every time the phone rang, but now she was a seasoned professional and even irate callers didn't upset her half as much as they used to. However, as she picked up the phone to ring the cattery, her hand ever so slightly shook and butterflies rushed into her stomach. At least she didn't have to go in person, she told herself. It was just an enquiry.

"Lorelei Cattery, Laura speaking. What can I do for you?" said the bright, efficient voice.

"Oh hello, I'm ringing about the advertisement you placed in The Bicester Advertiser. I would like to know a little more please."

"I see. Very good."

Although Elizabeth knew the 'Lorelei lady' by sight, she had never spoken to her and so the Scottish accent took her slightly unawares and threw her for a moment. Don't be so ridiculous

Elizabeth, she told herself. Why shouldn't she be Scottish?

"Well, let's see what can I tell you? As I stated in the advertisement, he is male. He's four years old, a chocolate point. Very nice temperament if a little nervy, but that's only to be expected in the circumstances."

"Oh, right," said Elizabeth, realising that she hadn't prepared any questions at all. Fortunately Laura seemed well able to impart the necessary information.

"So, you are probably wondering why he is in need of a home. Well the fact is his owner has sadly passed away and it's a condition of mine that if anything happens and they can't live with their owners for whatever reason they come back to me. So here he is. Now, he needs a very particular home. He has lived with his elderly lady as an only cat. He has never encountered children, dogs or boisterous people so far as I can tell. He will need someone who can devote all their attention to him. Do you see?"

"Yes, I understand," said Elizabeth, feeling a wave of compassion for this little lost cat.

"Now, before we go any further," said Laura, "have you any experience with Siamese at all? Because, as I always tell people, they aren't like other cats and they certainly aren't for everyone."

"Well, actually no," admitted Elizabeth. "I haven't had a pet before." Suddenly she felt deflated. She hadn't had experience of very much at all, really, had she?

"I see. Well then, he may not be the cat for you."

"But, I've always loved animals and when I have met any they have always loved me. Could I at least see him?" faltered Elizabeth. Something about the cat's story had really caught her imagination and she wasn't willing to give up just yet.

Hearing the nervousness in her voice, Laura softened a little.

"I suppose you could visit, see how you get on. Are you far away?"

"No, no just down the road in Newton Prideaux."

"Very well. This is what we will do then. You pop by and see me on Saturday morning at 10 o'clock and we'll see. Now, I'm not making any promises and you won't be taking him home with you or anything like that, you understand? It's just a wee chat, okay? Now then, what's your name and I'll put you in my book?"

"Thank you, thank you so much. I'm Elizabeth Menier. M. E. N. I. E.R."

"Thank you. Oh, Elizabeth in case you are concerned, he's not entire."

"Entire?" said Elizabeth, a little alarmed by the phrase.

"Oh, how can I say delicately? He's um without his wee bits and pieces, if you understand my meaning? So, I'll see you on Saturday then. Cheerio for now."

Flushed and embarrassed Elizabeth meekly thanked Laura and quickly put the phone down. Today was Thursday. She had all of Friday ahead of her to worry about it.

She decided not to mention the cat at work. For one thing, it may never happen and for another, although she loved her colleagues dearly, they did delight in teasing her, particularly Mark and Sandy. For now this would be her secret. She wasn't even sure it was a good idea. What if she wasn't a suitable owner? What if she didn't like the cat? There were so many unknowns. Elizabeth knew she would have no peace until it was resolved either way. All she could do was force it to the back of her mind for now.

On Saturday morning Elizabeth was up early. It was a bright October morning and the autumn light flitting and flickering across her bedroom ceiling had woken her long before the alarm clock. It was no use lying in bed once she was awake. A thousand thoughts rushed into her head and uppermost was the thought that today she had to go to Lorelei.

At a quarter to ten Elizabeth was parked outside the cattery. She hated to be late for anything, but on the other hand she didn't want to make a nuisance of herself by arriving too early. The clock on the dashboard hardly seemed to move. Would five to, be too early to go in?

As she sat pondering the best course of action, Laura came out of the cattery gate, straight up to the car and knocked on the window.

"Elizabeth?" she mouthed.

Flustered by her sudden arrival Elizabeth fought to undo her seatbelt, grab her handbag and open the door. When she finally struggled inelegantly out of the car, her hostess greeted her warmly.

"I saw you parked there. Nice to see you're in good time. I am early for everything, I hate tardiness." With that she strode back through the gate leaving Elizabeth obediently following on.

"So," said Laura, "I'll give you a quick tour and then we can talk about The Boy.

They headed for the back of the cottage and the tall wire pens that Elizabeth had glimpsed from the road.

"These are my stud boys, Rafferty, Dylan and Atticus," said Laura, proudly. The occupants of the cages regarded their guest with curiosity.

"The noisy one, there, that's Rafferty. He likes visitors."

A large cream cat with a dark grey face and paws let out a series of loud yowling noises that Elizabeth found quite alarming.

"Is he all right?" she ventured.

"He's fine, just showing off because you're here. Rafferty, treats in a while, eh?" Laura called and started to walk towards the cottage. "Now the other two," she continued. "Dylan, that's the Sealy and Atticus the Foreign White there. You won't hear a peep out of them until food time. They are happy to laze about, but Rafferty, he needs to be the centre of attention."

"Oh," said Elizabeth quietly. She hadn't understood a lot of what had just been said but she tried to look intelligent. Sealy? Foreign what?"

Perhaps sensing her visitor's bewilderment Laura said, "I'll tell you what. I won't show you any more just now. We'll go to the office, have a nice cup of tea and a chat about things."

Elizabeth nodded. She felt that she ought to be saying more, but she didn't really know what to ask, and her hostess seemed such a capable woman, she couldn't help but feel a little intimidated.

Sitting in Laura's office surrounded by portraits of slender, exotic looking cats did nothing to assuage her fears. She really was quite out of her depth. Perhaps she should not have rushed into things, waited for a normal cat to come along? She could almost hear her mother quoting from Proverbs "*Desire without knowledge is not good, and whoever makes haste with his feet misses the way.*"

"Now then," said Laura bringing in their tea. "You are interested in Lawrence?"

"Lawrence?" smiled Elizabeth. "Is that his name?" Instantly the reason she was there came back to her. A cat needing a home, and that cat's name was Lawrence.

"Yes, sorry didn't I say? Jean, that's the lady who owned him, named him after Lawrence of Arabia. Not sure why, but there you are. Anyway, he's a fine chap, but he does need a very special home."

Elizabeth nodded. She felt almost as though she was supposed to say something at this point but she didn't know quite what.

"He's been back with me for about three weeks now, and I don't want him to get too settled and have to go through another upheaval. So I'm looking to rehome him as soon as possible."

"Well, I could take him straight away," blurted out Elizabeth.

"Ah, now you see, I am a little bit concerned about that. You have been honest enough to admit that you haven't had experience with animals before, and taking Lawrence would be a huge commitment. Siamese can be tricky. I always think they are too intelligent for their own good, and they are sensitive. But they're loving and bond very closely with their humans. It's not a case of feeding them and away you go. They need you."

"No, I realise that. I did a little bit of research on the internet," said Elizabeth, fumbling in her bag for the papers she had printed off.

"Good, good, no matter. I don't need to see it. You seem like a sensible lady to me. Now, do you mind me asking, do you live alone? As I said Lawrence isn't used to a noisy environment."

"Yes, I do. It's very quiet. A bit too quiet I sometimes think. I lived with my mother, but now that she's passed away, it's just me I'm afraid."

"I see. And do you work?"

"Yes, I work at Pearson's in Crayton."

"The estate agents? Full time?"

"Yes."

"Now, normally you see, that would be a problem. But I take it you could pop home if necessary and see Lawrence at lunchtime say? Crayton isn't too far away. So, tell me why do you want a cat?"

Elizabeth was struck dumb for a moment. She hadn't expected to have to make a case for herself.

She swallowed hard. "I, I have always loved nature and animals. My mother didn't allow pets and so all I could do was admire from afar, if you see what I mean. Anyway, now…..things are um, different and I would love to have a pet. Something to come home to, something to care for, I suppose."

"I see, you are captain of your own ship now, eh? And what makes you think Lawrence could be the one for you?"

Elizabeth thought for a moment. She didn't really have an answer, she just felt she could help. He needed a home, she needed something to love and care for.

"Well, I just want to help him, I suppose. He's alone in the world and he needs someone to take care of him."

Laura put down her cup decisively. "Look, I can't say you were exactly what I was looking for, but perhaps we can come to some arrangement. Go and have a think about what it would mean to take him on. Read up as much as you can on Siamese. Ring me if you have any questions and we will take it from there."

Elizabeth's face showed her disappointment, and Laura quickly added, "I'm not saying no, you understand? I just need to be sure it could work."

"Could I see him?" asked Elizabeth, sadly.

"I'm sorry, at this stage I don't think it would be good for either of you. We'll both have a think and then we'll see, eh?"

****

As Laura closed the gate and watched her visitor drive away, she felt sure she was very close to breaking several of her own rules. There was something about Elizabeth Menier that had affected her deeply. If ever there was a lady that needed someone, it was her. Laura could almost feel the loneliness exuding from her and yet there was also a peaceful understanding about her that could be just what Lawrence needed.

Laura was also a great believer in fate. She had seen it so many times over the years. A cat came along and very soon its perfect match turned up. Coincidence or fate, she was never quite sure, but it was something she never questioned, she simply had faith in it. And she had faith that Lawrence had found his new mum.

She went back inside, closed the office door and walked back along the corridor to the cat room. She went over to a large chocolate point lying with his chin resting firmly on the arm of the chair. From his half closed eyes to his melancholy expression, his body spoke of dejection.

"Lawrence," she said. "I've a feeling things are about to look up for you, son."

Chapter Four

On the Tuesday evening following her visit to Lorelei, Elizabeth came home to find a message on her answer phone. It was from Laura and it started ominously.

"Well, hello, Elizabeth. Laura here. I was just ringing to see if you had thought any more about Lawrence. I do have another party interested in him, but I wanted to give you first option. Please give me a call for a chat anytime."

The fact was Elizabeth had thought about it a lot. What would it be like to have an animal relying on her? What if she wanted a holiday? What if he was ill and had to go to the vet? And then she realised that she had been looking through her mother's dark crystal. What about all the good things a cat would bring? What about the pleasure in helping another soul? Surely these things outweighed the bad. She was fairly sure she had come to a decision, but now this call was forcing the issue.

She had already semi decided that, on Saturday she would call Lorelei, and if Laura agreed, she would say she would take him on. She had already slipped a furry mouse cat toy into her weekly shop. But now someone else wanted Lawrence. She hadn't been expecting that and suddenly she felt slightly panicky. In her mind he was already her cat. She knew she had to ring straight away. Still in her coat and shoes she picked up the phone and rang. Her heart was thumping as she heard Laura's voice at the end of the line, "Lorelei Cattery."

"Laura, hello, it's me Elizabeth. It's about Lawrence. I'm returning your call," she babbled.

"Oh, yes good. So you got the gist of it then? Now what do you think?"

Elizabeth felt her throat tighten. This was it.

"I would like to have him, please," she said, decisively.

"Good, good. Well, as you know I've a few reservations, so how about you take him on trial, this weekend maybe, and see what you both think of each other?"

Elizabeth suddenly felt like a little girl and her heart soared. What would it be like to hold one of those slender cats? What would it be like to see one walking around her cottage? It all seemed such an exciting prospect.

"Now then, don't get rushing out buying things, I have plenty of bedding, food, trays, litter you can take, until you see how it goes. Would you like to see him before Saturday?"

Elizabeth had work to consider but at that point she wanted nothing more. "Yes, please," she said. "When could I come?"

"Well, whenever suits you. I am here nearly all the time, because of the cattery, so just say."

Like a laugh bubbling up inside her, Elizabeth found herself saying, "Could I come now?"

"Now?" said Laura. "Well, I don't see why not. He was having a wee snooze last I looked."

"Right, right, I'll just grab my car keys and I'll be there soon."

"Righty ho. Oh by the way, Elizabeth, I remembered why he is called Lawrence. Jean, the lady who owned him, had a father who was very keen on Lawrence of Arabia. It's a bit odd I know. But it might confuse him if you change it. This boy has had too much upheaval of late."

"Change it? Why would I do that?" said Elizabeth. "It's his name."

Elizabeth's stomach was full of butterflies as she rang the bell at Lorelei. She was about to see "her cat" for the first time. A little voice in her head was trying to spoil things, as usual, telling her to be careful, that "He might not like you, you know nothing about cats." Since the death of her mother, she seemed to have created this inner commentary to replace her mother's warnings. She closed her eyes and tried to shut it out. This was going to be a good thing!

Laura opened the door.

"Come in, come in. I've told him he is having a visitor. Go through, go through."

They arrived in the Cat Room just in time to see a kitten screech across the floor carrying a furry ball in its mouth, pursued by three even smaller kittens.

"This lot are lively bunch of hooligans," remarked Laura as the kittens skidded under one of the chairs. "Now, let's see, where is your big chap?"

Elizabeth's eyes quickly scanned the room. There were various grown cats in beds scattered around, all eyeing her suspiciously.

"Ah, here he is. Come and have a look at him," said Laura, beckoning Elizabeth to the far corner of the room. "This is Lawrence," she said.

Lawrence was a shock. Elizabeth had been expecting a lithe, slender cat with a coffee brown face, like the chocolate point ones she had seen online. But Lawrence was large and his face was the colour of dark mahogany.

"There, isn't he a beaut?" said Laura, proudly.

"He's very dark," said Elizabeth trying to hide her shock.

"Yes, I suppose. But they come in all different shades. His mum was a Havana and daddy a Seal, so he wasn't likely to be pale. I bred him myself of course.

Elizabeth looked at Lawrence. As she moved slightly to one side get a better view, his deep blue worried eyes followed her. Those too were odd, not the slightly slanted, almond shape she had expected, but huge, round and soulful, like deep blue tarns.

"Well then, Lawrence," said Laura. "Shall we get you out so you can see Elizabeth?" Reaching forward she gently lifted the big dark cat. Seeing him in Laura's arms only made him seem even bigger to Elizabeth, and the deep frown line between his eyes simply added to his troubled demeanour.

For all this, there was something so innocent and vulnerable about him that Elizabeth was immediately smitten. She understood Lawrence. He looked like she felt most of the time, unsure and a little afraid of the world.

"He is wonderful," she whispered.

"Stroke him, if you like. He is a gentle soul."

Elizabeth reached out and touched the cat's dark head. The fur was so short she could feel the bones of his skull. "Hello, Lawrence," she said. "Aren't you beautiful?"

A rumbling strange 'in and out' purr came from him as an answer to her comment and his long spotted whiskers pushed forward as he tried to sniff her hand.

"He's so big," said Elizabeth, wonderingly.

"You, think? Well, I suppose he's quite sturdy."

"Could I hold him?" asked Elizabeth.

"Of course. Here you are."

Laura placed the large, warm cat into her arms and to Elizabeth's surprise, he tucked his head under her chin and let out a long sigh. He was much heavier than she had imagined, like a little bear cub, but Elizabeth felt happiness infuse into her whole body. This was her cat.

There wasn't much discussion after that night as to whether or not Lawrence was going to live with Elizabeth. Both she, Laura and, they suspected Lawrence too, had decided that was the case. And so on the following Friday night Elizabeth arrived at Lorelei with a brightly coloured cat carrier and a heart full of excitement and nerves.

As promised Laura had prepared a selection of things for him to take away with him: a bed, a litter tray and litter, bowls and some food.

"I think that should start you off. See how he goes and try not to change anything too suddenly. Keep to the same food and litter especially. Anyway, you go and load those into the car and then we can go and fetch him. He knows you are coming for him today, I've told him all about it."

When Elizabeth returned and found her way to the cat room, Laura was holding Lawrence and gently murmuring to him.

"There you are," she said when she noticed Elizabeth. Suddenly she sounded quite business-like again, "Shall we get this boy on his way? Have you the carrier there? I'll pop him in for you."

Lawrence was silent on the journey home. He just sat right at the back of the carrier and looked out with enormous, anxious eyes. Elizabeth talked to him all the way back, reassuring him that all would be well.

At the cottage, she made sure the front door was closed securely and then, opened the plastic door of the carrier. She half expected a panicked cat to come streaking out and zoom past her, but nothing happened. Lawrence simply sat in the cage. Elizabeth gently put her hand in to stroke him, but he recoiled and seemed to squash himself even further into the corner.

Puzzled, Elizabeth went to make herself some tea, carefully leaving the kitchen door open in the hope that he would follow. But he didn't. Laura had said he might want to do things at his own pace, so reluctantly Elizabeth went about making her drink, putting some of his food down and trying her best to ignore him.

She sat down and put on the TV. She couldn't concentrate on it for thinking about Lawrence sitting in the hall, all by himself. After about ten minutes she heard a sound, like something moving very slowly on the hall floor, and went to investigate.

She was just in time to see Lawrence slinking along the floor, his belly pressed to the ground, heading back into the carrier. This was going to be a slow process.

Having returned to her armchair Elizabeth resigned herself to being patient. Whatever she heard, wherever he went, she had to ignore it, and let him explore on his own. It was what Laura had advised, so she just had to abide by it. What she really wanted to do of course, was to pick him up and hug him, but love is patient, love is kind, she reminded herself.

At around nine o'clock she heard him in the kitchen eating from his bowl, and it took all of her restraint to stop her running in to see him. Just let him be, Elizabeth, she thought. He is finding his own way. She imagined what her mother would have said about having a cat wandering about the house, and she smiled.

By ten, there was still no sign of Lawrence, just a few faint scuffling noises here and there, and so she decided to go up to bed. She would set the alarm at two hour intervals through the night so that she could come down and make sure he was alright.

She made herself her usual cup of hot chocolate, refilled the cat dish and made her way to her room. For a long while, she lay awake, listening out for the cat, but the house was as silent as ever, just the tick of the hall clock and the odd crack and creak from the woodwork.

Having read until she was completely tired, her eyes began to close and she dozed a restless sort of sleep. In fact it was barely sleep at all, more like a top layer of sleep, where her ears and brain were still active and listening. Eventually her sleep deepened until she was startled awake by something on her pillow. She opened her eyes

47

and in the darkness saw Lawrence right next to her.

His expressive face looked into hers. "Can I trust you?" was written all over him.

"Hello, Lawrence," she said, softly.

He held her gaze for a moment and then began pawing at the duvet.

"What?" she said. "What is it you want?"

Instinctively, she lifted up the covers and was astonished to find that within seconds, Lawrence had burrowed down inside the bed and was now lying at her feet, purring.

That was it, that was what he wanted. Perhaps he had been used to sleeping with his previous owner? It wasn't something that Elizabeth would have encouraged, and she imagined her mother having conniptions about such practices, but it seemed to give him comfort and his purring grew louder as he settled himself over her ankles.

Elizabeth switched off her alarm and went to sleep, trying to keep as still as possible, listening to Lawrence's purrs turn into delicate even snores.

That first night seemed a long time ago to her, she couldn't imagine life without him now. She and Lawrence had well and truly bonded.

Chapter Five

Now four months on, it felt as though Lawrence had always lived with her. He had filled up her life so completely that she couldn't imagine what she had done without him. He was at the forefront of her mind whatever she did.

However, outside her harmonious household, things were proving difficult and one thing in particular was about to loom large.

Elizabeth had always been good at ignoring unpleasant things; it was a defence mechanism she had developed as a child. Her mother would be outraged when she left her revision until almost the day of the exam. "Sticking your head in the sand, and hoping for the best won't do, Elizabeth," she would say. But it had become a habit. After the initial panic, Elizabeth had simply pushed the thought to the back of her mind until it had become absolutely necessary to think of it. In the meantime her mother had badgered constantly away at her and warned of dire consequences for her laziness.

The committee meeting had been just the same, a horrible black cloud on the horizon that she had pretended not to notice. But now it was time, today was the day. As soon as she got home from work, she fed Lawrence and made herself a ham sandwich, which she ate standing up. This was for two reasons, one because if she allowed herself to sit down it would be even harder to force herself to go to the meeting, and two because she knew that Lawrence would immediately assume she had settled for the night and jump up on her lap. Ridiculous though it was, Elizabeth hated to disappoint him. To move his comfortably curled warm body off her lap felt like cruelty.

This was a problem she had discovered since Lawrence arrived. She did so much less than she used to because she would frequently find herself "disabled by the cat". The circulation in her legs would nearly be at a standstill but she resolved that Lawrence must not be disturbed from his snoring slumber.

As she ate, she began to turn her mind to the meeting. What could she possibly bring to such an event? She had been trained to say very little, her mother had seen to that. She hated to sit in judgment and yet here she was, about to do just that.

The Cock was the one and only pub in Newton Prideaux. It was extremely old and to a large extent what everyone imagines a country pub to be like: whitewashed, beamed and covered in hanging baskets. It had been photographed and made into a rather brightly coloured jigsaw puzzle in the sixties, and nothing much had changed about it since then. Different Landlords had come and gone but the pub remained. It was rumoured that "the new man" was going to make big changes, but only time would tell.

Elizabeth didn't go into pubs. In fact, she didn't drink very much at all; another of her mother's deadly sins: "Your eyes will see strange things, and your heart will utter perverse things". It was to be avoided if at all possible. She had heard that The Cock had now started to serve tea and coffee, but a pub was still a pub and it made her feel uneasy. Now she had no choice but to go inside one.

She wondered, could her mother really have objected? It was to attend a meeting that would benefit the community. Even so, she still felt apprehensive about it. A woman walking into a pub, alone?

At that moment Lawrence jumped up onto the work surface next to her and enthusiastically head butted her. He always seemed to know when she needed encouragement and she rewarded him with a piece of her wet pink ham, which he hoovered up in seconds.

She had agonised over what to wear. After all, it wasn't a night out, but her work clothes may seem too business-like. She longed to be like those women who just threw something on and looked wonderful. Somehow Elizabeth felt she managed to make everything look just a little bit ugly.

In the end she went for a plain lilac crew neck sweater, with some smart beige trousers. It wouldn't win any prizes for style but at least it looked sensible and smart. "Smart" had been her mother's ultimate accolade. She never said people looked stylish, or fashionable, but "smart."

Just before seven, Elizabeth kissed Lawrence between his dark brown ears and tried to ignore the dipped head and reproachful blue eyed look he always gave her when he realised she was about to go out. Feeling full of guilt she put on her anorak, pulled up the hood and swapped her cosy home for the chilly evening.

She could almost see the lights of the pub from her cottage, but it still seemed a long silent walk to it across The Green. Looking around her at the lights of the other people's homes, she envied all those souls quietly passing the evening behind cosy drawn curtains. Glancing back, she could just make out Lawrence's slender shape sitting next to the lamp in her window, watching her go.

Elizabeth paused outside the pub with its big studded oak door for a moment and took a deep breath. Her stomach fluttered. This was all about having a new life and she had to get on with it. Take the plunge. So, Dina had said the meeting was in the back room..........Her courage wavered just a little, as she realised she didn't even know where that was.

Her heart began to beat a little faster as she lifted the door latch and walked in. She couldn't give up now, she had to do this. Inside she was surprised to find that the pub was virtually empty. There was no sign of Roger Hayden and just two old men sat on stools at the bar. When they saw her, one of them made a comment to the other. Steeling herself she walked to the bar.

She stood there for a while, feeling herself getting hotter and hotter. The open fire seemed to crack very loudly and she wasn't quite sure what to do. Then, one of the old men spoke to her. She hadn't recognised him at first, but now she realised it was Mr King from the garage.

"You, all right?" he said, nodding.

Before she could answer, the other man, who she didn't recognise, called out, "Roger! Young lady 'ere wants servin.' What you doin' out there? Growing the 'ops?"

Elizabeth cringed. She didn't want to make a fuss, she could wait, but within seconds the Landlord came out from a back room, carrying with him a towel slung over one shoulder and the smell of hot cooking fat.

"Sorry!" he said. "Just helping the old lady out. Got a late office Christmas party in at eight, and she's doin' her fruit out there."

Roger Hayden wasn't from the village or even from the county. He had taken over the pub last year after moving from London, and that had caused no end of speculation and suspicion.

He said he had "always fancied a *traditional* country pub." But within months he had started to change things. Most people found him a little abrasive and brash. They didn't like new ideas in Newton Prideaux.

He looked expectantly at Elizabeth, "What can I get you, love?"

"Water, please. Could I just have a water, Mr Hayden?"

His face broke into a big grin, and with an almost mischievous look he said, "Blimey, who's he? Don't call me that, you make me feel like I'm in court or sumthink. It's Roger."

She felt her face turn red.

"Now, what sort of water, tap, fizzy or flat? Not so straight forward, is it?"

Elizabeth often came up against this sort of thing. There was something about her that made people want to tease her, to have fun at her expense. As always, she found it best to ignore it.

"Just flat please," she said, calmly.

"Ice and a slice?"

"No, thank you."

"Plain and simple, then. Just like me," said Roger turning away to get the drink.

With his big grin and slightly craggy face he reminded Elizabeth of a mad old pirate, washed ashore in Newton Prideaux and determined to liven things up. She must have seemed very naïve she thought, standing there asking for water.

Taking her drink with a slightly shaking hand she said, "Could you tell me where the back room is please?"

"That'll be in the back, I reckon," piped up Mr King, laughing.

Roger Hayden ignored him. "Oh, so you're here for the meeting, I see. Well, nobody's here yet, but it's just through there when you're ready." He gestured to a frosted glass door at the back of the pub.

Disappointed at finding herself adrift, Elizabeth desperately wanted to get away from the bar, so she thanked him and took her drink to the wing backed chair, next to the fire where she could wait without being seen.

Sitting there in there in the dry heat from the snapping fire, she took off her coat and put it awkwardly on her lap. She tried to compose herself. She had come this far, she couldn't lose her nerve, she would just have to sit it out until the others arrived.

Roger and the two men continued to talk, sometimes just a little too quietly for Elizabeth to hear, and she fought to control the feeling that they were talking about her. They must have far better things to talk about, than me, she told herself.

Finally at around ten past seven Dina Watkins burst through the door, talking to someone, who Elizabeth assumed was the other leading light of the committee, Ron Pickard.

"Right," she was saying, "I've printed out as much as I can, but we'll have to do our best. Good evening, Roger. Shall I just go through?"

Dina was always in a hurry, always running slightly late, always talking and not listening.

"We have a new member coming tonight, don't we? Ruth Menier's girl. She seems a bit of a drip, but I thought it might do her good. Shrinking violets are all very well next to the fence, but we can't let her sit on it."

Most people would have been tempted to make themselves known at this point and thoroughly embarrassed Dina, but Elizabeth was not like most people and so instead, she ducked back as far as she could into the chair and held her breath.

She felt her eyes begin to sting. What she had heard struck an uncomfortable chord. That was her, wasn't it, bit of a drip? It was too late to go home now; the men at the bar had seen her but she wished more than anything that she could just creep back to Lawrence and her cottage.

After a decent pause she got to her feet, picked up her coat and made her way to the glass door. Roger caught her eye and shrugged. Elizabeth wanted to think it was in sympathy but a little bit of her thought she saw just a hint of amusement in his eye.

As she walked in Dina looked up from her bundle of papers and smiled. "Elizabeth! Good, come in. I have a little job for you. Just put these out on the table, would you? One to each chair."

Like a little girl laying the table for her mother, Elizabeth obediently took the sheets and placed them as she had been told. Was this to be her role as far as Dina saw it? A bit of a drip but useful? As she finished her "little job" she noticed that Dina couldn't help straightening a few of the papers for her.

"Well, it looks like we're first so we may as well sit down," said Ron, taking his place at the head.

"I chair the meetings," he told Elizabeth, "and Dina here is our Treasurer. But we are always looking for people to take on extra duties."

Elizabeth's heart sank a little further. She smiled, but said nothing. She wasn't at all sure she wanted to be there at all, let alone become "something" on the committee. Much as she loved St Martin's she had never volunteered for anything very complicated there either. Partly because she wasn't sure she'd be any good at fundraising etc. and partly because her mother was always keen to point out that they were looking for people with *experience* in these things.

And so here she sat wondering what the evening would be like. In theory, a couple of hours sounded nothing but at the moment it stretched out before her like a prison sentence.

She began to feel hot again, the three of them just sitting there was claustrophobic. She desperately felt as though she should say something but her mind was a complete blank.

Dina broke the silence "Shall I see if Roger has organized the tea and coffee?" she said. "I've bought some biscuits for us from Waitrose."

"Roger won't like that, Di."

"Well, he'll have to lump it then. He wanted to charge us a fortune for a few digestives, so I told him to stick to the coffee and tea."

Dina headed out into the bar and Ron and Elizabeth looked at each other silently. Thankfully Miss Elwell arrived at that moment and Elizabeth was able to hide again.

Shortly afterwards Dina returned with refreshments and the remaining two members of the committee, Clive Bescott from Bethesda's Tea Room and Susan Kosov from the Cottage Loaf Bakery.

After everyone was seated and suitably refreshed Ron called the meeting to order. He welcomed Elizabeth and everyone smiled nicely at her, making feel very much the new girl.

"Now," began Ron, "this being our first meeting of 2015 I would like to start on a positive note: Christmas. I would just like to congratulate everyone. I think the village looked particularly festive this year. I really feel that most people have made a marvellous effort. However, this inevitably brings me to the matter of Heron House."

A rumble of agreement passed around the table, as though most of them had been waiting for just this issue to be raised.

"Heron House?" said Clive.

"The first house you come to as you enter the village," said Ron, frowning.

"Not one single decoration," tutted Miss Elwell.

"Perhaps she's Jewish?" put in Dina.

"What's that got to do with it?" barked Ron, impatiently.

"Well, Jewish people don't celebrate Christmas, do they?"

"Are you sure dear?" queried Miss Elwell. "I mean Bing Crosby did sing White Christmas, didn't he?"

"Bing Crosby wasn't Jewish!" pointed out Ron.

"Well, he always looked Jewish to me."

"Jewish or not," concluded Ron, "she could at least put a Christmas tree up in the porch. Christmas trees are nothing to do with Jesus, are they?"

"Yes, but it's still a Christian festival, isn't it?" commented Susan. "I don't think it's reasonable to expect her to go against her religion. Anyway, do we know she is definitely Jewish?"

"Well, no," said Ron, sheepishly. "I didn't even know it was a woman living there until you said so, Dina."

"Do you know her, dear? Could you have a word?" ventured Miss Elwell, turning to Dina.

"I only know her by sight, I'm afraid. Anyone else?"

Bravely Elizabeth spoke up. At least she could contribute to this discussion. "Well, I don't know her exactly. I've spoken to her a couple of times. Her name's Maggie. She bought the house from Pearson's and I know she is away a lot of the time. Perhaps she was away at Christmas."

"Well," said Ron, "perhaps we could leave that with you then? Just a quiet, tactful word is all that's needed."

Elizabeth was mortified! She had only meant to offer some information and now she had been nominated to sort out the problem on behalf of the committee.

Before she could think of a reason to refuse, Ron had passed on to the next subject. "Now, I know summer seems a long way off but we will need to be thinking about Britain in Bloom again soon. So, who will be our bloomers?"

Elizabeth remained in a semi catatonic state for the remainder of the meeting, robotically chewing on one of Dina's Waitrose ginger creams and wondering how on earth she was going to deal with her task.

Eventually Elizabeth vaguely became aware that Ron was winding up the meeting, asking if there was any more business and tidying away his agenda.

"Oh, yes very quickly," said Dina, "if you can think of anyone who might like to join the committee, please let me know. We are a bit light on members at present."

Still in a daze Elizabeth blurted out Bryan's name. Maybe it was a subconscious attempt to find some protection behind his big character? She wasn't sure.

"We asked him once" commented Ron, "but apparently he can't leave his wife for too long. She's disabled."

"Anyway, we'd never get anything done, would we?" commented Dina. "He would be telling his tedious stories all evening."

Elizabeth went quiet again. All she had succeeded in doing was giving herself a very large problem and failing to recruit a would be ally. Few things are as bad as you imagine them to be, but the committee meeting had managed to surpass her worst dreads.

Chapter Six

Elizabeth woke early to wind and rain rattling against her windows. The huge gusts pummelling the ancient sashes made her glad to be safe inside. She pulled the duvet a little higher round her neck, hugging the warmth into herself.

Feeling the movement, Lawrence tunnelled up for air and gave her one of his silent, blue, penetrating stares.

"I'm not getting up yet, Lawrence, its Saturday," she said. "It's much too soon. Come and lie here with me." She reached out and wrapped an arm around the cat who immediately became fluid, slipped out of the way and hopped onto the floor. If she was awake it was time to get up, at least that's how Lawrence saw things. Elizabeth knew that very soon she would hear his scratchy Siamese voice calling up from the kitchen as he looked for food.

Just a few more minutes and then she would go down and see to both of their breakfasts. Saturday was the only day she allowed herself to be just a little bit lazy. From Monday to Friday she had to get up for work and Sunday for was for church and reflection.

Today there would be the normal chores to do, the weekly shop, and catching up with her ironing, but there was also something else she needed to think about.

Now that February was half way through she really ought to be organising things for her party. Many times since Kim's funeral she had regretted mentioning her plans to Dina, but at least it was an added incentive to go through with it. She knew it was only a matter of time before Dina started asking how she was getting on with the arrangements and threatening to get herself involved. This had to be Elizabeth's party, it mustn't be taken over.

Growing up Elizabeth hadn't had birthday parties. Her mother felt that they 'caused trouble', either because of who was invited and who was not, or because things 'simply got out of hand' at such gatherings.

And so, to that end Elizabeth was also not allowed to go to other people's parties either. Eventually her classmates stopped asking and it became established that she just didn't go to things. Her own twenty first had been spent having tea with her mother in Crayton.

Somewhat macabrely her mother's funeral had been the nearest she had ever come to hosting anything, and even that had been somehow taken away from her by well-meaning people who had assumed that she wouldn't be able to cope. It wasn't the time to complain or try to assert herself and so she had gone along with it. Dina *heroically* stepping into the breach along with the vicar's wife Maria, and Roz who made sure Elizabeth didn't have to do a thing. A kind gesture but one that only seemed to reinforce her childlike uselessness.

The funeral had only been a very small affair with a few cakes and sandwiches but Elizabeth had had to stand by and watch them efficiently made by others. Even poor backward Bunny Kitteridge had been allowed to put cress on her sandwiches, she thought despondently.

Having said that, she had no real idea about where to begin. Parties always looked so lovely on television, and she knew that was what she wanted hers to be like. Not timid or staid, as people would be expecting, but bright and fun. It had to have colourful decorations, plenty of food, a little drink and all her friends around her.

Since her mother had died she had attended some church social evenings and so she knew the basic ingredients, it was just how to go about doing it herself. She had to admit one of her main worries was Lawrence. How would he react to such an event? She had even wondered if perhaps Laura would have him back for the day. It was a hard decision. Which would upset him most? Going back to Lorelei or being locked away in the spare bedroom while his house was invaded?

There would be lots of difficult decisions to make. Even the day was a concern. Her birthday was on Friday 1st of March, but would people expect it to be on Saturday night? Wasn't that the traditional night to have a party?

She wished there was someone she could ask. Not Dina but someone who wouldn't try and run everything for her. Perhaps she could ask Mr Hayden at the pub? But he had already shown a tendency to tease her, hadn't he?

Just then there was a crash from the kitchen. She could tell from the sound that it was Lawrence's metal dish hitting the floor. He had knocked it from the draining board and now it was teetering round and round on the flagstones in smaller and smaller circles. It was time to get up.

****

As it happened, Elizabeth's luck was in, and as she was just about to leave the supermarket and make her way home, she bumped into Bryan, also on his way out carrying a bottle of scotch and a loaf of bread.

"This is what an Irish breakfast looks like," he told her laughingly. "Very traditional in parts of Ireland, you dip one into the other."

Despite the dark, windy weather, Bryan was one of those people who seemed to radiate good humour whatever the situation. Today was no different and he seemed quite happy to stop for a chat.

For some reason, despite his bluster she always felt quite at home with Bryan, there was something almost avuncular about him, as though he understood her shyness and wanted to put her at ease.

"So, then," he said, "how are things, with young Elizabet?" He always made the last 'th' in her name into a hard sound, but somehow she liked the uniqueness of it. No one else called her Eliz a bet.

"I'm fine thank you, Mr McConway, and you?"

"Ah, you know, not so bad. But not so good that I couldn't be better. Oh and I've told you before, it's Bryan. Just done your shopping then, so," he said, looking at her trolley. "Plenty for that cat of yours I see."

"Yes, I do spoil him a little."

Bryan smiled. "Maybe just a little," he said. "Ah well, I'd best be off." He turned up his collar against the rain and began to walk.

Plucking up courage Elizabeth said quickly, "Erm Mr Mc….. Bryan, I am having a party for my birthday soon and I was wondering, if you could give me any tips? I mean after all your years in hospitality?"

Bryan leant back slightly and considered the question.

"You want to know the secret of a good party?" he said after a moment.

"Yes, please. Any advice you can give me would help. I'm a bit of a novice at this sort of thing."

"Well, in my experience, the big thing is yer people. If you don't invite the right people it will fall dead on its arse. You see, if you get a load of quiet ones, it will be like a wake, but if you get all the noisy ones, chances are it'll end in a fight. No, the thing you want is a good mixture. Sure, I remember a party we had one night at the Grosvenor. My God, talk about out of hand. Do you remember a group called The Eagles, now? Well they were there, some of them anyway, and The Steve Miller Band, do you know them? and God knows who else was there, but anyway just after midnight the whole bloody lot of 'em decided that they would go up the road to Buckingham Palace and visit the Queen. The Big House was not that far away from us, you see. So, away they went, just like that, all off along the street like a bunch o' loonies wanting to meet Her Majesty.

Anyway, when they get there they are very disappointed, because they are expecting to see yer men with the bearskin hats and red jackets standing outside. But of course at night it's just the police.

In the meantime I've sent young Helen from reception to make sure they don't get into any bother and she comes back roaring o' laughing. Because apparently the police had told them *A top secret piece* of *information* that Her Majesty doesn't ever actually sleep in Buckingham Palace because she can't stand the noise of the traffic, and that's why the guards are only there during the day. The Met are just minding the building until she comes back in the morning. She actually sleeps in a small hotel in Hampstead. But they are not to tell a living soul.

So, good as gold, all these eejits come traipsing back to the hotel all pleased with themselves because they are now in the know about Her Majesty's secret sleeping arrangements. Ah, God you should have seen them hushing and elbowing each other and not a word to me when they came in. I shouted to them, 'Did you not see the Queen, so?' And to the man they all gave me knowing looks and went on their way like MI5's latest recruits. I'll never forget it as long as I live. Imagine that now, the Queen of England sleeping in a B and B!"

They both laughed at this outrageous notion. A lot of people in the village said Bryan made all his stories up and that they were complete nonsense, but Elizabeth liked to hear them. She didn't really know why. Maybe she liked to live vicariously through Bryan's adventures. After all her own life had been so very dull. Whatever the reason, and today was no exception, she always felt happier for seeing him.

It was only as she waved him off and watched him drive away, that she realised that she was no nearer to knowing how to organize her party than before she had asked the question.

Perhaps she would just have to do the whole thing herself.

Chapter Seven

When she had finished putting her shopping away and Lawrence had finished in his role as official bag inspector and plastic rustler, Elizabeth found that her mind had returned to her party fears. Bryan hadn't really given her much to go on, even though she had enjoyed his story of the rock stars and the Queen. What she really wanted was for someone to take her through it step by step, to help her capture all the important points about entertaining. Her birthday was getting closer and even for her, it would be a bit last minute if she wasn't careful.

She looked at Lawrence who was now chasing her shopping receipt around the kitchen floor and said, "Well, I shall just have to be brave and go and ask Mr Hayden, Lawrence, won't I?"

She spent the rest of the day pottering around under Lawrence's strict but kindly supervision, then at around three o'clock, just as the light was beginning to dim, Lawrence took himself to the back door and waited. Elizabeth immediately knew what he wanted and a loud whining yowl confirmed it.

Lawrence wanted to go out. At dusk, he liked to hunt in the fields that backed onto the cottage and as he had no cat flap as yet, it was up to Elizabeth to sanction it. As much as she detested his gruesome gifts of shrews, field mice and tiny birds, she knew it was his nature to seek prey and so reluctantly she opened the door.

Lawrence stood for a moment and sniffed the chilly evening air, drawing in long breaths with his mouth slightly open as though he was drinking in the various smells and then, he was gone, streaking down the path and through the whispering, dark hedge that marked the end of the garden.

With Lawrence out, the cottage felt strangely empty. When she had adopted him she knew they would be firm friends, but what she wasn't expecting was just how much she would love him.

Just his name passing through her mind made her smile and each night as she left work she felt a little rush of excitement at the thought of seeing him again. It was a little like she imagined falling in love would feel.

It was hard to let him wander but it was what cats do, even so a little bit of her feared for him out there. Newton Prideaux was probably one of the safest places he could be, especially behind the cottage in the fields and the woods, but she was always glad to see him home and hear his harsh voice at the door.

Rather than hang nervously about the house, she decided that it would be an excellent time to visit Mr Hayden. It was still quite early and she could catch him before the Saturday night rush started. She quickly grabbed her coat and went out before she could have second thoughts.

Even though it was barely half past three, Elizabeth was surprised to find the pub crowded. At first she thought the young men were a group of friends out on a trip but then she spotted all the equipment. Large black and silver cases and strange looking boxes on wheels. They must be a band. It had been rumoured that there was going to be live music at The Cock again.

She could see they were setting things up and so she decided not to bother Mr Hayden about her party. It really wasn't the sort of thing he would want to be troubled with on such a busy evening. But as she stood anxiously in the doorway, Roger spotted her and beckoned her over to the bar.

"What can I get you?" he twinkled.

Feeling herself flush under his very direct gaze, Elizabeth swallowed nervously. Just what was it about Roger Hayden that made her feel so unworldly?

"I wanted a little chat, actually, Mr Hayden, but I can see you are busy. I won't hold you up."

"So, no drink then? We can't tempt you to a little tipple?" he said.

Elizabeth had no idea of pub etiquette and failed to get the hint. "Oh, no thank you, Mr Hayden, I've just had a coffee before coming out to see you."

"Well, I'm glad not all my customers do that. Now what can I do for you sweetheart?" he said, good naturedly.

"No, really it can wait, you should be seeing to the band. It's a long time since we had a musical evening here in the pub. I hope people enjoy it."

Roger's face broke into a huge grin. "They ain't a band. Those are my ghost hunters."

Elizabeth found herself without words.

"Yeah," Roger went on, "I got 'em in to see what we've got in here."

"You think the pub is haunted, Mr Hayden?" said Elizabeth.

"Well if it is, these guys will find out. They are the real deal this lot. Doing the full thing: EVP, EMF, Flir cameras, all the whistles and bells. If there are any spirits about and they ain't the liquid variety, they'll find 'em."

Elizabeth recoiled slightly. The paranormal in Newton Prideaux, it was quite alarming. The Bible is very clear on the occult, it is not to be taken lightly or joked about. She didn't like the situation at all.

"Right, set up in the back rooms first lads, then you can come in here when we close. Anybody want a drink? On the house of course."

Roger's attention had drifted away from her and back to his ghost people. She could hear one of the young men asking if he had had experiences, any strange noises or cold spots around the place.

"Only if I upset the old lady," Roger was saying jovially. "Plenty of noise and cold spots then."

They all laughed and Elizabeth prepared to leave.

"Woah, 'old up," Roger called after her. "What was it you wanted, love? Just let me see to these guys and I'll be with you."

Elizabeth watched them go behind the bar and had half a mind to sneak away. Her brain was struggling to remember the quote about the occult and polluting your soul, but she couldn't quite bring it to mind. The whole thing made her very uneasy.

When Roger returned he was full of bonhomie, not at all like a man dabbling with the supernatural. "Right, then," he said. "Now I've got my Ghost Busters settled, what can I do for you?"

Elizabeth took the plunge, "I'm having a party for my 40th birthday and I was hoping you can give me some advice."

"Yeah, right, well the first thing you need is a good venue. I can recommend one, at a very reasonable price too."

"Oh, I've decided to have it at home, Mr Hayden. but thank you anyway."

Roger Hayden rubbed his ear thoughtfully. He wasn't used to such artlessness, and it amused him.

"So, you want me and Lorna to do you some food?"

"No, I think I shall manage that. I just wanted to know how to create the right atmosphere, how to keep everyone upbeat and happy."

This time Roger laughed out loud. "So there's nothin' in this for me then, not even an invitation? Not only that but you'll be competition that night. People won't be coming in here if they can get a free drink at your house, will they?"

Elizabeth was mortified, she had said all the wrong things and had made a complete fool of herself….again. She could feel herself blushing.

Roger smiled. "Just messing with you, you're all right. But I don't really know what I can tell you. I mean, give them plenty of booze, a good buffet and you should be laughing. It isn't rocket science, you know, keeping people happy? In my experience, most people want to have a good time. You get the odd miserable bugger, but that's up to them if they want to miss out." He gave her one of his pirate grins and put his hand on her shoulder. "Oh, and if you haven't got enough glasses, we hire them out."

She hadn't even thought about glasses, there was so much she didn't have a clue about. But she didn't feel at all comfortable standing there with Roger Hayden's hand on her shoulder and what amounted to a séance going on in the back room. It was time to make her excuses and leave.

"Thank you," she said moving away. "Thank you very much for your advice, Mr Hayden, and I hope they don't find any ghosts."

"I'm banking on them finding some! Nothing people like better than a haunted pub," he laughed "Ay, he's here again!" he said, suddenly looking at something over Elizabeth's shoulder.

At first she thought he was trying to scare her, pretending there was a ghost behind her, but when she turned around she was surprised to see a cat, sitting on the coconut matting just inside the door.

It was a silver tabby, much more stocky and solid than Lawrence and he was looking calmly around the pub with round amber eyes.

"Cheeky devil," said Roger. "He keeps turning up."

"Is he a stray?" said Elizabeth, getting down to cat height.

"No, he's from that cottage Leon and Rachael are doing up."

Elizabeth had reached out and was now stroking the cat's soft smoky, shaded head. "Hello," she said. "Aren't you handsome?"

He was a beautiful cat, his close plush fur and tigerish markings made him an impressive sight, sitting there on the welcome mat. He had that remarkable composure cats possess, that says, *I couldn't care less what you think of me, I am sitting here.*

Impulsively Elizabeth said, "I'll take him back to his home for you."

Having said this, she wasn't quite sure how she was going to accomplish it, but she needn't have worried. As soon as she pulled open the pub door and stood to one side, the cat walked out as though she was simply a servant doing her duty.

Together they sidled across the village in the direction of Yew Tree Cottage, the cat just a few paces in front with the odd glance over its shoulder to make sure she was still following.

The gate of the cottage was hanging off its hinges but Elizabeth managed to follow the cat through the gap and knock on the door.

Chapter Eight

At first Elizabeth was convinced that no one had heard. Loud rock music was coming from somewhere at the back of the house along with various scraping and hammering sounds. It seemed impolite to just wander in uninvited and so she stood not knowing quite what to do.

The cat, on the other hand, had a different idea and was weaving around her feet, wandering towards the rear of the cottage and then back again. He wanted her to follow him; she was quite convinced of that. After a very plaintive but silent meow, she gave in and went down the overgrown path at the side of the cottage.

There was no back gate and in the garden was a huge makeshift tent made of polythene sheeting lit up inside like a giant lantern.

"Hello!" Elizabeth called apprehensively, patting at the plastic wall. "Hello, excuse me! Hello!"

The noises and the music stopped and an arm swept aside the sheeting like it was a tent flap.

A large balding man in a well bobbled jumper and paint covered pale jeans appeared. "Hello?" he said.

"I'm Elizabeth Menier, I have your cat. He was in the pub." Realising how this might sound she added, "I mean, I popped into the pub to ask something and he was there."

The man held out a huge dusty hand that entirely engulfed hers.

"Delighted to meet you, Elizabeth Menier, and I rather think my cat has you." His voice was light and cultured, almost out of keeping with his bear like appearance. Seeing her obvious confusion he said, "He likes to collect people, you see? He brings them home. He really is the most sociable cat."

Elizabeth smiled. "I thought he needed help."

"No, not this chap, he knows what he's doing. He knows people gather at the pub and so he pops in for fuss. His name is Gilmour, by the way."

"Oh my, that's unusual."

"Yes, I suppose it is. We had his brother too, Hendrix but he died. Oh, don't worry, he didn't choke on his own vomit or anything like that. He had kidney failure."

Elizabeth didn't know what to say. Why would a cat choke on vomit? That was a horrible thought. She wasn't really following this conversation, and she was beginning to look for an excuse to leave.

"We've always named our cats after guitarists: Over the years we've had a Clapton, a Townsend, a Fripp. Anyway, I'm Leon, come and meet Rachael."

So saying he ducked down and disappeared into the plastic tent once more leaving Elizabeth with no choice but to follow. Inside the air was thick with dust and wood smells, and to her surprise she could now see that the back of the cottage was entirely missing and what was left of the kitchen had merged with the garden.

"Rachael, Rach, come and meet Elizabeth. Gilmour brought her round."

A slim, blonde woman came out from the cottage carrying a chisel and wearing an odd looking Andean style hat. She had an almost vague air about her, and seemed to regard this as an entirely natural state of affairs; to be called from a semi demolished house and introduced to a stranger didn't seem to bother her at all.

"Hi, Elizabeth," she said in a strangely flat voice. "Would you like coffee? There's plenty in the flask."

"Of course she'll have a coffee," said Leon. "I'll get it. Milk, sugar?"

"Just milk please," said Elizabeth, wondering why on earth she had just agreed to it.

The two women stood together under the sheeting, their breath smoking in the cold air while Leon went back into the shell of a kitchen to fetch the drink. Elizabeth was by now feeling very agitated and hoped that she wouldn't have to start the conversation, but Rachael just smiled from her seemingly tranquil bubble and waited.

Finally Gilmour wandered in front of them and went into the cottage too, carefully picking his way through the chaos, and Elizabeth saw her chance, "I have a cat, too," she said. "He's a Siamese, he's called Lawrence."

"I like Siamese," Rachael said gently. They are so aesthetically pleasing. I always think of them as Art Deco Cats."

Silence again. Elizabeth cleared her throat. As always she felt very adrift in social situations. "It looks like a big job," she ventured, nodding at the cottage.

As she did so Leon returned, handed her a chipped mug and picked up the conversation. "Oh it is, but it's what we've been dreaming of for years. Marrying the old and the new, you see?"

Elizabeth didn't see, so she kept quiet.

"Redemption, restoration and repurposing all in one go," said Rachael, who, despite these words was still not showing any outward signs of excitement.

"I've always liked this cottage," said Elizabeth, hoping that this would be a safe answer.

"Then you need not worry!" said Leon. "We plan to keep the façade exactly as it always has been. We just need to make it useable for contemporary living."

"We are passionate about this build, aren't we, Leon?" said Rachael in her listless tone. "It's what we do, who we are. We are both architects, so this place is in safe hands."

"I don't think the locals realise…we get lots of dirty looks. They just think we're wrecking the place," added Leon. "In fact, Elizabeth, apart from Roger at the pub you are really the first person from the village we have had a conversation with. Mostly they just glower, even when Gilmour brings someone home, they tend not to stay."

Elizabeth drank deeply from her mug. She was not at all sure what she was supposed to say. After all, she was on the residents' committee. They might not approve.

"Come on Elizabeth; let me show you the plans. You can be an ambassador for us in the village. Make sure they know our intentions are pure," said Leon, alarmingly putting an arm around her shoulder and guiding her into what was left of the kitchen. Elizabeth had no idea how to read plans but meekly she went along hoping she would make the right noises.

But to her surprise, on a rickety looking trestle table, instead of the flat one dimensional collection of lines she had been expecting was a black and white 3D picture of the cottage with its huge new extension.

"Marvellous, isn't it?" said Rachael. "The planners were delighted with our vision for the cottage. And as you can see, we have tried to make it as eco-friendly as possible, which counts for a lot these days. But I don't think that compromises the original design, do you?"

Elizabeth stared at the plans. "It's a wonderful picture, I can see exactly how it will be," she said.

"Ah, well thank God for Archicad," said Leon, inexplicably. "Rach, there are some biscuits around here somewhere aren't there? We should feed our guest."

"No, no really, don't worry. I have nearly finished my drink and I must be getting back. I was telling Rachael, I have a cat."

"A deco cat, Leon," added Rachael.

"Great, Gilmour could do with a friend. You must introduce them. Anyway, whereabouts are you in the village, Elizabeth? Are we close neighbours?"

"Er no, I live at the top of the village, Back Lane, the last cottage."

"Oh yes, I know, beautiful cottages. You could do a lot with those. Have you got much land at the back? You could extend like us."

"Quite a lot actually, but it suits us, as it is. We have enough room, Lawrence and I," Elizabeth smiled. She placed her empty cup on the draining board, which appeared to be floating in mid-air, having lost its cupboard. "Thank you for the coffee, it's been lovely to meet you. I do hope everything goes well," she said, nodding at the plans.

"I'll show you out, Elizabeth. Thank you for dropping in. Come and see us again anytime. You can see how we're getting on." Leon led her back through the tent, closely followed by the grey tabby and out into the front garden.

He shook her hand heartily, "Thank you for coming. It's nice to finally meet a friendly villager. We are not terrible people, are we, Gilmour?"

Elizabeth blushed. "No of course not. I'll see you again soon, I'm sure." With that she stoked the cat's broad head and made her way out.

Walking back through the village, Elizabeth began to feel quite proud of herself. An unexpected social encounter and she had done reasonably well, she thought. They seemed to like her! They didn't seem to notice how awkward she was. Perhaps she was beginning to get better at these things.

As she began to climb the hill back up to the cottage, a thought struck her. She had promised to go and see the owner of Heron House, hadn't she? Perhaps now would be a good time.

Bolstered by her meeting with Leon and Rachael she turned and headed down the road leading out of the village. Heron House was a rather grand building, it had belonged to a Doctor once upon a time and still carried an air of importance about it. Some of the older residents of the village still referred to it as the 'Doctor's house at the end'. It was much taller than any of the other houses in Newton Prideaux and sported a distinctive turret style tower at the front. This afternoon, it appeared to be all in darkness but Elizabeth bravely went through the gate and up the path.

The bell was one of the old fashioned ones that had to be pulled and deep in the house,

Elizabeth heard it solemnly ring out. No one was home at Heron House.

Chapter Nine

Sunday was always a special day for Elizabeth, not just because her mother had always insisted that they 'kept the Lord's day' but because she truly believed that there should be at least one day when people stopped rushing around and quietened their minds. A time to think about God and how to serve him. She knew that most of the world carried on as usual, but in her little corner of Oxfordshire at least, Sunday was still observed.

As usual, her Sunday began with church. Taking a last look at herself in the hall mirror before leaving, it occurred to her that she was one of the few women in the congregation who still wore a hat. She kept meaning to leave it at home. She knew it was an old fashioned notion but she just didn't feel right entering the church with her head uncovered and so today, as with every other Sunday, she put it on and made her way to St Martin's.

Elizabeth liked to arrive on time and go straight inside. She didn't care for chatting before the service like some of the villagers did. Socialising was for afterwards. It seemed almost impolite to keep 'Him' waiting.

St Martin's was quite a plain little church, with a neat square bell tower at the front and the nave stretching out behind it. Unremarkable you might say, but it was old, and the thought of all the people who had worshipped there before her gave Elizabeth a sense of peace. She was very fond of her little village church and she particularly liked it at this time of year.

Easter was coming and the church looked stark now, with its whitewashed interior, unadorned by flowers and the solemn purple cloth covering the alter. But soon lent would end, the cloth would be removed and the flowers would return. A happy hopeful time, when the nights would start to draw out and people would not be so closed off from one another. Or at least that's how Elizabeth saw it.

Inside the church she took her usual place and prepared to concentrate. *It isn't enough to attend church*, her mother used to say, *you have to listen to the lesson and apply it to yourself.*

The Reverend Donovan greeted his flock and started the service with a rousing version of

Immortal, Invisible, God Only Wise. When the last notes of the organ faded away and everyone had taken their seats, the vicar smiled out across the congregation.

"Well, good morning once again. You certainly sound in fine voice today." His Welsh lilting accent made him easy to listen to and his genial manner went down well with his flock. "Now, I picked that hymn for a reason," he said. "Not only is it one of my favourites but it also has a bearing on my sermon today. God only wise, it says, and he is wise, he knows our pasts and he knows our future. But that is for him to know, and not us. Deuteronomy tells us, *God alone knows the future. We have no business trying to divine what God has not clearly revealed.*" It seemed an odd choice of subject to Elizabeth but none the less she listened patiently as always.

The church was quite full today and Elizabeth wondered momentarily if she should have suggested to Leon and Rachael that they came along to a service and met a few more people, but then again, they didn't really seem the sort of people who would feel at home in St Martin's.

Amongst the familiar faces she could see Bunny Kitteridge and her mother Ellen. Like her,

Bunny was wearing a hat, the same black cloche she had worn to Kim's funeral, pulled down almost to her eye lids.

It sometimes felt to Elizabeth as though Bunny had been appointed to be her dark self, holding up a mirror to her idiosyncrasies and pointing out her peculiarities and oddities. She would leave the hat at home next Sunday, she decided. Perhaps Lawrence would like it as a bed.

During the sermon Elizabeth found it harder and harder to relate to what was being said. Reverend Donovan clearly had a point he wanted to get across, but she couldn't imagine what had set him on that course. As for applying it to herself, she wasn't one for crystal gazing. She didn't even read her horoscope.

As the service was coming to a close and they rose to sing one last hymn: *I Know Who Holds Tomorrow,* Elizabeth was surprised to see Bunny suddenly get to her feet, whisper something to her mother and slip quietly back down the aisle. The thud of the church door closing told Elizabeth she had gone.

It was most unusual; Bunny never went anywhere on her own. Elizabeth brought her attention back to the hymn. She would ask Ellen if she was all right afterwards. Perhaps she had just been feeling faint.

As the congregation filed out, a few people paused to comment on the sermon but Elizabeth simply thanked the reverend and hurried by. As she stepped out into the fresh air, a familiar voice called her. "Any luck with Heron House?" It was Dina Watkins and her husband Christopher. "Elizabeth! Elizabeth! Any luck with Heron House?"

Elizabeth reluctantly waited for them to catch her up.

"Well, how did you get on? Did you see Mary, or Maggie, or whatever her name is?"

Relieved that she had actually gone and tried to see her neighbour, Elizabeth said, "Sadly not, Dina, I did go but nobody was at home."

"Pity. Oh well, keep trying eh, there's a good girl."

"Elizabeth," said Dr Watkins, his face as usual, looking the utmost picture of calm. Elizabeth could only imagine that he had developed this unflappable demeanour after years of living with the impatient, demanding Dina. "How are you?" he enquired, smiling.

Before she had time to respond, Dina was talking again. "Well, what did you think of that sermon, then? Roger has really ruffled the Reverend Alan's feathers."

"Oh, has he? I thought it was an odd subject."

"Well, first he had the ghost people in and now he is holding a psychic fayre. That man will do anything for money."

"He's just trying to drum up trade, I suppose," commented Christopher, a remark that was completely ignored by his wife.

"Yes, I knew about the ghost hunters. I hadn't heard about the fayre though. Is it fortune tellers, that sort of thing?" said Elizabeth.

"Who knows, but Alan is not happy about it, and I don't blame him…….. " Dina stopped in mid-sentence. "What **is** she doing?"

All three turned to look in the direction of Dina's stare.

At the back of St Martin's was an uneven patch of lawn with huddles of leaning gravestones scattered about it. At one of these stones a figure was pacing back and forth, touching the headstone and then turning to look at the people as they were leaving the church.

It was Bunny Kitteridge and she was at her father's grave. "Is that Kim's grave?" asked Christopher.

"It is. What on earth is she standing there for?"

"Perhaps she is just visiting him," offered Elizabeth.

"Just as Church happens to be coming out? She's had all week to do that. I don't think so. And why does she keep touching it and looking over here."

"Perhaps she thinks we have forgotten," said Christopher.

"How ridiculous; he only died in December. What's the matter with her? Ellen should take her home."

"Well, she's certainly drawing attention to herself," said Christopher.

Just then Ellen did appear and ushered her daughter away. Whatever it had been about they would probably never know. But it was clear Bunny had something on her mind.

"Thank goodness for that. We'll have Roger's ghost people camping out here if they think something odd is going on," said Dina. "Come on, Christopher I want to get the chicken in."

As Elizabeth watched them go she heard the doctor say, "I wonder if they found any ghosts at the pub," and a wry smile passed over her face.

For the rest of the day Elizabeth spent her time at home with Lawrence. The business with Bunny had worried her, even more so as she was intending to write a list of invitations to her party today. Should she include Bunny? But yes of course she should. It would be unchristian to do anything else. Just because she made Elizabeth uncomfortable was no reason to exclude her. She felt ashamed for even thinking it.

Lawrence jumped up beside her and sat on the pad she was using for the list. He looked straight into Elizabeth's eyes. It was one of his most endearing traits and it was how he communicated. He could convey so much with his deep blue eyes that Elizabeth and he were beginning to understand each other completely without a sound passing between them.

His handsome, dark face and his huge fangs gave him a loveable but slightly goofy expression that Elizabeth adored. Sometimes she would just sit and look at him, taking in the intricacies of the fur patterns on his muzzle, their suede like change of direction on his nose, and his soft brown lip leather. If he was asleep she would watch the rise and fall of his brown flank and the twitch of his coffee bean paw pads.

It was true that she had fallen head over heels in love with him. She knew her mother would most definitely not have approved. She hadn't really liked people who doted on their pets; it wasn't Christian. She maintained that animals have no souls. That was the difference between us and them. God had given us souls. Animals didn't pass into The Kingdom of Heaven.

Looking at him now and seeing the life and intelligence in those sapphire eyes, she knew Lawrence had a soul. She could almost see it and she also knew if he wasn't there in heaven with her, then it wouldn't be heaven at all.

Chapter Ten

On the morning of the party Elizabeth woke to the sound of birds singing outside and a horrible half remembered dream in her head. It wafted away like smoke, even as she tried to recall it. It was something to do with Roger Hayden standing on top of his pub roof, bathed in flames that viciously licked and roared around his body. The rest of the dream faded quickly, until she was left with just that image. Why he was on the roof and why he was on fire was unclear but it hung over her like a cloud over the sun.

Getting out of bed and putting on her dressing gown, she told herself that today was a special day, a party day and she needed to shake off her dark thoughts and get busy. It was just a dream and dreams can't harm you.

Her actual fortieth birthday had been the day before, and it had passed with very little fuss. At work her desk had been decorated with helium balloons and her colleagues had clubbed together to buy her a rather lovely bouquet, which now sat unbecomingly in a bucket of water in her pantry. The evening had been spent quietly with Lawrence. It had been like any other Friday night and Elizabeth struggled with the idea that she really was now forty.

Perhaps the party would bring it home to her. But at the moment she just didn't feel forty. She didn't feel any different at all. In the lounge she had put up a banner saying *Happy Birthday! 40 Today!* And even that bothered her. For one thing it had been her birthday yesterday, and for another, was it really protocol to wish oneself a happy birthday? As she went downstairs with Lawrence rushing ahead of her down the narrow staircase, and purring loudly at the thought of breakfast, she couldn't help but wonder if this party was such a good idea.

In her little kitchen every surface was covered in party related things: paper plates, serviettes, cling film, and as she cleared a small space on the work top to serve Lawrence his food, she fought back the feelings of dread that had begun to creep up on her.

One thing that did still seem like a good idea was the appointment she had booked at the hairdresser's that morning. She had made up her mind to be daring and finally get that modern hairstyle she had been fretting about. Her guests would be so surprised to see her new look and inside she felt a tiny fizz of excitement.

Leaving Lawrence hunched over his bowl making happy little yumming noises she went upstairs to get herself ready. This would be the last time she would have to struggle with her mass of hair. Tomorrow it would be short and chic, just like in the magazines.

Crayton had been 'Town' for as long as Elizabeth could remember. When locals spoke of 'going into Town' it wasn't Bicester or even Oxford they were referring to, but Crayton. Comprising of two main streets and a large market square it seemed to hardly warrant such a grand title. But to Newton Prideaux and its surrounding villages, this was the hub of things.

Small though it was, it still boasted a bank, two pubs, an optician and a general store, as well as an assortment of small businesses that opened with a flourish, only to disappear a few months later. The exceptions to this of course, were Elizabeth's place of work, Pearson's and the hairdressers that she was now heading for.

Bogart's Stylists had been there in different guises for years. With its sun-faded, film star photos, and its bright advertisements for hair products, it added a slight glimmer of Hollywood glamour to Crayton. Elizabeth had never so much as crossed the threshold; today was a very big adventure. Bravely she pushed the door and went in.

As she entered the noisy, slightly acrid atmosphere of the salon, she felt that the staff had all turned to look at her, as though they knew she had never done this before.

"Can I help you?" said a young blonde girl standing behind a glittery half-moon counter.

Elizabeth cleared her throat. "Um, I have an appointment."

"With a senior stylist or a junior?"

"I'm sorry, I don't know, but I was told I would be seeing Scarlet."

With that the girl shouted out, "Scarlet, your nine o'clock lady is here!" It struck Elizabeth as odd, since the young woman who stepped forward was only about a foot away from her. In fact the whole salon was really quite a small space, and yet still she had to be announced by the 'sentinel' on reception. Feeling a little apprehensive she smiled as her stylist came to greet her.

Scarlet had a very long dark fringe over one eye, a stud in her nose and short blonde fuzz of hair covering the rest of her head.

"Hello," she said. "Aven't seen you before, 'ave we? What you avin' done today?"

"Well, I'm hoping you can help with that. I am going to a party and thought I would be brave and have a new look." Not for one moment did Elizabeth consider saying it was in fact her party; she hated fuss.

Scarlet frowned. "Oh, roight," she said, her Oxfordshire burr surfacing even more strongly. "Well, you just pop yourself in the chair for me and I'll 'ave a look."

Immediately Elizabeth sensed a lack of enthusiasm for her make over and she wasn't sure why. Obediently she sat in one of the white leather chairs and waited.

Scarlet was now talking to the blonde girl at the desk and glancing over at her. Did they really know she had never been to a hairdresser in her life before today? Was it written all over her?

When Scarlet returned she had adopted a professional smile.

"Let's see then. I'll just comb it out for you." She undid Elizabeth's bun and began to pull her hair down, separating it with her fingers. "Oh," she commented. "Ow long 'ave you been growin' it?

"Quite a while now," replied Elizabeth. "But I'm ready for a big change. Something more up to date."

"I see," said the young woman. "So, do you want it puttin' up? 'Ave you brought a picture?"

"No, I want it cut. Something short and easy to do."

Scarlet was frowning even more. "See, the thing is, if it's a restoyle," she said, "You 'ave to book a consultation first and there's nobody free to do one today."

"Can't you do it Scarlet? I'm sure we could decide what to do, couldn't we?" pleaded Elizabeth.

"No, 'as to be a senior, see."

Elizabeth felt suddenly deflated. She had been so excited about her new short hair and now it looked like she wasn't going to lose her plain grey mane after all."

"Please," she said, "I really do want to change my hair. I want to look different for the party. Is there anything we can do today?"

Finally Scarlet's frown lifted and she smiled. "Tell you what, we can talk about some stoyles that might suit you and Ill 'ave a think. Would you like a coffee, and we can chat and I'll show you our stoyle book?" An altogether more cheerful Scarlet went off in search of the book.

When the coffee arrived it turned out to be like beige milk in a cup that hadn't quite lost its sugar from the last drink it held, but polite as ever, Elizabeth forced it down.

"Now," said Scarlet, "this is our book. You 'ave a look through there and tell me what sort of thing you're looking for."

As Elizabeth flicked through the pages of impossibly neat bobs, geometric fringes and beautiful models with striking faces, she began to wonder what on earth she did want. She had thought the hairdresser would tell her that.

"Well?" said Scarlet, "anything you fancy?"

Elizabeth shook her head.

"I always think it helps to know who you like."

"Like?"

"And who you don't, of course. It's a bit more difficult for older ladies. I mean I saw that Angela Ripon on the telly the other night. I don't know who does her 'air but it looked like a mouse nest... Well, you wouldn't want it like that, would you?"

"What would you suggest?" said Elizabeth, feeling more adrift than ever. She had really imagined that she would place herself in the hands of the hairdresser and a few minutes later would be transformed.

Elizabeth looked around at the other customers in the salon. They seemed to be part of a clique, they all knew each other and more importantly, they all knew what style they wanted. As always, Elizabeth was the odd one out.

After a pause, Scarlet said slowly, "Now, I tell you what might suit you, short and flicked out at the back. I had a client, she had hair like yours. She's dead now bless her. Died the day after she came in to see us…..no connection, mind."

Scarlet laughed heartily at this, but it only added to Elizabeth's ever darkening mood.

"You know," said Scarlet, calming herself, "it's always a shame to cut really long hair, so how about I tong it for you for your party, give it a bit of body?"

Elizabeth could only guess this had something to do with curling tongs although no idea what it would actually look like, but by now she felt she would have agreed to anything just to escape from the situation. The salon was filling up and the heat, the noise of the hairdryers and the radio all combined to make her feel anxious.

Disappointed she agreed and was quickly whisked over to a sink where her head was thrust backwards while a teenager silently washed her hair and sprayed her liberally with water. As the drops ran down her neck Elizabeth knew this had been a mistake.

For what seemed like ages Scarlet worked on her hair, rolling and unrolling it around hot tongs and meanwhile assuring Elizabeth that people wouldn't recognize her with her new glamorous curls. When she had finally finished, Elizabeth looked at the reflection facing her in the mirror. She looked like a little girl in a Victorian picture with ringlets hanging down.

Scarlet ran her hands through it, trying to make it look more adventurous and unruly but with Elizabeth's plain face in the middle of the girlie curls it looked awful.

"There," said the young stylist. "Much better, isn't it?"

Elizabeth meekly nodded as she viewed the horrendous image looking back at her.

"Now, you'll need some product for those dry ends. I'll just start you with the basic shampoo and conditioner, and we'll talk about what products you might need when you decide on a stoyle. Okay? Right, I'll give you some spray to hold it until tonight and then you're good to go. As the pungent choking spray surrounded Elizabeth, all she wanted was to get outside and into her car before anyone saw her and her ridiculous curls.

As it turned out she need not have worried about that at all, because as she walked back to her car, the March winds did their work and by the time she had driven back to Newton Prideaux, her waves and ringlets had dropped out into odd kinks and rat tails.

Instead of returning to the village feeling liberated by her new look, Elizabeth felt deflated. As she looked back down the hill from her cottage, she just caught a glimpse of Roger outside the pub, gathering the night before's glasses from the tables, and just for a moment her dream came back to her, only this time Roger looked uncomfortably like the devil.

Chapter Eleven

Elizabeth knew she still had a lot to do for the party but she also felt the need to spend some time at church, just a little quiet time to calm herself and maybe even get some perspective on being forty.

Before she left the house she combed out what was left of her silly curls and pinned her hair back into its customary bun. Yes, it was plain but for now, it was what she had. And perhaps a new style was something for the future. She looked at her reflection and quoted out loud. *'Your beauty should not come from outward adornment, such as elaborate hairstyles and the wearing of gold jewellery.'* Quite right too, she thought, and putting on her jacket, she left for church.

She loved to approach St Martin's through the lych-gate in the side wall of the church. She had read, that traditionally this was the way the coffins entered for funerals, but to Elizabeth, it evoked images of country weddings and Sunday afternoon strolls.

This morning, she thought the church looked lovely in the early spring light. Daffodils had now begun to appear along the sides of the gravel path leading to the porch, and clumps of them shone out at intervals amongst the greening stones. Spring was definitely edging its way slowly in.

Inside, the church was cool and quiet. The smell of brass polish told her she had not long missed the "ladies who did" for St Martin's. She was grateful to have the place to herself.

She took her usual seat, knelt forward onto the hassock and prepared to pray. Elizabeth always closed her eyes very tightly when she prayed, as she had done since she was a child. Then, it had been to convince her mother how fervent and sincere she was, but now she just felt that the harder she concentrated, the more meaning the prayer would have.

She especially needed God to hear her today. She just wasn't sure how she should be feeling. He had given her forty years on earth and what had she really done with it? Her life hadn't followed the same pattern as most people's, and she wondered what God had planned for her. At forty, she had no husband, no children, nothing to reflect upon as people did on

116

these special birthdays and no big achievements. She was just herself, every bit as unexceptional as poor Bunny Kitteridge.

When she finally broke the seal between her knees and the soft leather hassock beneath them, she felt stiff and cold, but with a sense of peace. A confidence that things would soon be revealed to her, and all she really needed was patience.

Renewed, she headed home and to her party preparations. When she arrived, she found that Lawrence had been investigating the bouquet in the pantry and had managed to spread half chewed petals across the kitchen floor. He looked up as she entered and greeted her with a long questioning waaah sound. His worried, brown face watched her every move. Everything was different today and Lawrence didn't like it, it wasn't right, and Lawrence loved routine.

Elizabeth had reserved the spare room to accommodate her companion for the duration of the party. His favourite bed was already in there and later she would add a litter tray and fill his bowl with tuna as a bribe. She knew he wasn't going to like the noise and the people, but she just couldn't bring herself to take him back to

Lorelei for the night, just in case he thought she was returning him forever.

"Well, Lawrence," she said, "I wonder what tonight will bring?" But as Reverend Donovan had pointed out, it didn't do to try and look into the future.

Just before seven thirty Elizabeth stood staring down at the freshly made vacuum tracks in her carpet pile, lost in thought. Was everything in hand? Had she covered everything? She felt almost as though she had organised the end of term dance instead of her own birthday party. She still couldn't make it feel like anything to do with her.

She had chosen a very smart, bright pink dress from Marks and Spencer for the evening, and she had been very pleased with it until tonight. When she put it on, she noticed the label referred to the colour as *Cerise*. Cerise! It sounded ostentatious and even a little gaudy. Now she worried it might be a little too bright. When she had bought it, she had imagined herself with a new trendy hairstyle, but now she was afraid she might be just Elizabeth in an overly colourful dress.

In the end, the guest list had turned out to be much less difficult than her choice of clothes. In a village, much of the list is dictated by etiquette and so once she had worked out who she really **had** to invite, the others were easy. She had decided to include Bunny and Ellen after all, for as much as she found Bunny's mirror image of her failings disturbing, she liked Ellen and her gentle ways, plus it would have been very unchristian not to ask them.

The doorbell rang, shattered her thoughts and made her jump violently. It was seven thirty on the dot. Her first guests had arrived. They were the Vicar and his wife, Alan and Marie Donovan.

"Happy Birthday," said Marie, presenting her hostess with a large bunch of daffodils wrapped in slightly crumpled florist paper. Elizabeth silently hoped they were from the vicarage garden and not the graveyard as she feared.

The Vicar's reputation for being careful was well known in the village and although thrift was indeed a virtue, 'The Parsimonious Parson,' as Bryan called him, had certainly upset a few people with his lack of generosity. He now stood eyeing the buffet avariciously and declaring it to be a "splendid spread."

As ever Elizabeth struggled in such situations. Her mind was absolutely blank. She knew she should have said something, started a conversation, but her brain refused to think of a single interesting thing to say. So instead she smiled at her expectant guests.

"You look very nice," said Marie. "Very bright."

Elizabeth's fears were confirmed, the dress was too pink. Should she offer them something to drink? But then if she did, she would have to leave them alone to fetch it. This was horrible. The three of them stood awkwardly in the lounge, smiling.

The doorbell rang again and Elizabeth scuttled gratefully away to answer it. It was Bryan, and she couldn't have been more pleased to see him.

"Bryan!" she said. "So glad you could come."

"Aah, I was delighted to accept your invitation, but I'm here on my own. My other half, Maeve the Rave, well, she doesn't like these things so much these days, being unwell an' all. So how is it going then, Elizabet' this party of yours? It looks very festive in here and look I've bought a little drink to celebrate with," and he produced a huge bottle of champagne with a red ribbon tied round its neck.

Elizabeth had never tasted champagne, and she only drank wine very occasionally for that matter, but she thanked him anyway and it did look very glamourous with its bright yellow label and shiny gold top.

"Oh, thank you it's lovely," she said. "Please go in, Reverend Donovan and his wife are here."

Bryan made an "*Oh, how boring, face,*" winked at her and went in.

"Reverend, good to see you, and your lady wife too. Isn't this grand?"

Greetings over, Bryan was only too happy to take charge, chatting easily away, and leaving Elizabeth free to answer the door as more people arrived. Thank the good Lord for sending Bryan McConway.

By eight, almost half of the guests had turned up and Elizabeth was beginning to relax just a little and disappear into the background. She even allowed Bryan to hand her a glass of white wine.

"So Elizabet'," he said, "how does it feel to have reached the grand old age of forty?"

"Well, if I'm honest. I feel like it's not real. As though this isn't my party at all, as though I've just arranged it for someone else. Does that make sense?" Bryan rubbed his chin.

"Well, you know, birthdays can be odd things. They take people in peculiar ways sometimes. You know, I had a fella turn up at the hotel in Athlone once, he was convinced his birthday had a curse on it."

Elizabeth widened her eyes.

"I know, can you imagine that? Anyway, he's telling me this at reception as he checks in, so I say, now what would make you think you had a curse on you?

"*Well*" he says, "*it isn't so much just on me, but also the people around me. You see, they try so hard to give me a good time but it always ends up going wrong. For example, one year a friend drove all the way down from Scotland just to wish me a happy birthday and didn't he then run over my dog in the driveway and we spent the day at the vets.*

Another year, a friend set my hair alight trying to light candles that had gone out on my cake. Sure I still have the scars here on my forehead to prove it.

Then, there was this one time, my neighbour did a huge barbecue for me and the whole lot of us ended up with food poisoning. I'm not joking, it's been one thing after another. But then, what finally did it for me, was last year. I love the cricket you know, so my brother got us tickets for a day out at Lord's and the opening batsman hit a six into the crowd and knocked me clean out."

So, now I'm beginning to think he might have a point and that there may be something in this curse stuff. Because you know, we Irish are inclined a little toward superstition.

Anyhow, he says this year he is taking no chances. He's travelled over to Ireland and he's booked into our fine establishment. He has brought his own food and he will stay alone until the day is over. Nobody knows where he has gone and so he should be safe.

Do you know he even picked a ground floor room so he didn't have to risk the lift, can you believe that?

Anyway I wish him good luck and away he goes to his room. Well, about 11 o'clock, I get a call. There is a fuss going on at reception. The man's brother has turned up, demanding to see him.

I go down and explain we are not at liberty to discuss who is staying at the hotel and it would be a breach of privacy if we did so.

Well, he says, *I know he's here, I've seen his booking on his credit card. Look, will you just tell him I'm here.*

So, politely I say again, I'm sorry no, sir we are not able to do that. He has specifically requested not to be disturbed and we take our guests' needs very seriously.

Okay, okay, he says. *Well, you are spoiling his birthday, it's on your head. Will you at least let me leave him a gift?*

So I reluctantly agree and he hands me this little parcel. Seeing my look he says, "*It's just a few of his favourite chocolates.*" And off he goes.

"Now, I'm not joking, this package was tiny and I remember thinking it was hardly worth all the fuss, so I put it on one side to give to the fella in the morning.

About 7 o'clock that evening I take it upon myself to just call in on our guest to make sure he has everything he needs. I knock but there is no reply. After a while I'm concerned so I use my pass key and go in and there's ya man just lying on the floor.

Turns out he was a diabetic and had had a hypo, and died right there in the room. And you know, what stays with me is the last thing the paramedic said to me, *What a pity now, he didn't have something sweet on him like chocolate. It might just have prevented this.*

Well, I swear to God you could have knocked me down where I stood. All I could think about was that parcel, the one thing that could have saved him, sitting there in my reception."

"Oh Bryan, "said Elizabeth, "the poor man."

"You see, he was only allowed a small amount of chocolates because of his condition. If I'd known I'd have gone straight up with them, but like he said, everyone tried to help him but somehow it just didn't work out.

Elizabeth hoped fervently that this was just one of Bryan's outrageous stories. But something about it rang horribly true and she took a very large sip of her wine.

Chapter Twelve

The party would mark a kind of sea change for Elizabeth. Although she didn't know it then, during the course of that evening she was to learn a lot of things that she ought really to have known already, both about herself and about her friends and neighbours.

By eight-thirty, the gathering had stumbled past its awkward beginnings and was starting to look like a proper party. Most of the guests had arrived, Bryan had made a toast to their hostess at least three times, and the buffet was now beginning to look distinctly distressed and a little sparse.

Two of the last people to arrive were Sophie and Robin from 'The New Houses.' Their babysitter had turned up late and they came in, full of apologies. Sophie was carrying the most beautiful basket of lilies and both of them greeted Elizabeth warmly.

"Oh, they're beautiful," said Elizabeth, inhaling the heavy scent of the flowers. "Thank you, so much. I think you know everyone, don't you? Shall I get you some drinks?"

When Elizabeth returned from the kitchen she was surprised to see that the young couple appeared to still be standing alone, while a gaggle of villagers were deep in discussion about something.

As she passed by with the drinks, Miss Elwell's brother grabbed her arm. "Isn't that right, Elizabeth? I was just saying, the village isn't the same."

"In what way, Mr Elwell?" she said.

"The new houses," Miss Elwell said, in her slightly shaky whisper of a voice. Edward frowned. He was quite deaf and didn't catch what his sister had said, "THE NEW HOUSES!" she said again for his benefit.

"Oh, do you think so?" said Elizabeth, equably.

"I do. They have completely spoilt the look of the place. We used to win prizes for the most beautiful village, not any more."

"Aar, you're too hard on yourselves. It's still a beautiful place to live," said Bryan. "I've the loveliest views from my house."

"Well, you don't have to look out onto those red brick barnacles, do you?" said Miss Elwell, petulantly. "You live just outside the village."

"You mean carbuncles, Miss Elwell. It was Carbuncles yer Prince was talking about," laughed Bryan.

"Carbuncles?" Edward snapped, confused by the snippets of the conversation he could hear. "Who's got carbuncles?"

"Well, I'm afraid I agree with Miss Elwell," said Dina entering the conversation. "They don't really fit in, do they?"

All the time Elizabeth was growing hotter and hotter. This was a very loud conversation and Sophie and Robin must be hearing every word. Just for an instant she felt almost faint, as if her head had become elongated and the room was shrinking down around her.

And then Ellen Kitteridge spoke, "I think it's nice to have new people, especially families coming to the village, new life! Things would die out if it all stayed the same."

"Like what?" challenged Dina.

"Well, a lot of people from the new houses help out at events, at fetes and things. They get involved in village life. The cricket team would have gone a long time ago if it hadn't been for Magnus Tanquist. Kim said he saved it single handedly; he's done wonders."

"Is that the chap from Birmingham?" said Ron Pickard, suspiciously. "Hmm. He's keen, I'll give him that."

"We don't see him at church, though," pointed out Alan. "A lot of the young families don't come."

"Well maybe not every week," said Ellen "but it's so lovely to see all the children in the Easter Bonnet parade, and at Christmas, at the Kris Kringle service. Things like that," added Ellen. "It's what makes the village come alive."

"Yes, but it's a small village," insisted Miss Elwell. "We can't have everyone!"

"Well, we like it, don't we, Bunny?" said Ellen, smiling at her daughter, who was working her way through a plate of sandwiches.

"And we like parties!" said Bunny, holding up a sandwich to show the others.

Luckily people laughed and Elizabeth prayed the awkwardness would pass. Thank goodness Robin and Sophie were such nice people.

Behind her she heard a knock and voices in the hall as someone else arrived. Bryan appeared a moment later with Rachael and Leon, both looking as casually dressed as when Elizabeth had seen them working on the house, but minus the plaster dust.

"Hello!" said Leon, raising another bottle of champagne in a languid salutation. "Not too late, are we? We've brought along another guest, hope you don't mind."

Following them was a slightly bizarre looking elderly lady. She was dressed in the most extraordinary ensemble, which seemed to consist entirely of layers of chiffon, ranging in colour from lilac to deepest purple.

"Hi there," she said, waving a sun mottled arm covered in purple bangles. "Nice to meet you!"

"Elizabeth," said Leon, "this is my mother, Edith Esposito. She's over from the States."

With her mischievous green eyes and glamourous swept back blonde hair, she was a complete contrast to her son and daughter in law's rather casual dishevelled style.

For a moment Elizabeth feared their arrival would start another conversation about outsiders ruining the village, but she soon realised that all eyes were now on the woman they had brought with them.

There was an uncomfortable silence and then the lilac lady, said "Good to meet you, Elizabeth. You know, this is so nice, a party on my very first night! I get to meet everyone and have a blast too! Who's in charge of drinks around here?"

The strange mid Atlantic accent was fascinating, Elizabeth couldn't quite get to grips with it. There was something altogether peculiar about it. Something not quite right.

"I'd be happy to do the honours," volunteered Bryan. "What will I get ya, Ee-dit?"

"How about a shot of rum, Mr Irish," she said with a twinkle.

The assembled guests could not have been more surprised if a pterodactyl had landed on the village green and strolled into the cottage. No one said a word.

"So, you're forty, huh?" went on Edith, clearly oblivious to the effect she was having. "Well, you know, it's no big deal. Don't listen to people telling you, your life's just beginning, or it's all over now. You know what? It is what it is…… a birthday! Just like plain old 39 and a little like 41 too. That's the deal."

Edith Esposito put her head back and laughed. It was obviously something she did a lot, there was an unselfconsciousness about it, a simplicity about it. This lady found life all a bit ridiculous.

As she listened Elizabeth realised what it was that was so very strange about her accent. It reminded her of the way Americans spoke in old black and white movies. It was just a little bit corny, as though she might come out with an archaic phrase like, *That's the way the cookie crumbles*, or *them's the breaks, honey,* at any moment.

"Oh, sweetie, don't look so shocked. I'm not gonna bite ya," said Edith laying her hand on Elizabeth's arm.

"No, no I'm not, Mrs Esposito. It's just I didn't expect you to be, um I didn't know you were from……"

"The States? I'm not, I just live there. When I divorced Leon's father I married an American. Uh huh, I know, it's the accent, right? Kinda throws you. Guess I'm just a sponge, I pick things up real quick. I'll probably go home talking like I come from Ox-ford-shire if I stay too long."

"So, where are you staying?" said Bryan. "Surely not amongst the rubble at the cottage."

Leon laughed at this notion. "Can't imagine Mother in with us really, can you? No, she's with Roger over at the pub. He's just started taking in B and B guests."

"Something else," muttered Dina, darkly.

"Has he now?" said Bryan. "Good for him, but what about the ghost? How do you feel about that, Ee-dit?"

"Oh, please honey, call me E or Aunty E. Edith is such a little old lady name, donchya think?"

"Well then, E you must call me Bryan."

It was obvious that Bryan was enjoying every minute of his encounter with the newcomer. Meanwhile the other villagers stood well back and observed in a slightly sullen silence.

"So, the ghost. Yeah, Roger told me about that, but you know, I'm just too damn old to worry about the booger man. And if he wakes me before eight, I guarantee, I will be a whole lot scarier than he is!" Once again Edith laughed loudly.

She was such a forceful character that Elizabeth actually found herself flinching and backing away a little. She was feeling very conscious of just how quiet the other guests had become. She really didn't know how to handle the situation.

Fortunately, the situation began to handle itself and while Bryan went to get another drink for his new ally, people started to look at each other and make surreptitious little "going home" gestures.

Miss Elwell and Edward were the first.

"Well, we must be getting back. Thank you so much for inviting us Elizabeth, it was very nice. Thank you." And like two little grey mice, they gathered their coats from the hall and left.

"We must away too!" said Dina "Mustn't we, Christopher?" As always the slightly befuddled looking Christopher Watkins followed in his wife's wake, aware something was going on but not quite sure what.

"Well, Happy Birthday once again, Elizabeth," he said, as he passed.

It was clear that the party was breaking up, as one by one Elizabeth's guests made their way to the front door.

"It's been lovely, Elizabeth," said Sophie, kissing her hostess on the cheek. "Thank you for asking us. You will come and see Ellie and Ruby soon, won't you? They both keep talking about you and Lawrence."

In the end the exodus had happened very quickly, leaving only a few survivors still afloat amongst the debris of the party: Edith, Rachael, Leon, Bryan and Elizabeth.

"Well," said Leon "was it something we said?"

"Ah no," commented Bryan, "that's just the village for you. Look, I would love to stay and enjoy your company for just a little longer, really I would, but I should be getting back to Maeve, you know? It's been good to meet you though. You take care now. And, E I shall be looking out for you, over at The Cock."

Elizabeth saw him out and wondered what she should be doing with her remaining three guests. Without Bryan she had no idea what to say to them. However, when she went back into the lounge, she found them busily clearing things away.

"Oh please, there's no need to do that. I can sort it out tomorrow."Edith Esposito stopped and put her hands on her hips, "Look honey, I have given so many parties and I know, nobody really wants to come down to a whole lot of tidying, so let us help. It won't take long. We'll put the leftover food in the refrigerator, dump all the garbage and we'll do the dishes together, how's that?"

Chapter Thirteen

"So, like I said, never kid a kidder. Nobody really likes the mess after the night before. This way you get to go to bed, leaving everywhere fine for the next day." Edith Esposito was standing in Elizabeth's kitchen, looking for all the world like a lilac fairy Godmother, dishcloth in hand and a satisfied smile on her face. "So now, what say we all have a night cap?"

A little perturbed, Elizabeth stood wondering what to do. She had already had champagne and now more drink had been mentioned. She really wasn't even sure there was anything left over from the party, and she certainly didn't want to get tipsy.

"Excellent idea, Mother," said Leon. "Now, let's see, have you got any brandy or whisky, anything like that? Just point me in the right direction and I'll sort it out."

Ushering the ladies into the lounge, Leon followed Elizabeth's mumbled directions to a rather ancient bottle of brandy that sat in her pantry for the sole purpose of Christmas baking.

Concerned though she was, she went along with the plan. The last thing she wanted was to reveal just how very unsophisticated she was to the glamourous Ms Esposito.

Politely taking the glass from Leon, she inhaled. She knew the smell from Christmas of course, but as she took her first sip, the harsh, fiery taste took her completely by surprise. Apart from making her cough as it hit her throat, she was surprised to find that it was oddly warming and comforting.

Whether it was the family's enviable ease, Edith's warm nature or the mix of champagne and now brandy, Elizabeth didn't know, but she found that she was actually feeling quite comfortable for once. It was as though they had often sat there talking together in the cosy lamp lit lounge.

Edith swirled her drink and said, "I think people had a good time, honey. And there wasn't much food wasted, was there? You know that vicar guy even took home a doggy bag. You did good, Elizabeth."

It was an odd sensation to be praised and Elizabeth didn't know how to respond, but feeling mellow she just let the phrase run around in her head, *You did good, Elizabeth*. Edith carried on talking. "You know, Bryan is an interesting guy. He was telling me he used to run hotels all over the world and he loved it, he's been pretty much everywhere. But his wife didn't enjoy the life. She felt left out and lonesome with all the long hours and so on, so he gave it up, just like that - for love. Then they ran pubs together until she got sick. If that isn't a love story I don't know what is. He gave up his happiness for hers. How come I never meet guys like that, huh?"

Elizabeth smiled. "Really, did he? Bryan has never told me that."

"That's my mother for you, Elizabeth. She will get your life story out of you in under ten minutes," said Leon.

"So, shoot me! I like people, I like their stories! What's wrong with that? People are interesting. Now about you, Elizabeth? You know, I think I'm gonna call you Betty. I can't get my head around El-iz-a beth, it's too long. Yeah, Betty, like Betty Bacall.

"Uh oh, here we go. Be careful, Elizabeth," said Rachael. "She will wheedle all your secrets out of you."

"So, honey you live by yourself here, huh?" continued Edith ignoring the jibe.

"She has a cat," said Leon pre-empting Elizabeth's reply.

"You don't say?"

"A Siamese in fact. I was hoping we might be introduced."

"Yeah, bring him out. I love Siamese!

"I'd love to show you, but Lawrence, is well, a little shy. He's in the bedroom at the moment."

"Nothing wrong with being a little cautious of folk," commented Edith and for a moment Elizabeth felt like the comment was directed at her. "He's probably just choosy with his company. Can't say I blame him. Go get him, he'll be fine. We'll just ignore him until he feels comfortable. Oh, and honey, if you got a cat those lilies are a no, no. You need to dump them."

Reluctantly, Elizabeth left her brandy on the side table, opened the door at the bottom of her staircase and went up. She knew Lawrence would hate being paraded before the visitors, and she also knew that getting rid of the lilies seemed

141

very ungrateful, but she wasn't sure how to refuse her charming guests on either count.

In the bedroom, Lawrence was sitting on a chair hunched up and wide eyed, looking nervously behind her as she came in.

"Hello, Lawrence," she said. "I'm so sorry about the party. Are you all right? Did all those people worry you?" She ran her hand over his dark head and down along his slightly ruffled spine. As always, his expressive face and deep sapphire eyes spoke volumes. Lawrence was concerned. People were in his house and he didn't like it. But somehow, even in his agitated state, he managed a purr for her. "Now," she said, picking him up and cradling him, "I have to take you downstairs to see some people. Come on."

He buried his head in her armpit and folded down his ears to his head and, as they made their way slowly down the narrow wooden stairs, he barely moved a muscle.

She nudged open the door and stepped down into the lounge. A collective *Aahh* went up as the cat made his appearance. And that was quite enough for Lawrence. He shot out of Elizabeth's arms, twisted completely round in mid-air and streaked back up the stairs, claws skittering on the wood as he went.

"I'm so sorry," said Elizabeth. "He's very shy. He's used to it being just the two of us….."

Edith flapped her hand. "No problem. Let him go, it's fine."

"Such a pity," said Rachael. "He looked beautiful, what little we saw of him."

"Gilmour would have been in like a shot, showing off to all and sundry, wouldn't he, Rachael?" remarked Leon, gesturing with his glass. "More brandy anyone?"

"You know?" reflected Edith, "I'd forgotten just how polite and deadly we English can be. They are so much more direct in the States. Here it's all little acid drops, isn't it? A little snipe here, a little comment there, or maybe even just a look."

"Mother, please! Don't assassinate all Elizabeth's guests. Have some more brandy."

"Just sayin,'" said Edith, holding out her glass.

"Well, I suppose we are a little restrained here in the village. It's a very quiet sort of place," Elizabeth explained.

"So, who was the weird girl?"

"MOTHER!" exclaimed Leon.

"Whaat? I'm just asking. Okay, okay, let's talk about something else. So, Betty you were saying, it's just you and the cat, right?"

It felt so strange to be addressed as Betty, it was probably the diminutive that her mother would have detested the most of all, but it seemed to please Edith enormously to use it.

"Yes, I lived with my mother, but she passed away last year."

"Wow, you must really miss her."

Elizabeth didn't reply.

"So, you looked after her, right? What a good daughter. She was one of the lucky ones."

"Well, we looked after each other, really. Mother had a very strong personality."

"Uh huh, and you never married? Was that cos of Mom?"

Elizabeth was spared having to think of a tactful answer by a sharp "Shhh" from Rachael. Lawrence was now at the bottom of the stairs peeping into the room.

"Okay, okay, everyone. We don't see him, right?" whispered Edith.

They all sat silently, as very, very slowly Lawrence dropped lightly down from the bottom step and made his way into the room. At first he stood and looked at them with anxious eyes, and then Edith leant forward and spoke to him. "Hey, Lawrence, you okay honey?"

To Elizabeth's total amazement, Lawrence not only went towards Edith, but promptly flopped over on to his back and started rolling around in front of her. Suddenly he had transformed from a shy, slinking shadow to a cuddly, cute cat, happily revealing the soft, coffee coloured fur of his underbelly and luxuriating in the attention.

"Hi, big guy, you are SO beautiful," said Edith, stroking his flank. "I knew you would come see us."

"Oh, Elizabeth," said Rachael, "he's adorable. Look at those fangs!"

Lawrence continued to squirm and squash the backs of his ears into the carpet pile. He was obviously in seventh heaven basking in Edith's praise.

"You know, your Mom is one lucky lady to have you."

A little flame of delight sprang up in Elizabeth. She had desperately wanted to call herself Lawrence's mummy, but she worried it would seem a little peculiar and old maidish, and now Edith was saying it like it was the most normal thing in the world.

"Look at all that panther baggage," said Leon, smiling. "That's a fantastic belly."

"Betty, he's pretty special, isn't he?

"Well, I think so, but I suppose I am a little biased. I can't believe how relaxed he is. He normally hides if anyone comes to visit."

"Well, that's the Esposito effect," said Leon. "I always say, it's impossible not to like my mother, it even works on cats."

Edith Esposito was hard to dislike and it appeared, hard to resist, because when the family finally left the cottage that night, Elizabeth had somehow managed give her the bouquet of lilies, and agree to meet her for coffee in Crayton and show her "The sights". Not only were there no sights in Crayton but Elizabeth wasn't even sure where they could get coffee on a Sunday, such was the power of the lilac fairy Godmother.

Chapter Fourteen

Elizabeth was more than a little apprehensive about taking Aunty E into Crayton. Although it was home to her, she was aware that it was quite a dull place. It lacked the village charm of Newton Prideaux but wasn't really big enough to consider itself a market town.

Crayton was functional. It had 'amenities' as they said at Pearson's but it certainly wasn't a tourist destination. As she waited outside The Cock she wondered what she would find to show her guest in such a hum drum place.

Just after midday Edith fluttered out of the pub, dressed in dark leggings, high heeled ankle boots, a bright crimson woollen wrap slung casually about her and carrying an oversized black patent shoulder bag. It was quite a startling effect and much too glamorous for a day in Crayton.

She tottered down to the car wiggling her fingers in a wave as she came. "Hi, Betty. Ready to hit the road?" she shouted. Elizabeth opened the passenger door and welcomed her guest. "So, let's go see the town."

"Erm, E wouldn't you rather go to Oxford or even Bicester village? It's marvellous for shopping, you know. Crayton really isn't that exciting," said Elizabeth.

"No, I've seen Oxford many times. I want to see **your** town, honey. I want to see where you work. I just want to have a look around I guess."

"Well, if you're sure, Crayton it is, then."

As they drove along the green winding lanes, Aunty E commenting on the loveliness of the scenery now and again, it felt awkward and polite. Elizabeth was now having very serious doubts about this venture and was wishing it was just a normal Sunday. She had been to church that morning but by now she would usually have been at home cooking lunch while Lawrence sniffed hopefully at the oven door. This was a trip into the unknown and she was feeling more and more anxious.

As she expected, Crayton was virtually deserted when they pulled up in the market square. Most shops were shuttered up or in darkness with the exception of Crayton Stores which seemed to be the only lively spot in the town, as people came and went carrying newspapers.

"Well, here it is," said Elizabeth. "Not much to look at, I'm afraid."

"So this is your main town, right? You work here, right?"

"Yes, you see that building. That's Pearson's, I work there."

"Real estate, okay. So you always worked there?"

"Yes, Mother knew the owner Mr Pearson and she got me a job there after I left school."

"Right, and so you like it, huh?"

"Well, yes I suppose so. The people are nice. You saw a couple of them at my party."

"Okay," said Edith. "What else ya got to show me? Two pubs. Which one is the best? The Lamb or the King's Head?"

"Oh, I don't know. I have never been in either, I'm afraid. That's the hairdresser's over there; that's been here forever."

"You go there?"

Elizabeth laughed. "Well I tried to go there. They wouldn't cut my hair."

"Whaaaaat!" exclaimed Edith. "You're kidding me, right?" her green eyes opened in amazement.

"No, they thought it was too long."

"HELL, now I've heard everything. A hairdresser who doesn't cut hair. It's *your* hair, honey! Go someplace else. Get it cut and maybe get some colour in too. You don't want all those greys peeping through, now do you? Good hair is a must if you want to feel good about yourself. We'll sort something out before I go home. Okay, so does this place have a market day?"

"We used to, but there is a big farmer's market in Bicester, so people go there."

Inside, Elizabeth was getting more and more agitated. She wished she hadn't mentioned her hair at all because now she felt sure Edith was going to frogmarch her off to another hairdresser and make a scene. Why had she agreed to come into Crayton? It was an enormously embarrassing experience. As though someone had walked into her home, taken one look and said, 'This is how you live? Oh my goodness!' She felt parochial and dull next to her glamorous companion.

"So," said Edith, "wanna get out and walk a little? It's a nice spring day."

Elizabeth didn't want to walk. She didn't want to extend this excruciating experience any longer than was absolutely necessary, but she also hated the thought of offending E.

"Come on, we could grab a coffee and you can tell me more about yourself."

Leon had been correct about Edith getting people's life stories from them, but at this moment Elizabeth saw an escape. "Oh dear," she said. "It's Sunday, I don't think there will be anywhere open for coffee."

To her relief, Edith twisted round in her seat, looked hard at Elizabeth and said, "Okay honey. Right, well I guess we came to Crayton and it was closed. You wanna go back to Newton Prideaux, and we can get coffee there?"

Snatching the reprieve, Elizabeth immediately started the engine and turned the car round.

"I think that's a good idea. Perhaps we could go to Bethesda's," said Elizabeth thankfully. "They have very nice fruit teas."

Edith sat back and was uncharacteristically quiet on the return journey, as though she was mulling something over in her mind. Was she just disappointed in Crayton? Or was she judging Elizabeth and her shamefully dull life? Either way, Elizabeth felt she had let her enthusiastic new friend down.

By the time they reached the village, Edith's gregarious nature had resurfaced. "Well, here we are back in Paradise," she said. "Leon and Rachael just love this place and I can see why. It probably is THE most English village I ever saw. You know, I keep expecting to see Miss Marple go by on her bicycle." Her laugh rang out and Elizabeth almost felt that she had been forgiven for Crayton being such a disappointment. "Now," she went on" I don't think I'm in the mood for fruit tea. Let's go see Roger at the bar."

Reluctantly, but by now determined to make it up to E, Elizabeth agreed.

As they walked into the pub, the comforting smell of Sunday roast greeted them. It was carvery day, another of Roger's ventures which had been condemned out of hand by the locals, but had actually gone on to be very popular. Carvery at The Cock was now a regular feature for Newton Prideaux and the surrounding villages. The truth was, Newton Prideaux residents would have preferred to see their pub close than to see it prostituted by its current Landlord.

The carvery was due to begin at two, but as yet the pub was still quite empty, apart from the diehards who could be found sitting at the bar whatever time of day one visited.

It struck Elizabeth that there was something strange about the place in the day time, as though the warm, evening glamour had drained out of it and left behind a slightly sepia tinted version of itself. Until recently she had not put a foot over the threshold and now she felt she was here all the time.

She looked around at the horse brasses, dark red wallpaper and ancient fireplace, and she could understand why the villagers disliked the brash new landlord. Signs covered the walls advertising all sorts of events: Psychic Fayre, Salsa Classes, Beer Tasting, Live Music and Quiz Nite. The final one, made Elizabeth smile. How her mother would have hated to see it spelled like that.

"Roger, Hi!" called Edith. "Can we get two of your special coffees, please?

"Of course you can, Lady Edith. And when you say special, you mean made with love, of course," he said, grinning like a schoolboy.

"I MEAN MADE WITH WHISKY, as well you know, Roger the Dodger."

Roger placed his hand on his heart and bowed his head in defeat. "Two Specials coming up, ladies"

Elizabeth was about to say she just wanted coffee but something told her to go along with the game. She already felt like the backward country cousin without adding to it. "So, have you been out and about, ladies?" Roger asked, returning with their drinks.

"We went to Crayton - it was closed," said E flatly.

"Don't worry," said Roger. "It always looks like that." The two of them laughed and Elizabeth managed to force a smile.

"You should have gone to see The Rollright Stones…..you can't count 'em, you know? It's a fact – spooky, really."

"Oh my! I thought you said you should have seen The Rolling Stones", laughed Edith. "Don't tell me you charmed them into playing here."

"I'd like that," said Roger. "Old Mick up on the bar, giving it some. No, I'm on about the standing stones. We are in a bit of a paranormal hot spot here, you know? Ghosts, crop circles, the lot."

"Is that so?" said Edith, sceptically.

Elizabeth stayed silent, admiring the ease with which E handled the wolfish landlord. They obviously got on and Elizabeth could see him thinking, *What is "Lady Edith" doing with that dull mouse of a woman*? She had started to think that too, if she was honest. Why was Edith bothering with her?

They took their coffee over to a window seat. Edith threw down her bag, sat down and immediately relaxed, whilst Elizabeth perched neatly on her chair and stared at the net curtain blowing in the draught from the ancient sash window.

She felt miserable. Crayton was a mistake and now she was sitting in a pub drinking a coffee with whisky in it on a Sunday, The Lord's day. What was that phrase people used now? Out of your comfort zone? This was certainly out of hers.

"Now that's better," said Edith, savouring the first sip of her coffee. "You know, I miss England, especially the spring and summer - the winter, not so much."

"How long have you lived abroad?"

"Most of my adult life, I guess. Gregory, my first husband, was a college lecturer, so we went all over. Vancouver, New York, Barcelona. Then, we divorced and a few years later, I married Bryce and wound up in Miami. That's my home now. You should come visit. You'd love it."

"Oh, I've never really been abroad," mumbled Elizabeth. "You must be very brave to move from place to place like that."

"Brave? I don't know. When you have no choice you get real brave. When I divorced Greg, I was so scared. I had never been on my own but after a while you realise that you just have to get used to doing stuff alone. Each little thing is a victory. Of course you must know that, after your mom passed."

Elizabeth nodded, but couldn't help thinking that choosing which jam to buy in the supermarket wasn't really what E was talking about.

"And," E went on, "you learn. You learn that you have instincts and the best thing to do is to trust them. So, what do you want to do? Where do you want to go, Betty? Now you have your freedom?"

"I'm quite settled here, really and now I have Lawrence, of course..." she trailed off. Edith put her head on one side and looked at her with a mixture of disappointment and understanding.

"You know, you and Lawrence are alike. You are both afraid of the world. Hell, you're afraid to breathe. You just gotta throw yourself out there. If it goes wrong, you'll survive. Hiding and playing safe isn't the answer: life will just pass you by. Move somewhere else, take a chance."

"Oh, I couldn't leave the village. All my friends are here."

"Friends? Or just people you are used to living with? And honey, why are you scared of that weird girl? I was watching you at the party. Why does she make you so uncomfortable?"

"Bunny Kitteridge? I'm not afraid of her, I just… "

"Just what?"

Elizabeth swallowed hard. She was shocked that E had noticed her reluctance to mix with Bunny, and it felt wrong to say anything about the poor girl.

"Well, Betty?"

"I think….. I'm like her?"

"Whaaat! Why on earth would you think a thing like that?" shouted Edith, alarming the two bar flies at the far side of the pub. "You're kidding me? You two are nothing alike."

"E, we are the same age, neither of us married, both of us live with our mothers. Well until recently of course. I look at her and I see me."

E suddenly looked sombre. "Look, I'm only here for a short time, but the least we can do is get your hair sorted out and make you feel a little better about yourself. You need confidence, honey. When I go back to the States, we will keep in touch. I wanna know how you are doing."

"I'll write, I promise," smiled Elizabeth, feeling strangely hopeful and just a little bit scared.

Aunty E threw her head back and let out one of her magical laughs. "Get with the programme, Betty. I mean email, Facebook! You kill me."

Chapter Fifteen

Elizabeth looked at her reflection in the hall mirror. Edith's all too brief visit had certainly changed her.

Her hair was now fashionably short and parted at the side, subtle highlights blended with her greys, giving her an altogether more youthful look, and even a little bit of mascara had found its way onto her eyelashes.

E had called it a very low key make-over, "*Kind of a make under*" but to Elizabeth it was a dramatic change. She was particularly pleased with her hair, which now took no time at all to dry and style. A complete revelation after years of her heavy, long locks. She had to admit she had been worried about cutting 'her glory.' It felt slightly unchristian, but E had laughed at her and said, "*You know, I never could figure out why religious people think God frets so much over how they fix their hair! He's interested in your heart, honey not your damn do!*"

However, cosmetics were entirely another matter. Edith hadn't quite convinced Elizabeth that she should also be wearing make-up. She had agreed to try various products, but foundation made her face feel stiff and unpleasantly caked, while the jammy, greasy consistency of lipstick meant that she constantly rubbed her lips together to get rid of it. *"You look like you just sucked a lemon,"* concluded E. And so she stuck to just a little mascara and a dab of what her mother would have referred disparagingly to, as rouge, but what Edith called blush stick. She felt immensely grateful to E for taking her under her wing. During their week together, E had little by little encouraged Elizabeth to become more of her own person and do what she wanted rather than what she had been told she should do. It was a wonderful feeling of liberation.

And it wasn't just about her physical appearance, she now felt much more able to trust her own feelings and follow her heart. But those bright days came at a price. Now, with them behind her and Edith having flown home to Miami, Elizabeth's world was suddenly a lot less brightly coloured than it had been.

In some ways meeting Edith had made her life seem even emptier, as though it had only served to heighten the loneliness and the flatness of her existence. It was a feeling, that in her mind, Elizabeth had started to call *stillness.* Edith Esposito had done so much with her life compared to her: she was still living in Newton Prideaux, still working at Pearson's, still unmarried, and still childless. All she could do was try and carry on where E had left off. But she didn't know where to start, just how to throw herself out there! It all seemed much more difficult on her own.

She was definitely trying to be assertive but at the last residents' meeting, she found that wasn't easy either. Yes, she had bravely spoken up when she disagreed about the new litter bins. But once she had said her piece and been roundly dismissed by the other members of the committee, she felt she couldn't say any more on the subject and sank back into her shell, only to be reminded a few minutes later about her failure to speak to the resident of Heron House.

Elizabeth was left with a feeling of restlessness and frustration that had not been there before. She had had a glimpse of what she might be and she didn't want to sink back into her rut. Edith had disturbed her peace and now there was no going back to her fool's paradise of familiarity.

Easter came and went and although Elizabeth enjoyed it as always, the weather seemed to fit her low mood. It was extremely miserable, not like spring at all. At the beginning of April, spiteful flecks of icy snow dashed across the village and as the month wore on, the cold gave way to rain.

The local weather forecasters were already predicting that it would be one of the coldest and wettest springs on record. Villagers longed for the first hint of warmth and farmers worried about the Rapeseed crop sitting soggily in their fields. The winter looked set to continue right into May.

One Friday afternoon at the end of April, Elizabeth returned from work to discover she was getting low on treats for Lawrence. It was a miserable drizzly day and if it had been anything for herself, she would have stayed safely at home. But it wasn't fair to make Lawrence do without, so she put on her anorak and decided to make a dash for the village shop before it closed.

She set off with her hood pulled up and her hands in her pockets, hoping not to meet anyone. As she passed by The Green, something caught her eye. The village children had made a kind of den, right in the middle. It seemed to be nothing more than a few sticks covered with reinforced blue plastic sheeting. As she neared it, she could hear the raindrops landing heavily and dying on it.

Elizabeth smiled to herself at the thought of the fun the children would have had despite the awful weather. She wished, not for the first time, that she could have been someone's mother but that was something that had long since passed her by. She was Lawrence's mum and that would have to do.

As she neared the shop she saw Ron, half hidden by a golfing umbrella, coming down from the direction of the Old School House with Mollie, his Jack Russell, plodding miserably behind him through the rain.

"Could do without this eh, Elizabeth?" he called. "But better than the snow, I suppose."

"Yes, that's true," replied Elizabeth, anxious to keep moving.

"Tell you what, He'll have to go, won't he?" Ron said.

"Who?" replied Elizabeth, puzzled.

"The tramp!" said Ron, nodding his head towards The Green. "Can't have missed him?

Right in the middle, he is. Cheeky beggar."
Elizabeth made the connection. The children's
den wasn't a den at all, it was a tent!

"Oh," was all she could think of to say. The
thought of an old tramp setting up home on their
green came as quite a shock. "I didn't realise. Oh
dear," she added.

"Anyway, I'd best get on, but don't worry,
he won't last five minutes. We'll soon move him
on."

As Ron and his dog walked away Elizabeth
stood in the fine drizzle still picturing what it
might be like inside the blue shelter. A person
living on The Green! She wasn't sure why, but it
had had a big impact on her. She knew people
slept rough in the towns, but here? In their
village?

She went into the shop feeling numb and
picked up a packet of Lawrence's favourite treats
without even looking at them. At the till, she
responded to Mrs Wilson's cheery chit chat
automatically, but all the time, the image of the
blue tent was in her mind. She couldn't explain it,
but its arrival made her feel as though dark
clouds had just drifted across her sun.

She stuffed the treats into her pocket to keep them dry and hurried off up the hill towards her cottage. Try as she might, she couldn't help but glance over at The Green. Nothing was moving except the flap of the blue sheet in the wind. She didn't want to think that a man might be sitting out there on The Green in the rain and dark. It chilled her to her very core.

As she thankfully closed the front door, Lawrence came running from the kitchen, where he had been sleeping next to the radiator, and started rubbing around her legs. Even he didn't want to be outside tonight.

Elizabeth chose soup for her evening meal. It was quick and comforting and with crusty bread it was as good as any restaurant dish as far as she was concerned.

As she sat at the table with her food and Lawrence sprawled across her lap, she sent up a silent prayer to thank God for her blessings. Her efforts to get more out of life seemed less important now, compared with the fact that she already had so much: a home, a job, food, and of course, her cat. That poor soul out on The Green had nothing.

It was a terrible state to be in, she thought, going from place to place with just those few plastic sheets to keep you dry. Why hadn't he got anywhere to stay? Hadn't he any friends or family? It all seemed very sad.

After her meal Elizabeth couldn't help but dwell on the tramp, he invaded her thoughts constantly. She tried to rationalize the situation a little. Some people chose that way of life, didn't they? They didn't like houses. They enjoyed their freedom too much, at least that was what she had heard, and it did give her comfort to believe it. All the same, as she drew the curtains against the rainy darkness she couldn't help looking towards The Green and the forlorn blue wigwam at its centre.

By bedtime the high winds had started to rattle around the cottage and periodically, what sounded like hail, rushed to the windows and pattered on the glass.

At ten o'clock Lawrence was waiting by the door to the stairs. He was a stickler for bedtime, and his nightly routine of treats and snuggling down at the bottom of Elizabeth's bed. He chirruped with excitement as she made her way towards him.

"Well, up we go, Lawrence. We are lucky to be indoors tonight. Think of all the poor cats out there with no home to go to," she said.

Lawrence answered her immediately with what she liked to think was agreement. Then he ran up the first three stairs and waited for her. As she reached him he ran ahead up the next three and so on to the top. It was his nightly ritual and Elizabeth loved it.

She tried hard that night to settle down and sleep, reminding herself that the tramp was probably used to being out in all weathers, and that it was most likely his choice to camp out. But as Lawrence drifted off into a blissful sleep, snoring delicately, she lay awake listening for every gust of wind and every lash of rain as the wild weather continued.

Having eventually dropped off to sleep in the small hours, she awoke exhausted. Putting on her dressing gown she went straight to her bedroom window. Peeping out at the rain washed village she could see that the tent had survived the night, although part of it was now flapping violently in the wind. Something had to be done, this couldn't go on. It was inhuman.

It was Saturday morning, and so as soon as she was dressed, she decided she would go and see the vicar. This man needed their Christian charity, not Ron Pickard's threats to move him on. As Edith had told her, "You have instincts and the best thing to do is to trust them."

Chapter Sixteen

Later that Saturday morning Elizabeth rehearsed the words in her head as she quickly made her way in the direction of the vicarage. She would tell Alan that as Christians they must do all they could to help …… the, well the… the ugly old fashioned word 'Tramp' had been put in her head by Ron and now it wouldn't leave. Homeless person. She must say homeless person. That was what they were called now, homeless.

As she made her way up the long drive to the squat, little Vicarage she was surprised to see Alan emerging from the front door, wrestling himself into his ancient green wax jacket as he came.

"Elizabeth!" he called. "Are you here to see me?"

"Well, yes. I was hoping to. It's about the ….. homeless person," Elizabeth said.

"Oh, I see," Alan said, frowning as he unlocked his car door. "Well, I'm on my way to St

Philip's at Little Rollright to take a marriage service but rest assured it is in hand. I shall be attending the Residents' Meeting to talk about it."

"Good. Thank you," she said, feeling relieved. "In that case I'd better let you get on. I was just concerned nothing was being done. I'll see you at the meeting then. Thank you." The vicar got into his car and started to reverse down the drive. Seeing that Elizabeth's concern was still evident, he rolled down the car window and said,

"Please try not to worry. We'll get him moved on in no time - asylum seeker most likely." His round beige face beamed reassuringly as he drove away.

Bewildered, Elizabeth wandered down the path again. Alan's wife Maria saw her and knocked at an upstairs window of the vicarage. She waved to Elizabeth and smiled. It all seemed very unsettling. The Vicar talking of 'getting him moved on.' and Marie looking like she didn't have a care in the world. Was Elizabeth the only one who felt awful about the man who had come to live on their village green?

Having him removed was not the sort of help she had come for. She did what she always did when her spirit was disturbed, she popped into St Martin's to sit quietly and calm herself.

This morning she was not alone. Ellen Kitteridge was sitting in one of the front pews with her head down. She stood up as soon as she heard Elizabeth enter.

"I'm sorry," said Elizabeth. "Did I disturb you?"

"No, not at all. I was just talking to Kim. I'm going to see his sister today and I just wanted to let him know."

Elizabeth smiled. She didn't know what to say. She couldn't very well ask how he was, and so she just nodded.

"Right," said Ellen, "I'll be off. I want to be there and back before it gets dark. I hate driving in the dark and I don't want to leave Bunny too long. Take care."

Elizabeth had so desperately wanted to mention the tent on The Green, but there hadn't really been an appropriate moment. When Ellen had gone and the church door had thudded shut, she knelt in prayer. At that moment she felt so alone, both physically and mentally.

Elizabeth closed her eyes tightly, breathed out and began. As always she felt calmed just by the very action of prayer, but this time, she was hoping that in praying she would also learn what God wanted her to do. As she sat silently in the chill of the church, with just the clicking and settling of the wooden pews for company, she knew what she had to do. It was the hardest thing God had asked of her but it was definitely there in her heart as clearly as if she had been spoken to.

She got rapidly to her feet and went out into the damp spring day. She walked directly towards The Green without thinking. Her breath was coming in short surges and her eyes became fixed on the flimsy blue tent. As she got nearer, she wondered if anyone was watching her. But she had to trust her instincts. E wouldn't have given a hoot about what other people thought, she would just have done it, and Elizabeth must find her courage too.

Walking across the sodden village green her heart was pounding and she felt as though her face was burning with anxiety. As she drew closer to the bivouac, a black and white speckled snout appeared for an instant, poking out from under one of the makeshift walls. It sniffed the air and was suddenly gone. Elizabeth came to a standstill.

Then a young black and white collie bounded boisterously towards her, barking excitedly. She froze as the dog circled her. A voice from the tent called out, "Pal. Stop it!" and the dog instantly dropped to its stomach in the grass and was silent.

Elizabeth's heart was still fluttering wildly and she stood uneasily with the dog behind her as if it was rounding her up. The flap of the tent opened and a tall, heavily built figure emerged. To Elizabeth, he appeared to be completely grey in colour and as though he had recently been expelled from a vacuum cleaner dust bag.

As she focused on his grimy face she was surprised to find he was quite young. She had always imagined tramps to be old and wizened people, but this man couldn't have been more than thirty. The tiredness on his pale features, coupled with his huge overcoat and heavy boots reminded her of pictures she had seen of exhausted young men in the trenches of the First World War. The same kind of weariness hung about him. "'Ow do," he said, nodding questioningly in her direction.

"Hello," she said, shyly. "My name is Elizabeth Menier, I…" her voice tailed off. What had she come to say? Edith would know and God knew but unfortunately she did not, and so she just stood there.

"Mick Latimer," said the man, extending a large blackened hand. Elizabeth took it briefly in hers, feeling at a loss. When nothing more was forthcoming, the man said, "What is it, then? 'ave you been elected to tell us to go? Is that it?"

"No. No. It's nothing like that," said Elizabeth, hurriedly. "I just came to see if you were, well, in trouble or anything." The grey figure burst into a husky laugh from deep in a bubbling chest, making the collie bound towards him in excitement. Fondling the dog's soft black ears, he said,

"We're always in trouble, in't us, owd lad?" Glad of the distraction, Elizabeth admired the dog. "E's me best mate. We teck care of each other, Pal and me," explained his owner.

"Is that why you call him, Pal?" Elizabeth asked.

"No, it were me kids as give him that name, like the dog food?" replied Mick Latimer. Elizabeth

176

looked up sharply from patting the dog and met the man's steady gaze. He had children somewhere! Her heart lurched horribly and she suddenly wanted to get away. She was simply not up to the task. She was out of her depth.

She turned before he had chance to say anything else and fled.

"I'm sorry, Mister Latimer. I really have to go now," she mumbled.

Elizabeth walked away feeling light headed and disturbed. She had failed. She didn't have the courage to help. She couldn't just go back to her cottage and close the door, she needed to walk off her agitation. This was an awful situation. Why wasn't she more like Edith? She would have been laughing and joking with the man by now and finding out all about him.

She had no clear route in mind and so she just walked, hoping she wouldn't meet anyone who wanted to chat. Perhaps she needed to go back to the tranquility of St Martin's until she felt better. She chose a quiet route skirting the cricket pitch fields at the back of the church.

As she passed Ellen's cottage a movement at the window caught her eye. She saw Bunny standing in the lounge drinking tea and talking to someone in a very animated way, throwing back her head and laughing. Elizabeth knew Ellen had gone out, so who could be visiting Bunny?

Something didn't seem right and it just added to her agitation. It was a very strange world this morning and everyone seemed to be behaving oddly. She thought of Lawrence and how, when he was perturbed, his eyes widened, he ducked his head down and made a grumbling sound deep in his chest. Everything about him said **I don't like this, it's not right,** and that was exactly how she felt now.

She was just about to turn into the back gate of the church when a thought came to her. A terrifying thought and one which she really wasn't sure she had the courage to do. But she stopped. She really, really didn't want to do this, but now it was in her mind, she couldn't ignore it. She was doomed either way.

Almost in a daze, Elizabeth went to The Cottage Loaf Bakery and having exchanged polite conversation with the owner Susan, about the wet weather, she bought two large Cornish pasties and without hesitating walked back to the blue tent.

Once again Pal came barking out to meet her. Shaking inside, Elizabeth called, "Mister Latimer! Mister Latimer! It's me again. Sorry to disturb you but I thought you might like these." As she spoke, the young man appeared looking slightly bemused. "Please," she said, handing him the warm paper bag. "Please take them." Without even waiting for a response, she had handed over her gift, turned and ran back the way she had come, her head whirling with thoughts, questions and a terrible overwhelming feeling of sadness.

****

The following morning Elizabeth attended Church. She looked and felt drained. She had hardly slept, going over and over in her mind the exchange with Mister Latimer and wondering what she could do to help him.

Reverend Donovan greeted them all and as he spoke of the blessed time of Pentecost, she felt herself sink into the familiar, soothing routine of prayers, hymns and praise. But she had to admit that she found it hard to concentrate when it came to Alan's sermon. She just couldn't help thinking of their conversation at the vicarage.

At the end of the service, as the congregation filed out, Elizabeth hoped she would be able to slip past Alan as he said goodbye to his flock, but it wasn't to be. As soon as he saw her he beckoned her over.

"Elizabeth, no hat today?" he smiled. "I just wanted a quick word. Oh don't worry, not about your hat" he laughed. "No, its good news! Our prayers have been answered and as usual God has taken us all by surprise."

Elizabeth looked blank. "Good news. How do you mean, Alan?" she asked.

"Well, with all this rain you see, The Green is beginning to flood. So our friend will be forced to go elsewhere without any sort of confrontation or unpleasantness."

He was obviously very pleased with this solution and wished Elizabeth a very happy Sunday.

She headed home from Church, with a mixture of fear and sadness bubbling up inside her. She could see that Alan was right; much of The Green was in fact disappearing under huge pools of water. The outer edge had already gone and toward the centre just the very tips of the grass could still be seen poking out of the water.

There was only one thing to be done. She went home to prepare.

Chapter Seventeen

Back at the cottage Elizabeth sat in a state of agitation. Every instinct was telling her it was the right thing to do, but she was afraid. She wished she could have talked to Edith at that moment and asked her what she thought, but Edith was four thousand miles away in sunny Florida, and it was Elizabeth who was in rain soaked England deciding what to do.

Could she ring Edith? She had no idea what time it was in America, it could be the middle of the night! Thoughtfully she glanced toward her PC. She could send an email. But the same problem applied. She would just have to do what she thought and tell Edith afterwards. It wasn't comfortable but it was the choice she was faced with. The rain wasn't stopping and she just couldn't pass by on the other side.

As she stood in the hall changing her shoes, Lawrence pitter pattered down the steep staircase and entwined himself around her legs. He pushed his soft muzzle into her calf and wiped his face across it.

"Hello, Lawrence," she said, struggling with her shoes as the cat's persistent head butting continued. "Lawrence, I really have to change these. I have to go out." Purring enthusiastically he rolled over onto his side and started pawing at her sock. "Lawrence!" She said, "Stop it now. I have to go and do something important. Please don't make me stay and play with you or I will lose my courage."

She got up, disentangled Lawrence and determinedly shoved her foot into her boot. "Right, I shall see you later," she said, kissing her fingers and placing them on Lawrence's silky dark head. Disappointed, the cat lay down. This was a 'going out' gesture.

Ridiculously, as she marched resolutely towards The Green, her blue Wellingtons sploshing through the brown water, she found herself singing Dare to be a Daniel in her head. It was so long since she had even thought about that Sunday School favourite and yet there it was, resonating around in her mind: "Standing by a purpose true, heeding God's command."

She was now almost at the bivouac and she called out, "Mr Latimer! Mr Latimer! Hello!"

She had expected the dog to come dashing out to meet her as he had done on her first visit but this time Pal didn't come. As she drew closer to the tent she spotted him, head lowered, looking disconsolately out of the flap.

"Hello, Pal," she said. "I'll bet you don't like all this water?"

"Too bloody right," said Mick Latimer, splashing up behind her. "Me boots are soaked. Did you want us, Ms Menier or are you just out for a paddle?"

It was strange for Elizabeth to hear herself called Ms. The villagers were only too aware of her unmarried status and so never bothered with titles. She was just Elizabeth or Ruth's girl.

Despite his circumstances she was pleased to find Mick's good humour remained. It made her feel even more convinced that she was doing the right thing. She had to help.

She plunged in, "Well, I just came to see if you are alright, really and….," she hesitated, "and to see if you and Pal would like to come and use my garage to keep dry in." There, she'd said it. Mick did not reply so she hurried on, "Well, I know you probably prefer it out here but it really will be flooded soon and I can't very well ask you to stay with me, it wouldn't be right but I can't leave you both out here in the rain, can I and……?"

"Whoa, whoa, whoa. Just hang on a minute," said Mick. "Let's get this straight. You're offering for me and the lad to come and stop in your garage for a bit?"

"Well, yes," said Elizabeth. "If you wouldn't be offended?"

"Offended! You must think I'm bloody daft. Who'd want to stop out 'ere if they could be under a roof? We'd jump at it. Give us five minutes to get our things put up and we'll be there. Where are you?" Elizabeth smiled. It really was the right thing to do, she had no doubt of it now and as she pointed out her cottage at the top of the hill, she felt both happier and more fearful than she had in a long time.

Carefully Elizabeth reversed her little car out onto the lane and parked it. The now almost empty garage felt chilly and uninviting but at least it was clean and dry. With plenty of room for Mr Latimer and his friend. Leaving the door pushed open she went back inside the cottage and waited.

It was Sunday and still quiet in the village, and she was glad that most people would not have noticed the heavily set figure walking slowly up the hill, his backpack rattling like a one man band and his dog springing at his heels.

To avoid any attention Elizabeth slipped into the garage via its back door. "Well, this is it!" she said as her guest scuffed wearily towards her "It's not much but at least you'll be dry in here. There is an old privy at the bottom of the garden; you are welcome to use that, if you don't mind sharing with spiders."

She tried to sound bright and calm but in reality her heart was pounding. It seemed the most ridiculous thing to be doing. Inviting a complete stranger, a man at that, into her home and yet she couldn't have done otherwise.

Pal immediately began to go about the floor, nose down, taking in all the new smells, like a Bloodhound on a trail he was intent on investigating.

"This is grand, is this. It'll do me and the lad just fine in 'ere. Thank you again, Ms Menier, this is really kind of you, you know?"

Feeling embarrassed Elizabeth said briskly, "Well, I'll leave you to it, then," and went quickly back into the cottage. A few minutes later the grating metallic noise told her that her guest had closed the garage door behind him.

Lawrence was noisily chewing and pulling at his back claws when she went in and he paused at the sound from the garage and looked at Elizabeth for reassurance.

"Nothing to worry about, Lawrence," she told him. "Just a visitor. I'm just going to email Edith and tell her all about it."

Those first few hours with Mick Latimer and his dog out in the garage were some of the most uncomfortable Elizabeth could recall. She had acted purely on instinct and now the reality had started to sink in. She really hadn't imagined what it would be like, how it would feel to have a man camped out in part of her home. Her mother would have been utterly appalled at her reckless behaviour, but then, her mother was appalled by most things.

Elizabeth's snug little blue and white kitchen had always been one of her favourite rooms in the cottage. Even as a little girl she had spent many hours in there sitting at the pine table, swinging her feet noisily against chair legs and drifting away in her own childish world of thoughts.

It had always seemed a soothing room, full of well used implements and homely, domestic knick knacks, but tonight as she started to cook her evening meal, she felt ill at ease. Her eyes were constantly drawn to the white net curtained door leading into the garage.

Lawrence had already refused to eat near the door to the garage and was now tucking into his food at the other end of the kitchen with one wary eye on the door. He was definitely aware of their visitors and at any moment Elizabeth had expected to hear the low grumble from him that meant all was not to his liking.

As for herself she tried her best to go about things as normal but she was horribly aware of each clank of a pan or chime of a plate. A whole new problem had now come to light. Would he smell her food cooking? Did he have anything to eat? She had offered him shelter but she hadn't really considered eating arrangements. She hated to think of him sitting out there hungry with the cooking smells from her kitchen drifting in.

She continued to prepare her food, stoically ignoring the call of the 'white door'. She was just about to scoop her potatoes onto her plate when the sound of the garage door scraping, jolted her and sent Lawrence commando crawling out of the kitchen.

Making sure he was secure in the lounge, she took the keys from their hook and unlocked the white door. Despite promising herself she would stay calm, she rushed in like a flustered hen, only to find her placid young visitor sitting in her mother's wing backed chair casually preparing a meal on his Primus stove with the dog looking on.

"'Ello, 'ope you don't mind. I've just opened t'door a bit to let fumes out while I cook. Dangerous you see, in an enclosed space."

Pal wagged his tail in greeting but was far too interested in the food to be bothered to move. "No, of course, I don't mind. It's very……sensible," she said, feeling inadequate and silly, as though she had rushed out and made a fuss. "Just checking you were settling in," she said, feebly.

"Oh, don't worry about us, Ms Menier, we're fine. Damn sight drier in 'ere, eh?"

"Please call me Elizabeth," she said. Ms Menier made her feel even more uncomfortable with the situation, as though she was lady of the manor bestowing largesse on the poor.

She returned to her own cooking feeling rather annoyed with herself. This was a leap of faith and trust and she was failing miserably. She couldn't invite him in and then be afraid of his every move. Somehow she had to find it within herself to trust him. That would be uppermost in her prayers tonight.

When bedtime finally did come, she felt no better. Having spent a restless night trying to watch TV while with tumultuous swells of anxiety threatening to drown her concentration, it was difficult to imagine that she would be able to go to bed and sleep at all. Lawrence had kept her company, his long brown body extended along her outstretched legs. But even he seemed to be more alert than usual, just that little more watchful.

Before deciding to go to bed, she checked three times that the adjoining garage door in the kitchen was securely locked. On the last occasion, she was deeply embarrassed to hear Pal on the other side snuffling noisily at the gap at the bottom of the door. He knew what she was up to......checking up on him and his master.

Ashamed, she and Lawrence made their way up the narrow wooden staircase.

Chapter Eighteen

That Sunday night was very long indeed; every creak and every crack of the old cottage bringing Elizabeth back to consciousness, and the realisation of her situation. Sometimes she was convinced she had just dreamt it all, but as the greyish pastel light began to brighten her room, she understood it really had happened and that Mick Latimer and Pal really were, asleep in her garage.

Happily Lawrence appeared to have forgotten all about it and was singing The Siamese Song of Breakfast very loudly whilst walking to and fro on the end of the bed and treading agitatedly from one front paw to the other.

Elizabeth usually went down stairs in her dressing gown to feed Lawrence before going back to get herself ready for work. Today she paused. What if she went down and had to see Mr Latimer for some reason? He would see her in her night clothes! She quickly went into the bathroom and closed the door, leaving a bewildered Lawrence yowling loudly on the landing. Even as she climbed into the shower, she could imagine his big round blue eyes looking astonished at this change in routine.

Afterwards as she sat eating her own breakfast and watching Lawrence carefully dragging his, piece by piece, onto the kitchen floor to make it taste better, she remembered her email to Edith.

She turned on her PC and there was a reply. It was hard to imagine what she would say and it was much too late for Elizabeth to change her mind now, and so she opened it gingerly.

Hey Betty, I guess you will have already decided what to do by now and you sure don't need me to tell you. Get out there and do what you think is right. But just be careful, honey, don't let him take advantage. And don't be afraid to ask Leon for help either. Just tell him "Mom sent you."

Love E.

Don't let him take advantage? How could she do that? She had never been very good at telling when she was being used, and being a Christian also meant she had to be trusting. It was all so difficult. If only The Reverend Donovan could advise, but it was clear what his view was. He was the last person she could ask about her guest.

Before leaving each day Elizabeth had what she called 'snuggles' with Lawrence. This morning as he sat on her lap, slightly swaying and purring, she tried to articulate her thoughts.

"I had no choice did I, Lawrence? You can't leave someone outside in the cold and rain," she said, pushing his soft velvet ears back. "I couldn't have lived with myself. We'll get used to it. I'm sorry there's a dog. I will make sure you don't meet and I won't give him more attention than I give you, I promise."

The cat listened intently, puffing out his cheeks and whiskers with each purr, and Elizabeth found herself wanting to smile at his dark solemn face. Lawrence really did seem to take things very seriously.

As she refreshed the cat biscuits in the bowl and turned off all her electrical appliances (an old habit from her mother's time) she knew she had one more obstacle to overcome. She had to go and leave her lodger there alone. He wasn't exactly in her house but it still felt strange all the same.

"Well, here we go!" she said, picking Lawrence up and kissing him.

"You be my good brown boy. Mummy will be home later, and don't worry about our guests, they won't harm you." As soon as she released him Lawrence ran up the stairs and she knew he would be under the quilt in her room before she could even put on her coat. At least he would be safe.

Nervously she knocked on the door into the garage and called out,

"Hello! Hello! It's only me!"

As she entered she was embarrassed to find that Mick Latimer was still in his sleeping bag. Although fully clothed it still seemed wrong to be talking to a man in bed.

"Mornin', Elizabeth" he said, pushing his long hair back from his face. Pal immediately got up and came for attention, waving his feathery tail in excitement.

"Good morning. Did you sleep well, Mr Latimer?" she said, feeling her face begin to redden slightly.

"A damn sight better than I would 'ave done out thee-ur," he nodded towards the closed door. "Oh and by the way, call me Mick, not Mr Latimer. That sounds right formal." He smiled. "Mecks me sound like me Dad."

"I just came to make sure you are all right. I'm going to work now," she said.

"Oh aye? Well, thanks again for the night's kip. I'll be out your way by the time you get back."

"Oh," said Elizabeth. "I didn't realise, I thought, you … I mean I didn't think you had anywhere to go."

"I don't, but this were just for one night, weren't it?"

Elizabeth was confused. She hadn't really had a long term plan when she had gone marching across The Green and now she felt in a quandary.

There was an awkward silence and then she said, "Well, I think it's still raining so, er you might want to erm."

"Oh cheers, Elizabeth. Thanks very much. That'd be great. Ta," Mick said, stretching out a little bit more. "We'll see you later then, eh?"

Not feeling quite at ease with what had just transpired Elizabeth retreated back into her kitchen, locked the door and grabbed her work bag. It was done now and she couldn't take it back, but she couldn't help thinking that she might already have been taken advantage of, just as Edith had said.

As she walked down the path towards her car, she felt a little more sure of her decision. Looking at the slanting windblown rain that was now rushing across the village, it was still an awful time to have no shelter.

To ease her anxiety on her way to Crayton she tried to hold the utterly disarming picture of Mick in her mind -as she had just seen moments before, lying propped up on one elbow in his sleeping bag, his tousled hair drooping over his eyes and Pal curled up on his outstretched legs. He had reminded her of a sleepy little boy and not likely to cause her the slightest bit of harm.

At work, Elizabeth found it extremely difficult to concentrate. Time and time again her mind was called back to her cottage, now no longer sitting there peacefully with just Lawrence at home. Now she had a lodger. But the Meniers had never been ones to share their worries. *We don't want every Tom, Dick and Harry knowing our business,* she had been told, and so she kept her anxieties to herself and went about her day as normal.

Several times it had been on the tip of her tongue to tell someone, to just make sure it was okay, that she had done the right thing, but time and time again she just stopped short. She would talk to someone, the only one she could talk to about Mick Latimer, and that someone was God.

As five o'clock approached she found herself making excuses not to leave. She tidied her desk and watered the office plants, not wanting to go home in case... in case of what? She didn't know, just fear of what might have happened.

When she finally parked outside her little cottage, before she could even think about going inside, she knew she had to go to the garage. All day she had had time to think through the worst possible outcome and it seemed her mother wasn't the only one who had a dark crystal when it came to predicting the future.

As she approached the metal door she had made up her mind that Mick would be gone, taking with him her valuables and worst of all, her beloved Lawrence as well.

Panicking she lifted the creaking metal door and looked in. Mick and Pal were both there. He was sitting on an old camping chair, smoking a ragged looking cigarette with long strands of tobacco hanging out of the end. Pal wandered over to greet her and rolled over at her feet, tail thudding on the floor.

"All right, Elizabeth?" he said, casually from behind his haze of smoke. "'Ave you just come from work? What is it you do?"

Relieved, but still with a huge knot of anxiety in her chest, she managed to smile. "I'm an office administrator at the estate agent's in town. It sounds very grand, but I'm a glorified typist really," she said, self-deprecatingly.

"Good for you. Ay don't knock it, a job's a job and if it keeps the wolf from t' door," Mick replied. There was a slight pause and she wanted to ask about why he didn't work and if he had ever had a job in the past, but before she could decide how to broach it, the moment had passed and she merely smiled at him and said,

"Have you been alright today? Here, all by yourself?" It was a fatuous thing to say. He was always by himself, wasn't he? Mick laughed his husky laugh,

"Oh aye, me and the lad are used to it. We had a quick walk to do what we had to do, if you understand me and that were it. We stayed in 'ere out of wet. So, you worked there long then, at the estate agent's?"

"Yes, since school."

"Oh, aye. So you've lived here a long while, then?"

"Yes, a long while."

"And not married?"

Elizabeth paused. It always upset her when her marital status was referred to by a stranger. She never knew what to say. It wasn't her fault and yet she always felt that she needed to excuse it somehow.

Seeing her expression, Mick remarked, "Oops, sorry, none of my business. It 'appens to the best of us. So, you like living here then, in Newton Prideaux?"

"Yes, I do. It's a lovely place," she said simply but the conversation was already over in her mind. She didn't want to talk any more. She wanted to go inside and close her door. She turned to leave.

"Does it mean owt?" said Mick.

"Sorry?"

"Newton Prideaux?"

For a moment the words didn't register....... Did it mean anything? The village name? Yes, it did - she had been told at school, all that time ago.

"It means, The New Settlement by the Water, I believe," she said. "Now, please excuse me, I must go and feed my cat. He will be waiting."

As she closed the garage and walked to her front door, she felt despondent and yet she didn't really know why. Did Newton Prideaux mean anything? It meant the world to her.

Chapter Nineteen

Tuesday passed uneventfully. Elizabeth didn't quite know what else she was expecting to happen, but it was all very normal. She went to work, she came home, just as she had done for the last umpteen years. Mr Latimer and his dog continued to live in the garage and she continued to feel a little uneasy about it. And now she sat in her lounge with Lawrence on her lap, trying to shut it from her mind.

She hadn't been to see him when she got in that day; the previous night's conversation had perturbed her a little. One question in particular, why wasn't she married? He must have thought she was a bit odd or at best divorced. Either way, she didn't feel comfortable about it. She was also worried that he might be trying to find out about her for his own reasons, whether or not there would be a man around. It all felt quite worrying and not so innocent any more. Maybe she needed to email Edith and ask her what she thought.

She looked at the calendar on her sideboard. It would be the 1st of May next weekend and it still hadn't stopped raining. Somebody had told her once that it never rains all day, but in Newton Prideaux it felt as though it had been raining all day every day. At least it was a little milder, warm rain instead of cold as Mark, at work, had pointed out.

There would be Mayday celebrations over at Crayton on Saturday, she thought. She really hoped they would have nice weather. She had been involved in the festivities herself as she grew up but mostly what she remembered now, were limp tissue paper flowers and little girls in white pumps, with corned beef legs trying to dance around the maypole.

There was something else on the calendar, written in capitals, RESIDENTS' MEETING. Those Wednesday nights seemed to come around so quickly, but as usual Elizabeth ignored them until the last possible moment. They were generally a torture and if it hadn't been for Dina making such a fuss she would have resigned. She didn't really feel as though she contributed anything and the one task they had trusted her with had been an abject failure. She had not managed to talk to the occupant of Heron House.

She had dutifully trailed to the end of the village several times but always found the house empty. On one of these occasions she had seen the occupant driving away and had tried to wave her down, but she had just waved pleasantly back and driven on. Now, Elizabeth was worried that if she did eventually get to see Maggie or whatever her name was, it would be very strange to begin a conversation about Christmas decorations in the middle of summer.

And so, she felt resigned to go and sit in the room at the back of the pub and say very little. The door of the garage scraping open made her jump. Mr Latimer was on the prowl. She heard him speak to Pal. Oh my goodness! Mr Latimer! What if he was mentioned at the meeting?

As her mother had often observed, she was very good at burying her head in the sand and so Elizabeth switched on the television, stroked Lawrence and put it from her mind. A comfortable hole in the sand was always the best place to be when things looked difficult.

All through the day on Wednesday Elizabeth stayed well embedded in her sand pit. Work was very busy and she was able to immerse herself completely. She diligently worked through her lunch break, to avoid conversation or time alone with her thoughts. The residents' meeting was coming whether she thought about it or not.

As usual when the time came to leave her home, she felt it was a tremendous wrench. Not only was she leaving Lawrence and would have to contend with his sad face as soon as he realised it was 'That Night again,' but she now had the added worry of leaving Mr Latimer. She miserably ate her ad hoc dinner of cracker biscuits and strawberry jam and wished something would happen to prevent her going. But of course it didn't, it never does when you really want it to and so just before seven she was reluctantly putting on her coat and pulling up her hood.

Utterly miserable she trudged across the village and into the pub. Roger greeted her cheerfully. "Dina said to tell you she was running late sweetheart, so make yourself at home."

Elizabeth's mood sank a little lower. Now she had to wait for her torture.

"Drink? One of those special coffees?" enquired Roger. It seemed so long since she had been drinking coffee with Edith in the bar, it made her sad to remember it.

"No, no thank you. I'll just take a seat and wait," she said. As she sat down in a high backed settle to wait, Bryan appeared from one of the back rooms, wiping his hands on a bar towel.

205

"I thought it would be the Crypto RC10 that you'd have. You can get parts for them no problem. Probably just needs a new knife block. Did I ever tell you about the time I saw a fella in a restaurant kitchen, using a blow torch on a dead rat. Ah God it would turn your stomach if I told you half of what I've seen."

"Get on, was he? What for?" said Roger.

"To get the hair off. They were using them little buggers for meat in their dishes. The punters hadn't a clue they were eating rat. Aw God I could tell you some things. Now, Maeve, she won't hear anything about it. She says she'd rather not know."

"How is Maeve, by the way?"

"Ah you know, not great but what can you do?"

"You'll have to bring her down here one night. Might do her good."

"Well, maybe you know, if it ever stops raining that is. Do you think perhaps we should be building an ark, Rog?"

"Yeah, bloody weather. Me beer garden looks like a lake."

"And The Green, that's flooded too I notice. By the way, I see yer man with his blue tent has gone."

"It was strange that was. He just vanished; I said to Lor, he's found somewhere to go. Pound to a penny he's in somebody's shed and they don't even know he's there."

"Imagine that now, you go down there to check on your bits of wood and your old cricket bat and there's some fella sitting in there."

"He'd soon have my toe up his backside if I caught him hanging around here," said Roger.

At this point Elizabeth found herself becoming more and more flustered. Mr Latimer's presence was a hot topic and she didn't like the conversation one bit. She certainly wasn't prepared to defend herself and if she went into that meeting, the likes of Ron and Dina would be like dogs with a bone. She simply couldn't face it.

"Mr Hayden!" she said loudly, although he appeared not to hear and was now talking to Bryan about a family fun day he had planned for the summer. She got up and went over to where the two men were standing. "Mr Hayden, I'm feeling a bit poorly. Would you tell Dina I had to go home?"

"You can tell me yourself," said Dina sweeping in. "What's the matter with you?"

Elizabeth was caught. Could she face the meeting and the possibility that talk would turn to Mick?

"I have a headache," she lied.

"I've got a couple of paracetamol in my bag; I always carry them. Would you like them?" said Dina, already beginning to search for them.

"No, I think I just need an early night. I'm so sorry about the meeting." Elizabeth stepped a little closer to the door. Desperation had made her lie.

"I'll make sure you get the minutes," said Dina, as though it was a threat not a helpful promise.

"Thank you. Yes, that would be very kind."

"Oh, Elizabet'," called Bryan, "Before you go, have you seen him hanging around anywhere?"

"What, that grey cat?" interjected Dina. "Yes he's outside now. I've just shooed him off."

With that Elizabeth made her escape. Her head really was beginning to pound now, but it was more to do with fear than a headache. She closed the pub door behind her and walked thankfully out into the fine rain.

Under one of the wooden tables outside The Cock, Gilmour was waiting. His eyes lit up with unearthly green fire as the pub lights caught them.

Cats are very knowing creatures and Elizabeth felt certain he knew she was running away. "Hello, Gilmour," she said. He came straight to her and as she ran her hand over his soaking, silver fur, she wondered why he chose to go back time and time again to where he wasn't welcome. As before, he started to walk towards his cottage, making sure that she was following.

"Look, I'll walk you home, but I won't go in," she told him. And even though he had been forewarned, Gilmour still looked a little forlorn as she left him at his gate. "Not tonight," she said. "Not tonight, Gilmour."

Elizabeth knew where she needed to be and it wasn't exchanging pleasantries with the laid back couple at Yew Tree Cottage. The day might come when she would need their advice, but tonight she needed to be where she felt at peace.

The evening service would have started but it wasn't too late to creep in. She knew it would probably get back to Dina that she had been to church instead of going home, but at that precise moment her need outweighed her fear of the Doctor's ferocious little wife, and she made her way through the drizzle towards the lit stained glass windows of St Martin's.

When the service ended and the congregation had all filed out, Elizabeth took her usual seat. It had made her feel calmer just sitting there amongst fellow worshippers and feeling the strength of the love when they sang to God. But now that the church was quiet she could concentrate on listening.

She needed to ask the question that was in her mind. Why had Mick Latimer been sent to her? As usual of late, her connection to God wasn't a clear one, as though he was just that little bit too far away to hear clearly. She asked, anyway. What was she to do?

Many times in the past she had asked God to send someone into her life, a husband, someone to make a life with, away from her mother and her dominance, but he had never come. She had waited and waited but no one had arrived and now God had sent someone, but this young man was not meant as a partner. So, what was his purpose in her life? Should she take him in completely and let him live in her cottage? Like a son? Was that it? She had already lied because of him and until she knew what she was supposed to do, she would be forced to keep on lying and keeping him a secret.

She gazed upward hopefully, looking about the church for some sort of sign. Her eyes came to rest on the sad elongated figure of Christ, his head hanging painfully to one side, vivid red blood splashed across his torso. What is it? she thought. What have I got to do to help Mick Latimer? Tears of frustration blurred Jesus' sorrow-filled face and Elizabeth was at a loss. It was as though God wasn't listening. After a moment she dabbed her eyes, she must be patient a little longer. She breathed deeply, stood and walked determinedly to the door. She did not know what was going to happen next but she had no choice other than to face it head on.

Chapter Twenty

Whatever God had, or had not got planned for Elizabeth, one thing was certain, nothing could remain a secret for long in a village. May had finally decided to dry up and act a little more in character. The vermilion rhododendrons in the churchyard had opened, and the birds were at long last sorting out their living arrangements.

Though only a short time had passed since she had invited Mick Latimer to use the garage, they had already fallen into a kind of routine. Elizabeth would go and say good morning before going to work and they would exchange pleasantries along the lines of wishing each other a good day and commenting on the weather, and then in the evening when she returned she would pop in again to check all was well.

It was very polite and English and even a little eccentric perhaps, but Elizabeth was quite content to leave things as they were. As always she didn't go looking for trouble, but in a small village like Newton Prideaux, it was never too long before trouble found you.

Elizabeth knew full well that Mick would be spotted soon and it was probably better if she said something first. But the question was how should she go about telling people? Should she bring it up at the next residents' meeting? Or should she just start mentioning it to friends and let it out by the usual osmotic village process?

As it turned out all this would be immaterial because as Elizabeth reached her gate one morning, she bumped into Ron Pickard and his dog Mollie on their way back from fetching the morning paper.

"Morning, Elizabeth," he said. "Nice to see the sun at last."

"Yes, isn't it? It certainly lifts everyone's spirits, doesn't it?"

As she was about to climb into her car Ron said, "I've noticed you've been parking on the road? Is there something the matter with the garage? I should watch that if I were you, that brewery wagon really swings 'round this corner, you know? I've seen him clip the wall a few times. Wouldn't leave it there, if I were you."

And there it was, the opportunity that presented itself and backed you into a corner at the same time! Now she had to explain.

"Yes, thank you. Yes, I know he does," she began. There was no going back now. She couldn't lie again and so she said as casually as she could. "The thing is, I'm letting Mr Latimer, our homeless person, use my garage for a while. It's been much too wet to leave him out on The Green."

Ron's habitually genial countryman's face clouded in an instant. "You've got that vagrant in your garage and you've been leaving your car out here in the wet?" he asked, incredulously. "I'd have thought you had more sense than that, Elizabeth, I would."

"It seemed like the right thing to do," said Elizabeth.

"Did it? Well, I remember that vicar over at Thornbury who let one of our homeless brethren in and he ended up being killed in his own vicarage. Imagine that! He probably thought he was doing the right thing as well. He could be anybody, this tramp. What were you thinking? What would your mother have said?" he added to hammer home his point.

Taking up his stick he strode off up the hill without another word, dragging his little white dog behind him and his spine bridling with indignation.

Elizabeth felt her eyes sting with emotion. Did she really deserve such a reaction? A little shaken, she got into her car and drove away. On her journey she reviewed the exchange and thought of various things she should have said in her own defense, but the moment had passed. She had handled it badly and there would be no second chance. By now Ron would be spreading the word.

It was strange though, that Ron Pickard thought it made more sense for the human being to be out in the rain and the car in the dry. She decided not to say anything about her lodger at work. This at least could be a haven away from the impending trouble at home.

But as luck would have it, work did not shield her completely that morning. A national charity for the homeless had contacted Pearson's looking for donations or sponsorship. This inevitably led to discussions that made Elizabeth more than a little uncomfortable.

Out came the usual apocryphal tales of millionaire beggars who sat on the streets of Oxford all day before returning home in their Mercedes each evening, the beggar by the railway station who always had the latest trainers on his feet, or the beggar who received thousands in benefits but still begged. All the stories that people tell themselves to feel better. Elizabeth could not bring herself to join in. She didn't claim to know if Mick Latimer was a genuine case or not, but she certainly didn't want to discuss it with her colleagues.

When the office had closed, Elizabeth sat outside in her car for a while. It just felt like the safest place to be. All day she had endured people coming dangerously close to her 'secret' which was exhausting enough, but now she had to go home to her cottage and face her neighbours.

As she turned into her lane, she half expected to see a protest, led by Ron Pickard blocking her gateway, but nothing seemed different. Lawrence, having consulted his watch, was sitting on the windowsill waiting for her return and everything else seemed to be just as she had left it that morning.

Thankful that she was finally home she walked up the path and sighed as she turned the key in the front door. Inside, Lawrence would be there to greet her and she could hide away for a while with no one to please but herself. She was still considering getting a small television for her bedroom so that she could retire early if she wanted to, and tonight she wished she had done just that. The thought of a warm bed, TV, closed curtains and Lawrence purring next to her seemed like heaven.

But having fed Lawrence she found herself sitting gloomily in front of the television, wondering what to have for tea and flicking from channel to channel, unable to find anything sufficiently distracting. Lawrence huffed and rearranged himself ostentatiously on her lap as she fidgeted.

"I'm sorry, Lawrence," she said. "I'll just have to pop and see Mr Latimer. I won't be long. Instantly the cat jumped down from her lap and walked away on disapproving stiff back legs, and with one final flick of the tail he left the room.

Elizabeth knew she couldn't rest until she had told Mick that people would now be aware of his presence. She tapped on the connecting kitchen door and went into the garage.

She found her lodger sitting on the old laundry basket eating a sandwich from a triangular plastic package.

"Eh up, I treated meself," he said, raising the food to show her. "I've not got much contingence left now. I'll 'ave to be looking about for a few odd jobs soon."

Elizabeth now felt that her news would be even more unwelcome. If he had had any ideas of looking for work in Newton Prideaux, she was about to burst the bubble.

"So, Elizabeth 'ave you 'ad a good day?" As he spoke Pal got to his feet and came to greet her. He was more excitable than usual and jumped up at her. "Ere, wi's tha goin?" said Mick. "Come 'ere, lad." The dog reluctantly returned to his master. "E's bin a good walk today; 'e's full of 'imself."

"I see," said Elizabeth. "Well, I just thought I'd better tell you that people know you are here now. One of my neighbours caught me on the hop this morning and I had to tell him.

"Oh, I wouldn't worry too much. Folk will 'ave seen me and Pal about. They're not daft."

"I just felt I should tell them properly."

Mick laughed his chesty, laugh. "Ow do you do that, then? Announcement in't local paper? Or just say, oh and by the way I've got a fella livin' in me garridge wi' 'is dog, Pal. Nowt to worry about but I just thought I'd mention it, like."

She didn't feel inclined to laugh, it was serious.

"I'm just afraid you might have difficulty with people, if they know you are staying here in the village," she said.

"Now, it's funny you should say that. I met some locals today. Give me a bit of lip and ripped me coy-it."

"Ripped your what, sorry?" said Elizabeth.

"Me coy-it," he said, holding, up the pocket of his shabby overcoat. "I wouldn't 'ave minded, but it's me best, is this. Three young lads, fancied theirselves as 'ard men."

"Oh, Mr Latimer, I'm so sorry. Are you all right? I bet it was those Yarrow boys, they're always hanging around. Were there three of them? Fair haired?

"Look, it dun't matter. Me and the lad's fine. It were nothin.'"

"Even so, it might be better if you just walked at the back of my cottage, at least for now. I'm so cross with those boys, you haven't caused any trouble."

"Well, it's nice of you to be concerned, Elizabeth, but 'e needs a good walk, does Pal. It's 'im being a collie, you see. 'E needs to be on the go all't time and a garden wouldn't be big enough for him. But thanks anyway. I'm sure I'm owd enough and daft enough to teck care of meself."

"No, not in the garden, Mr Latimer. I know that would be too small. I mean the land beyond that. It belongs to me; well it belongs to the cottage I should say. All that at the back as far down as that old beech tree is mine. He could have a good run around down there and you shouldn't meet so many people as in the village. Just make sure Lawrence isn't about, won't you?"

"Lawrence?"

"My cat. He sometimes likes to hunt in the field."

"Oh, yer cat. Don't worry, Pal won't 'ave nowt to do wi' cats. He just ignores 'em."

"That's settled then. You and Pal are more than welcome to use the fields."

Mick Latimer shrugged. "What can I say? Elizabeth you've shown us real kindness ….. I don't."

The hard edge had all but vanished from his voice, and not wanting to hear his faltering 'thank yous', Elizabeth turned to go.

"Well, you know what they say, Mr Latimer? A stitch in time. I'll go and get my sewing box and I can mend that pocket before it gets any worse.

"I wish you could save it though, eh, Elizabeth?"

"Save what?"

"Time. Just stitch it up and save it."

Chapter Twenty One

Shopping in Newton Prideaux or even Crayton was no longer the same for Elizabeth. Now she felt, rightly or wrongly, that there was an underlying feeling of mistrust, an edge to every conversation. At times she told herself that she was just over thinking everything, that these remarks were not directed at her. What was that phrase Edith had said in her last email…"Honey, it isn't always about you."

Today, standing in the Cottage Loaf Bakery, a mundane conversation about the weather seemed to take a strange turn. Elizabeth knew Susan from the residents' meetings but she didn't seem 'herself.'

"I always think June is such a clean month," said Elizabeth, and having not received a reply, she said, "It's not too hot, just fresh."

"It's better now all that rain has stopped. Two pounds and ten for your loaf please, Elizabeth, "said Susan, briskly.

"Well, I must get on," smiled Elizabeth. "I'm going to get some bedding plants from Forgrove's this afternoon.......for the hanging baskets." Her words fell into a void. Susan was quite clearly not in the mood to chat. "I'll see you at the next meeting, then," proffered Elizabeth as she turned to go.

"If you think it's a good idea," commented Susan, polishing an already spotless counter.

"The meeting?" said Elizabeth "Why?"

"Sorry, just ignore me, ignore me," said Susan, hurriedly and bent down behind the counter to rearrange the cakes.

Outside in the late spring sunshine, Elizabeth felt even more convinced that she wasn't imagining things. By now it was common knowledge that Mick Latimer was staying with her, and instead of the outrage she had feared, she was getting a strange sense of being at war....A cold war.

The looks of disapproval, the mutterings and the odd conversation like that one. If they were trying to make her feel uncomfortable they were succeeding. This was her home and this growing sense of disquiet was something entirely new. At times in the past she had felt stifled and even a little buried by Newton Prideaux but never disapproved of. This was a hard development to accept.

When she reached home, she could hear that Mick was where she had left him, cutting the back lawn. This was the first time she had allowed him to do a chore for her. She had always hated the heavy lawn mower and it seemed to make perfect sense for him to do it, and in return she would pay him. Mick was always very keen to point out that he was no beggar and got his money honestly.

She went through the garage and out into the sunny back garden. Pal immediately barked in greeting and pranced on the spot with excitement.

"Ge ower, Pal!" Mick ordered.

"Mr Latimer, hello! How are you getting on?"

"Fair to middlin', I'd say. Just got this last bit to do. I din't think people 'ad these old mowers any more. You want to get yourself an electric one, Elizabeth. Go mad."

"Mother liked the stripes. Would you like some lunch when you've finished, Mr Latimer? I've just bought a loaf and there's ham."

She knew it was a risk asking him inside, but it was a warm day and with the back door open she felt reasonably safe. After all, Pal and he had been with her for some time now, she had to show them some trust.

Mick grinned. "That'd be very nice, Elizabeth, but please will ya stop callin' me Mr Latimer? Could you manage Mick or Michael even? I've said to you that many times, and it's still Mr Latimer this, Mr Latimer that. I feel as though I'm on't bloody African Queen.

Elizabeth felt her cheeks redden. "Yes, of course I will, Mick," she said stiffly. "I shall go and start the sandwiches."

When she went inside she was surprised to see that Lawrence was back. She had let him out first thing and he was now inside, watching Pal very closely from his observation post on the draining board. When he saw her he stretched and let out the tiniest little squeak of greeting. "Don't worry, I'll save you some ham," she said, running her hand along his slim, dark back.

225

About ten minutes later there was a knock at the door and Mick poked his head in. "I'll just teck off me boots," he said.

Elizabeth was about to politely thank him, but the thought of his feet and socks made her blurt out, "No, please don't worry. Just come straight in."

"Well, if you're sure. Pal, sit! Stay there, now, stay." The dog obediently sat at the threshold and fidgeted himself into a comfortable position.

When Mick sat down at the table, Elizabeth was struck by how very alien it seemed. There had never been a man about the house in her life time and now there was Mr Latimer about to have lunch with her.

In his crumpled shirt, sleeves rolled up, he looked like any number of farm workers who went into Crayton on market day and yet, he didn't belong. His accent, his pallid skin, and slight guardedness all marked him out as a stranger.

Lawrence knew it, and after pacing back and forth along the sink unit, jumped down and left the room. He didn't care for new people invading his patch.

The meal was an uncomfortable half an hour. Elizabeth knew she should not have suggested it as soon as she sat down opposite her guest.

"Nar then, cheers for this, Elizabeth," he said, before biting into his sandwich. This was Mick's version of saying grace, she supposed.

"So," he said, through mouthfuls, "will your lawn be alright for ya?"

"Thank you, yes. It looks much better, now. It's a job I always hate."

"Well, if you've got any more jobs you don't fancy, just gi' us a shout."

They sat in silence for a moment or two, before Elizabeth said, "What brings you to Oxfordshire?" It sounded ridiculously polite, as though she was conversing with someone she had just been introduced to at a party.

"We go where the fancy tecks us, me and Pal. We like the countryside, int' spring and summer, towns and cities int' winter. Other than that, we aren't too fussed."

"Where did you come from originally?" asked Elizabeth. She felt sure that Aunty E would have found a much better way to chat to him than her stilted questions. This seemed to be turning into more of an interrogation than a conversation.

"God's own country, Yorkshire. I'm a Sheffield lad, a Tyke" added Mick.

"Oh," she said. Having had no experience of anywhere outside Oxfordshire, she had no idea what to say about Sheffield.

She ate a little more of her sandwich and hoped she would be struck by inspiration, but all she could find to say was, "What did you do for a living?"

"This an' that. I were a chippie, mostly. I liked that, meckin' stuff for people. Never fancied steel, preferred wood."

Most of this meant little to Elizabeth and so she chose to nod in lieu of a comment, which might just highlight her ignorance about the world. If only she had Edith's gift for making people feel at ease. What she really longed to know was why he was, as he was, homeless and jobless, but how does one ask a question like that?

"So, what about you then Elizabeth? You've lived 'ere a long time, then?" said Mick.

"As I said, all my life, Mr Lat...."

"Oh, right, well, it seems a nice enough sort o' place. Bit different to where I grew up, but never mind. So what is there to keep you occupied 'ere then? I know about your job, but what else do you do?"

"I have Lawrence, of course. I'm on the residents' committee and I have St Martin's. So I stay quite busy really."

"Oh aye, I can see that."

"Don't you miss having a home, Mick?" she said suddenly. For at that moment it struck her just how awful it must be, to not have any sort of foundation in your life, a place where you hid from all the hardships, a place where you went to recover. Mick had nothing.

"Now and again, I s'pose, but sometimes you're better wi' out."

The sadness of his statement cast an immediate shadow over them. Like the sun going in.

"When you said, you would like to stitch time up and save it, the other day, was there a piece of time you were thinking about in particular? Were you thinking about your home?"

"No, it were nowt like that. Just thinkin' about when me kids were very little, I s'pose. When I were still their infallible dad.

"You must miss them," she said, but before she could pursue this further, Mick smiled.

"Tell you what I do miss," he said, rubbing his straggly beard. "Northern friendliness and sense of humour. Nobody has a laff down here. They don't speak to you, or say 'ow do. It's not what I'm used to. That dark 'aired woman that's about, always looks daggers at me whenever she sees me. I've done nowt to 'er, so far as I know."

"Dark haired woman?" queried Elizabeth.

"Aye, sometimes, wears 'at pulled right down."

"Oh, Bunny! You mean Bunny!"

"That 'er name? I saw her goin' along singin' at top of 'er voice, t'other day. As soon as she saw me, she got a right face on."

"Poor Bunny. Don't take it personally. She isn't, well, she doesn't mean any harm."

"Not the full shillin'?" commented Mick, almost to himself.

"She's like me. We have always lived here, part of the fixtures and fittings. I suppose we are both quite odd in our own ways."

"If you say so. Now, Elizabeth, sorry to trouble you, but is there any more tea in that pot?"

She reached over and poured him another cup. "Eh, Elizabeth. Did you 'ear about owd fella, walkin' through Sheffield wi' 'is wife? Well, they come to this fancy restaurant and 'is wife says, 'Oh, smell that. Dun't it smell grand.' So, fella thinks to 'imself, you only live once, and we've been married goin' on forty year. I'll treat 'er. So they walked passed it again."

Elizabeth waited for the next part of the story. She looked at Mick, who by now was grinning expectantly.

"So, what did they do, Mr Latimer?" she enquired.

"Oh, Elizabeth- it's a joke!"

"I see. I'm sorry, I didn't quite get it….."

"Not to worry, it's northern humour. Like I said, you all seem so serious down here. You should laff more, you know? It does ya good, to have a right good laff now and again."

Embarrassed, Elizabeth began to tidy the plates from the table, "Yes, you are probably right, I know I can be a little serious."

"Its bein' on your own so much. You just need a bit of practice, that's all," said her guest, leaning back and stretching. As he did so, Elizabeth noticed the huge sweat patches under each arm and couldn't help but stare.

"Would you like to use my kitchen to have a wash in?" she said. "Yourself, your clothes. I mean if you want to…?" She had not even considered this sentence before it left her mouth; it just felt the obvious thing to say.

"Really? I mean, I do me best, but that would be great. Obviously you'd not want me tramping in when you are 'avin' your tea but if I could use it sometime."

"I'll let you know a convenient time then, Mr Latimer."

Sensing that this was the end of the conversation he got to his feet.

"Right then, cleanliness is next to Godliness or so they say. Not that I'm one for God these days. We've not spoken in years. I'll be off now then."

"Oh, Mr…. Mick, I've left some money for you, on the work top there. Thank you again."

As her lunch guest went out, leaving a lingering smell of sweat, biscuits and cigarettes behind him, Elizabeth wondered for the millionth time if she had really been wise offering to share her home with this stranger and his dog.

Chapter Twenty Two

Flaming June had turned into a barely smoldering July. Each day the grey clouds swept in from the east and sat stubbornly over the village and surrounding countryside, making it feel more like autumn than the height of summer. Elizabeth had been looking forward to the lighter evenings but under that dull canopy it barely seemed to make a difference at all.

Spring's heavy rain had at least moved on, but Elizabeth's lodgers had not. Mick and Pal seemed quite content to stay in her garage and as each week passed, more and more little routines began to establish themselves. Mick now came in to wash just after Elizabeth left for work each morning although the rest of the cottage was still closed to him. They had taken to sharing a cup of tea and a chat on Saturday and Mick had done a few small jobs about the place, like mending old furniture and fitting a cat flap for Lawrence. It all felt both very strange and yet familiar at the same time.

Sometimes Elizabeth thought that she really ought to ask about his long term plans but that would have meant confronting the situation and that was something she didn't really want to do. Similarly she had chosen to resign from the Residents' Committee rather than face any fuss or unpleasantness. She knew Dina and Ron had been furious and so she typed a letter of resignation and furtively slipped it under Ron's door early one morning.

Once it was done it came as somewhat of a relief to her. She would have those Wednesday evenings back again and she certainly wouldn't miss Dina's attempts to 'bring her out of herself' or Ron and his obsession with Newton Prideaux Bloomers. She knew her mother would have said it was cowardice on her part, but as always Elizabeth chose the peaceful option.

She also found that she now preferred to go to the evening service at St Martin's. There were fewer people there at that time and on Sunday mornings she always felt just a little afraid of being buttonholed by someone about Mick. One gloomy evening, as she was returning from Church, something shining on the road caught her eye. It was just next to one of her front tyres and as she got closer she could make out little fragments of amber glass. One of her headlights was in pieces and the surrounding paintwork was scuffed and scratched.

And so Ron's prophecy had come to pass. She had no doubt that the brewery lorry had clipped it, just as he had said it would. Sadly she patted the bonnet of her poor car and promised to restore its 'eye' as soon as she could. It had been a bad place to park, but what else could she have done in the circumstances? For a few days at least she would now be walking down to the main road to catch the Oxford Bus.

Life had been very strange since her mother had died. Elizabeth had imagined that it would go along much as before, but with her taking baby steps into the world of independence. She had been afraid and thrilled about being on her own but as it turned out, life had not taken that path at all. She now had a Siamese cat who she worshipped and a virtual stranger living in her garage. Both of these things would have seemed so unlikely to the 'old Elizabeth' that it gave her a strange bubble of laughter inside when she thought of it. Given that she had discovered she had no talent for guessing what the future might bring, she now wondered where life might lead her next.

Aunty E, of course, was jubilant. In her e-mails she could almost hear her laughing as Elizabeth's life took each new turn. Going out for coffee and a visit to the hairdressers now seemed very mild changes indeed.

You certainly seem to pick up strays honey! Good for you. Let your heart tell you what to do. It's all part of living! Edith had said in her last e-mail. And it was true. At least Elizabeth felt alive, even if it was a little disturbing at times.

On Saturday morning Mick knocked on the back door, having finished weeding the side borders for her.

"Eh up, Elizabeth, are you there?" he called.

"Yes, yes, come in. I'll put the kettle on. Have you finished the borders?"

"I 'ave, I forgot what it's like to 'ave a garden."

"Really? You miss it?"

"You're joking, all that work? No, it's a pain in the arse, is gardening!"

237

There was a silence for a moment, as the words sunk in. Elizabeth cleared her throat and Mick said quickly, "'Scuse my French."

He sat at the table and waited.

"I've got cake for us, today. I hope you like coffee and walnut."

"Cake's cake in my book. I'll 'ave what's goin'," he said, smiling. "You know what we call this?" he added. "Avin' us snap"

"Snap?" said Elizabeth.

"Aye, your food. A small meal, I suppose."

"I see. Well then, here is your *snap* and a cup of coffee," Elizabeth said, awkwardly.

They both stayed silent for a few moments, Elizabeth pondering on the bad language and how shocked she had been when it had slipped into the conversation. Did it really matter that much? It was just a word. She was distracted from her thoughts though, by Pal wandering in from the garden and flopping down at her feet. He offered his soft underbelly up for fuss. "Ay! 'Oo said you was allowed in 'ere? Go on, back out on't yard!" said his master.

"It's all right, Mick let him stay. Lawrence is sleeping upstairs. He'll probably have a good sniff around later, but it's okay. Let him sit with us."

As she stroked the slightly gritty fur and pulled out a couple of dried leaves from its shaggy whiteness, Elizabeth felt at peace. The thick doggy smell, mingled with the cake and coffee made her feel strangely serene and safe, as though this was how things were supposed to be. It felt that both she and the cottage were truly alive. She pictured Lawrence sleeping peacefully on her bed upstairs, and listened to the mellow sound of the kitchen clock keeping time. It seemed to her that this was one of those fleeting magical moments when everything seems to be right.

She looked across at Mick. What had God got in mind when he sent him to her? Yes, it had brought trouble into her quiet life, but it felt like a good sort of trouble. Pal's head shot up and he looked at her accusingly with soft brown eyes. She had been so lost in thought, she had stopped stroking him. "Sorry, Pal, I was miles away," she said, soothingly.

"You were, weren't you, Elizabeth? Penny for 'em?" enquired Mick.

"Oh, just wondering about God and his plans," she replied.

"I see. Well, as I said, me and him fell out years since, so I can't help you there, I'm afraid."

"Mick," she said, changing the subject, "when you are on the road, where do you normally stay? I mean, people don't usually take you in, do they?" Her companion exhaled and pulled a wry face.

"No, they don't. In fact, this is the first time ever, if I'm 'onest. I normally sleep rough, you know? If I'm in a town or something, I'll find some cardboard, thick stuff is best, and settle somewhere. A doorway, a public loo even, just a bit of shelter. I've got me tent but it's not warm enough for winter time. If I've managed to get some cash in the day, sellin' Big Issue or summat, I'll travel on the night buses for a warm. Bus stations are good as well. The cities are best in winter. Countryside's too cold, no shelter. We survive, Pal and me. You learn, you know. You pick things up from other street folk. The biggest worry is being attacked and that's 'appenin' more an' more. But 'e's pretty handy to have by," he said, looking at Pal.

Elizabeth was appalled, he spoke about it in such a matter of fact way. Sleeping on the cold streets, being attacked, it was a world away from her upbringing. Restrictive though it may have been, she was never afraid, never in danger, or even very cold for that matter.

"But what about hostels and things?" she said. She had given money to support hostels, they must help people like Mick, mustn't they?

He laughed and shook his head.

"Well, apart from the fact a good many of 'em are run by God botherers - no offence…… they won't teck him," he said, nodding down at Pal, "and we come as a pair, the lad an' me. Anyway after three days or so they meck you put in a claim to the social and I won't 'ave that, you see, Elizabeth?"

"Too proud?" she enquired, raising an eyebrow.

"No, nowt like that. It's just, if I own up, if I register for owt I can be found, can't I? And I don't want to be found. I wish to remain anonymous," he declared with a heavy touch of irony.

"Found? But why not?" said Elizabeth. "Why don't you want to be found? What about your children? Don't you want them to find you, ever?" For a moment Mick Latimer was silent, his hand resting across his mouth. Then he raised his eyes to Elizabeth's and smiled the weary grey smile she had seen on that first day on The Green.

"No, I don't want 'em to find me. They're better off without me. Their mum, she's much stronger than me. She'll teach 'em 'ow to cope wi' life. What they should want and 'ow to go about gettin' it. I could never do that. Look at me, all as I've got is 'im." He smiled down at the sleepy dog at their feet.

In that moment Elizabeth's little golden moment had passed and been engulfed by harsh reality. Whatever Mick's full story was, she had just seen a very sad little snap shot of it.

"Any road, I'd best crack on. Thought I might teck this lad a good wander this afternoon and we can play a few games," he said, ruffling the dogs head affectionately.

"Yes, I should go too," said Elizabeth, automatically gathering the cups and plates together. "I have to take the car to the garage."

"Oh aye, your 'eadlight. I noticed that."

"It'll have been the brewery lorry delivering to the pub. I was warned."

"I don't reckon it were, you know. Its bin dead quiet up 'ere. We 'eard it go, din't we Pal? There were no lorry about."

"Oh," said Elizabeth "Well, how could it…"

"I reckon it were deliberate. I reckon somebody 'ad a go at yer car?"

"Who would do that, for goodness' sake?" said Elizabeth, beginning to feel uneasy.

"Well, I didn't see, but you 'ave got some odd uns about. What about that Bunny lass?"

"Bunny Kitteridge? No, Mick she's harmless, like a child really. She wouldn't do something like that."

"You're probably right, but kids can get up to mischief, you know?"

Mick left the kitchen and the last few embers of Elizabeth's glow were extinguished.

Chapter Twenty Three

Over the last few months, as Elizabeth had driven home from work, she had developed a guilty habit of looking towards Heron House. She automatically checked for signs of life, - lights on in the house, wheelie bins out for collection. It was only tonight that she realised that she was no longer under any obligation to visit its occupant. She had resigned from the committee and so it was nothing to do with her any more. If Maggie wanted to festoon her house with decorations or not, it was up to her and Elizabeth felt liberated.

She was still feeling relieved when she arrived home. Just her, Lawrence and a nice cup of tea was all she required to make her happy. Sometimes she even felt guilty that she was so happy to just stay at home. It didn't seem very exciting, this new life she was forging for herself, but what did people do, really? Nobody in Newton Prideaux seemed to have a very exciting life and so for now at least, she was happy to hide in her rut.

As she went into her cottage and closed the front door, Lawrence came running from the direction of the kitchen. Clearly he had had a busy day and had a lot to tell her. He reached up with his front paws, like a little boy wanting to be picked up and Elizabeth was happy to oblige.

Holding his warm, brown fur next to her face, she drew in his scent: musky, with just a hint of moss and grass, all mingled together to make the intoxicating fragrance peculiar to Lawrence. She kissed his head and held him a little closer. She would not have believed just how much she could love another living being.

After a few moments Lawrence decided he wanted to get down and began to wriggle his head down and under her elbow. It was a classic Lawrence 'get off mum, you are being too soppy' move and so, reluctantly she let him go.

As she did so the phone began to ring and Elizabeth went to answer it. Before she had even managed to say hello, Dina's voice flashed out of the receiver! "What's all this nonsense Ron tells me about you resigning?" she snapped.

Feeling much as she had done, when her mother had used that tone of voice with her, Elizabeth recoiled, "Yes, I'm sorry," she mumbled, nervously, "but I just don't think I was really much good at being on the committee."

"Well, you've hardly given it a chance, have you? You can't expect to be good at something straight away. You need to join in more, say your piece. But I don't think that's really it, is it?"

"Sorry?" said Elizabeth.

"I don't know how to say this. But I think you are just doing this to avoid the issue of your…….. , well, that young man in your garage. I'm sorry but it's appalling of you. You must know the village is up in arms over this. It's time you sent him packing. I know you think it's being Christian but it stopped raining a long time ago now and you need to think of your friends and neighbours. That would be truly Christian. Love thy neighbour, Elizabeth!"

And so it had finally happened. Dina had broken the British taboo and mentioned the unmentionable. Elizabeth knew it would probably happen at some point, but as always, she had been hoping it would somehow pass her by. She had prepared no defence and so she merely said, "Yes, yes I know, Dina. It's only temporary. I'll sort something out."

"Good. It really does need to stop, you know? Anyway, I expect to see you at the next meeting. Goodbye for now."

Elizabeth looked at Lawrence sitting tidily on the rug. His brown whiskers were pushed forward with interest and his frown lines deeper than ever. He knew, it was quite clear from his expression - he knew that she was going to defy Dina.

On Thursday evening as Elizabeth was returning from Church, she was forced to take a detour, having spotted Dina watering her tubs and tidying her already immaculate garden. Although it was true that she had decided to ignore her ferocious little neighbour's orders, she didn't want a face to face confrontation and so, as it was a pleasant summer evening, she took a slightly longer way home.

As she crossed The Green she met Bryan McConway heading for The Cock. He smiled when he spotted her. "Just off for my medicine, Elizabet'. I don't suppose you'd care to join me?"

She was about to say no, when a sudden rebellious thought came into her head. Why not? She didn't have to drink alcohol and she was sure

Auntie E wouldn't have wanted her to turn down a drink with her old friend 'Mr Irish'.

"Thank you, Bryan," she said. "I think I will." It wasn't all about rebellion of course. For a while now, she had felt very alone with her 'Mick situation' and she welcomed the chance to talk, especially with Bryan. He had that knack of always making her feel comfortable.

The pub was beginning to fill up as they arrived. Roger had declared Thursdays were Curry Club Nights and they were proving popular, at least with people from neighbouring villages. Elizabeth didn't see any of her neighbours there.

"What'll it be then?" said Bryan as they reached the bar.

"Could I have a cola, please?"

Bryan nodded and shouted out to Roger, "A Jamieson's and a Coke, please when you've the time, my friend." Then to Elizabeth he commented, "He's not too happy at the moment, you know?"

"Well, he seems very busy."

"No, it's not that, he loves it busy. It's yer village committee, wanting him to change the name of the pub."

"Change it? What to?"

"Aren't you on the committee, yourself? I thought you'd know. Well, apparently The Cock is vulgar, and they don't like Roger having a bit of fun with the name, like he does. They want it called The Prideaux Arms or some such nonsense."

"But it's always been called The Cock."

"Well, that's the latest I heard. It's too vulgar and needs to go. So how are tings with you, Elizabet'?

Roger arrived with the drinks at that moment. "All right both?" he said.

"Your curry night is going well, so," said Bryan.

"Yeah, I regret sayin' a free drink with each curry, though. I must have been feelin' generous," he grinned.

As he disappeared to the kitchen Bryan said, "It's a shame, you know. He works his balls off to make this place a success!"

Again Elizabeth found herself trying not to flinch at the expletive.

"Anyway, you were about to tell me how the world is treating you."

"Very well, thank you. Myself and Lawrence are in the pink."

"Aah, that cat of yours, he has a good life. I think I might just come back as a cat next time. I would love that, sitting on the ladies' laps and getting totally spoilt. And how is your, well, what'll I call him?"

"Mr Latimer?"

"Yer man in the shed."

"Oh, he's fine."

"You know, I think that was a very Christian thing that you did there, taking him in."

"Hmm, not everybody is happy about it I'm afraid. I really don't know if I was foolish."

"For what it's worth I think you are doing a grand thing. I remember a tramp I knew, Bish, was his name, or at least that's the name he went by. He used to turn up at the hotel in Birmingham regular as clockwork. Always came to the back door and we'd help him out wid a little bit of food from the kitchen. Bits and pieces, even a few bob when he was stuck. Ah God, I can see him now. Big shock of dark curly hair, he had and a face as white as a sheet. You know he had such big blue eyes, any girl would have loved them. But he worried me. He always look liked a good puff of wind could have blown him away.

I suppose like most people, I didn't give him a lot of thought, not as a person I mean. He was just a homeless man I helped out. I took him to be on drugs or something, clearly things weren't right with him. You'd ask him a question and he'd go rambling off about something totally different. And then other times, he'd turn up and shout at ya, even as you were trying to help him. I used to think it was terrible what drugs could do to you. But ya know, we all have our weaknesses, don't we? I wouldn't judge.

I remember, the staff, myself included, used to talk about Bish a lot. We liked him but they did wonder why he didn't just sort himself out. He

251

was a bright a young man. When he was off the drugs his mind was sharp and quick. He could have had a career or at least a job.

And then one day his sister came to find me. Bish had passed on. He died of pneumonia. Apparently he had been carrying a serviette from the hotel with my name written on it when they found him.

She said Robert, that was his name it turned out, had told her about us at the hotel. He had schizophrenia. It wasn't the drugs that made him like he was. It was the lack of them, well proper medication at least. She told me people like him just fall through the cracks. It's not like having an addiction where you can go on a programme and get clean. They aren't always self-inflicted wounds.

She said to me, when he left home he told their mother he was going to find his lost tribe. She didn't think he found it. But at least he found a little bit of kindness from me and my staff, and she was grateful for that. You know, that girl stuck in my mind. It's true what she said, they aren't all self-inflicted troubles. They just fall through the cracks. So, if you can help your man and stop him falling, I say good luck to you, Elizabet'." He raised his glass.

252

"Thank you, Bryan," she said. It was unusual to hear him tell a story that wasn't funny or didn't have a nice tidy ending, and it made her inclined to believe it. Perhaps she really was helping Mick and not just being used. "I know he'll have to move on at some point, of course. But I want it to be when he's ready. When he's got something else lined up. Does that make sense?"

"Indeed, it does, Elizabet', indeed it does. And in the meantime, here's to helping our fellow men, eh? Roger, same again over here when you've a moment."

"No, no, no, not for me, Mr McConway," said Elizabeth, finishing her drink. "I have to get back, but thank you for telling me about that young man."

As she turned to leave Bryan leant over and kissed her on the cheek. "You're a good soul, Elizabet'. Don't let anyone persuade you otherwise."

Chapter Twenty Four

Around midday on Saturday, as Elizabeth was returning home with her weekly shopping, she found herself beginning to feel quite agitated. She had got used to Mick popping in for lunch at the weekend and this was the first time in weeks she hadn't had any little jobs for him to do. She knew that it was perfectly fine of course, but all the same, it had left her feeling a tad guilty.

As she unpacked her groceries, the fresh bread caught her eye and she couldn't help wondering if she should have invited him in as usual, just for a chat. It was so difficult to know the right path to take.

As it turned out, Mick solved her dilemma by sticking his head in at the back door and saying, "Eh up. Are we 'avin' a bite t' eat together, as usual, Elizabeth?"

She felt a strange mixture of emotions, both comforting and disturbing at the same time. She was glad to see him, but it was also worryingly familiar, as though she was being taken for granted. With things as they were, she couldn't begin to see herself raising the subject of him moving on.

Mick Latimer slumped down at the table and ran his hand through his hair, "That couple doin' the cottage up seem all right," he said. "'Ad quite a chat with the bloke the other day. He's a bit posh but, there's no side to 'im at all. Quite down to earth, I thought."

Elizabeth didn't answer. She was still thinking how strange and difficult the situation had become. It had seemed a simple enough thing to invite someone in from the cold and rain, but she was beginning to learn that the freedom to make her own decisions came at a cost.

She knew she should have to talk with him about his plans soon, especially after Dina's complaint, but what Bryan had said had stayed in her mind. She couldn't take the chance of letting Mick fall.

"Yaw right, Elizabeth?" enquired Mick.

"Yes, yes I'm fine. I was just concentrating, sorry. So, you are getting to know our little village a bit more then?"

"S'pose, I am, yes. Tell you what I do find odd, where are all the kids? It's all old folk. Did summat 'appen? Were there a pied piper as come and took 'em all off?"

Elizabeth handed him his sandwich. "There are children. They just tend to live in the houses on that little estate. The new houses are almost like a separate village of their own. We only come together for special events, like fetes."

"Why don't they live in't village? I'd a thought it would be better for the nippers?"

"Houses are too expensive around here, Mick. Young people can't afford to buy them."

"That's one thing I 'ope for my kids. That they can afford their own homes one day. If you've got that, you're safe."

"What are their names? Your children."

"Ernie and Willow. I've a photo in me pack, I'll dig it out for you. I'm not in touch with the ex now, so it's not an up to date picture but I'll show you anyway. They are great kids. Best thing I've ever done in my life was 'avin them."

Elizabeth felt baffled to hear him speak like this. He didn't live with his children and it seemed that he had abandoned them, and yet he spoke like that about them. She wanted to ask why, but her courage failed her so instead, she said, "I grew up without a father. It's difficult. You always feel different from your friends. Like you are missing out."

"I s'pose it all depends on what sort of father, dun't it?" Mick said, biting into his sandwich.

This time Elizabeth's curiosity got the better of her and she said, "But why do you feel you were so bad for them, Mick? It seems such a shame not to see them grow up. How old would they be now?"

"Well, Ernie, he'll be ten in October and Willow is just turned eight. It is a shame. You're right, but it just weren't working out with me and the Mrs. It were no good for them kids, seeing us argue all't time. An' anyway, their mum has a better grip on things than I ever 'ad. I'm a bit of a dreamer, yer see. Never was that good wi' reality. I can see that now, but at the time, I were young. I wanted us to go travelling, as a family, see a bit of the world, yer know? Before they 'ad to go to school."

"Is that practical with very young children?" said Elizabeth.

"No, not at all. But I thought it were. And I thought Mandie did too. That's the thing wi' you women, no offence intended, but you pretend a lot."

"Pretend, Mick. What do you mean? What do we pretend about?"

"Loads of things! Take Mandie. When I met her at Tramlines Festival, she were a proper wild child, full o' fun. Then, once we'd moved in together, it were all different and once the kids came along, well, that really did change things. All of a sudden she wants a posh 'ouse, somewhere like Gren-ill, or Totley……."

Mick stopped because at that moment they both became aware of a curious noise coming from outside. At the same time Pal began to howl outside the back door and Lawrence came into the kitchen with his tail bristled and lashing, and then went to hide behind the washing machine.

The sound was coming from the front of the cottage. Both Mick and Elizabeth got to their feet and went into the main room closely followed by a barking Pal.

Looking through the window they could make out a cluster of people staring at something on The Green, but they couldn't see what was holding their attention.

"What on earth is going on?" said Elizabeth. "Let's go and see if everything is all right?" She opened the front door and the wailing sound grew louder.

It was a human voice and it was 'singing' a song. At least it sounded like one, a tune that Elizabeth felt she almost knew but not quite. It rose in dramatic crescendos and trailed off to tender, quieter passages, all without seeming to have any discernible words.

Bunny Kitteridge was there on The Green, 'singing' at the top of her voice, flinging her arms out and throwing back her head like a spangled diva.

"Chuffin' 'ell," said Mick, in bewilderment. "What's she doin'?"

People stood and stared, and Elizabeth became more and more uncomfortable. It really was horribly embarrassing and nobody seemed willing or able to stop it.

"Do you do requests?" someone called out, obviously feeling this was a chance to be witty, but Elizabeth shrank inside. Should she go and talk to Bunny? Try and stop her?

Finally, Ellen Kitteridge arrived, walking across The Green toward her daughter, with her head down to avoid meeting anyone's eye. She was the embodiment of embarrassment, a slight figure, barely big enough to cope with this huge responsibility.

"Bunny," she called softly. "Bunny, that's enough singing now. Come on. Come home with me". She reached out and took her daughter's stubby hand in hers, only to have it snatched away. "Bunny! Please, it's time to go now."

Like a huge, angry toddler, Bunny shook her head and folded her arms across her chest.

Elizabeth could stand it no longer. "Come on Mick," she said, "let's go and help."

She walked over to where Bunny was standing resolutely and said, "Hello, Bunny. Would you like to come to my house?" Bunny glowered out from under her brows but remained silent.

"Oh, it's a shame is that," said Mick, in a voice very unlike his usual gruff one, "cos, Elizabeth has just med me a lovely sandwich and

I bet she'd meck one for you. And I tell you summat else an' all, my dog, Pal 'ere would love some fuss, if you've got time. We could have a little party." Bunny considered this and looked at Pal, who was helpfully wagging his tail encouragingly.

"A party?" she asked.

"Aye, if yer like."

"That would be very nice, wouldn't it, Bunny?" soothed Ellen, gently trying to guide Bunny towards the cottage. "Shall we go in?"

Elizabeth was relieved to see Bunny begin to move and make her way towards the cottage, leaving the curious and the callous standing, disappointed that the show had ended.

"Mick," Elizabeth whispered, "well done. She loves parties."

"Bloody mad 'atters tea party," Mick hissed back, with just a hint of his usual husky laugh in his voice.

Inside the cottage, Ellen's relief was obvious. She sat down on the kitchen chair and almost appeared to melt into it. "Thank you so

261

much, Elizabeth. This is so kind of you," she said, wearily.

By now Bunny was stroking Pal and talking quietly to him.

"I just thought this would be nearer for you than home," said Elizabeth, "and I'm sure you didn't want all those people standing about staring. I'll make Bunny her sandwich and if I can find any, we can all have some biscuits too. This is Mr Latimer, by the way, Ellen. My guest."

Mick and Ellen briefly exchanged polite smiles. "Of course I know why she is doing this," said Ellen, abruptly. "We went into Oxford a few weeks ago and she saw a man busking. He was singing opera and she was absolutely fascinated. I couldn't get her away from him. He did have a beautiful voice and he had drawn quite a crowd, but it did make life very……. difficult."

Elizabeth handed round a plate of sandwiches, noting Mick was happy to take another one, even though they had just eaten.

"Well," he said, "I'll leave you to it, ladies. I'll share this with Pal.   Nice to 'ave met you both."

And with that he was gone.

As she watched him shamble down the garden with Pal jumping up at his side, she couldn't help reflecting on how good he had been with Bunny. How unlike his usual self he had seemed, not so gruff. He hadn't sounded like the Mick she knew…. He had sounded like a father.

Chapter Twenty Five

That year the autumn mornings began to arrive early. It was only the end of August, but already the Rowan tree's orange berries had turned to a deep red and the light had taken on an altogether more hazy and golden quality almost overnight.

Looking out of her kitchen window across the fields, Elizabeth could make out the shimmer of yellow leaves here and there amongst the green. Could it really be that the year had passed its prime so suddenly? It hardly felt as though they had had any summer at all. Next month the harvest would begin, and once that happened Elizabeth always got a sense that the countryside was drawing in on itself, retreating until the winter had passed.

Moving her gaze from the glimmering fields, she finished packing her lunch for work, and told herself that there may still be chance yet, for an Indian summer, and that she had things to look forward to. It was Friday and the weekend ahead was a long one. Monday was a bank holiday and unusually she had received two invitations: Sophie and Robin had asked her to a barbeque on Sunday, and Leon and Rachael had asked her to come and view the cottage on Monday. It made her feel quite excited having two social events. It was almost like being a normal person.

As she passed through the hall to get her bag she became aware that she had trodden on something. It was a little early for the postman but someone had pushed a note through her letter box, a small piece of lemon coloured note paper folded sharply in half. Another invitation?

Elizabeth picked it up, unfolded it and read the type written message,

"Do-gooders like you don't deserve

to live amongst decent people. Get

rid of him."

After staring at it for a few seconds she felt its contamination seep onto her fingers and she dropped it hurriedly down on the hall table. Who on earth would do that? Its sly, spiteful nature shook her and her stomach fluttered in shock.

Afterwards, as she went about her day, the letter kept creeping into her mind, a dark little sliver of unease. Who would have done such an awful thing? She wasn't hurting anyone and neither was Mick. Why were people so very concerned with what she chose to do with her own garage?

The day at work that followed was a difficult one. She felt jolted and anxious, as though she was only half present. At lunchtime she sat and brooded. She tried to read her book but in fact spent the time wondering what, if anything, she should be doing about the note? Some people would have gone straight to the police of course, but that seemed such a serious thing to do, over such a small thing. It wasn't as if there had been a threat in the letter, it had just made her feel uncomfortable. As always, Elizabeth concluded that the best thing to do was to ignore it. Tonight she would put it in her wheelie bin and forget all about it.

But that evening, before she had a chance to remove the offensive note, her phone rang. For just the briefest of moments, she irrationally thought that the person behind the note would now be on the end of the line. Her heart quickened as she picked up the phone. To her relief, Laura's smiling voice greeted her. "Hello there, Elizabeth. It's Laura. How is that wee boy of yours doing?"

"Laura, he's absolutely fine. He's here with me now, wanting to be picked up as usual." Lawrence was indeed stretching up her leg and patting her with his paw.

"Well, I should think so too! How dare you be talking to me instead of paying attention to him? He is a SIAMESE, after all," joked Laura. "Now, the reason I'm calling is because I've received some information about Lawrence. Apparently, the family were going through his previous owner's things and found some of his paperwork."

Elizabeth couldn't imagine cats having 'paperwork' and so she just said, "Oh, really."

"Yes, I've his pedigree here, his registration details and his vaccination record. Would you like me to post them on to you?"

"Thank you, yes. I'd better have them, hadn't I?"

"His vet's, are over near Bicester. Do you know Smullen and Scott?"

"I can't say I do. But if Lawrence goes there, I'll find it."

"Good girl, that's the spirit. Better for them to go to people they know. And they're a good practice."

After chatting for a while, Elizabeth felt that, like a doting mother, she was boring Laura with details of Lawrence's cute little foibles, and decided it was time to politely 'let her get on'. She must hear these tales from adoring owners all the time.

Picking Lawrence up and holding his lean body over her shoulder like a baby, she went to make their evening meals and the letter was completely forgotten. It remained so, until on her way to bed that night she caught sight of the yellow folded sheet still sitting on the hall table. Decisively she scrunched it up and tossed it up the stairs.

"There you are, Lawrence," she said. "You can have that."

****

Elizabeth had never been to a veterinary practice before, but clearly Lawrence had, because he had wailed non-stop since his cat carrier appeared in the hall. Now he was in the waiting room he had turned his volume up a few more notches, and was making a heart rending cry. It clearly told everyone he had been kidnapped and brought here against his will. Brought to this awful place that smelled peculiar and where dogs were free to wander up and look at you! The other pet owners, scattered around the room on plastic chairs, smiled indulgently and one lady even remarked, jokingly, "Someone isn't happy."

But Elizabeth couldn't laugh and join in. She hated hearing Lawrence so distressed, and yet if she spoke to him, he shouted all the louder.

"Woe–ooo, Woe--oo! Woe-oo!" His screaming had now reached gale force and he was scrabbling at the door of the carrier.

Trying her best to wait calmly, Elizabeth busied herself by looking at the vaccination record she was holding tensely in her hand. She had been delighted to find that Lawrence had a pedigree name and a proper official birthday. She didn't know why but both of these things gave her enormous pleasure.

Pet's Name: Lorelei Brown Bournville.

Breed: Siamese

Date of birth/age: 1.2. 2011

Sex: Male

Description: Chocolate Point

Learning things about Lawrence's life before they met seemed so exciting. Things that of course he could never tell her. She wondered how he had looked, when he came into the world on that 1st day of February four years ago and what his first owner, Mrs Whiting, had been like. It was like solving a puzzle.

The vet came to the door of his consulting room and called for "Fluffy Stubbs," and a large lady with an ancient looking cat basket creaked to her feet. Elizabeth relaxed, it wasn't her this time. But no sooner had she resumed looking at Lawrence's papers than another vet came out and said sharply,

"Lawrence Menier? Would you come through please?"

Elizabeth went into the consulting room and the door was closed behind her. She put

Lawrence in his carrier onto the examination table and waited. The silence grew until she found herself fidgeting and fiddling with her watch. At length the vet turned from his computer and said,

"Hello, I'm John Smullen. I've just been reading Lawrence's records and I see his vaccinations are late."

John Smullen was a tall man with closely cropped grey hair and what her mother would have described as patrician features. In his spotless button across blue top, he looked the epitome of sterile efficiency and competence, and Elizabeth found him utterly intimidating.

"Yes, I'm sorry, Mr Smullen. I have only recently been furnished with that information," she said …… *Why on earth was she talking like that? Furnished? She never used that word!* There was something about this sharp middle aged man that made her feel the need to be very formal.

"I see. Well, let's have a look at him. He has seen my colleague in the past I see, but I won't hold that against him."

Skilfully John Smullen extricated the now silent cat from his box and stood him on the table. Elizabeth almost felt she had to stand to attention for this solemn moment. This vet really was a very curt man. She wondered if he was the unpopular one that no one wanted to see.

But Mr Smullen surprised her. As he turned to his patient, his whole demeanour changed. His upright stance altered and his voice softened noticeably.

"Hello, Lawrence," he said, gently running his hand along the cat's back. "That's a fine name, my friend. A good name for a good cat, hmmm?" As the examination proceeded he continued chat to Lawrence. "You know, I have always rather liked you Siamese. Apart from your good looks, of course. I think it's because you are somewhere between a dog and a cat. You have personality and you love your humans." It seemed that Elizabeth was no longer required, that Lawrence and the vet were now in their own private little conversation and so she stood awkwardly looking on.

Finally the examination was over and the vaccination had been administered to the back of Lawrence's neck. To Elizabeth's amazement he hardly even seemed to notice it and went on happily purring at the vet.

"There," said John, filling in the vaccination card. "He's in good condition, nothing really to worry about. He has marvellous fangs, doesn't he?"

Elizabeth was completely taken aback. "I'm sorry his vaccinations were late," she said, not knowing what else to say.

"Oh, don't worry. There is always about three month's leeway with these things. By the way, his teeth might need attention in the future. It's the breed I'm afraid, narrow jaws. A small op will sort that out."

Elizabeth was horrified. An operation! She hadn't considered anything like that. She made a little sound somewhere between a gasp and a gulp and instinctively reached out to touch Lawrence.

John Smullen looked up. "It's nothing to worry about. It's very routine," he said. This was the first time he had actually looked her in the eyes. He smiled. "Is this your first cat by any chance?"

"Yes, he's my first pet actually."

273

"I see. It's frightening being responsible for another living soul, isn't it, Miss Menier?"

Elizabeth felt herself relax. Some of his previous abruptness had left his voice.

"You can ring the practice for advice any time, you know? My nurses are very good, but if you would rather speak to me, I'll call you after surgery. Here's my card. That's me, John Smullen."

As he handed her the little white card, he appeared to blush and clear his throat.

"Yes," said Elizabeth "I know."

Noticing how ill at ease he was talking to her, she realised something important. The intimidating John Smullen was really rather shy, and she of all people could understand that.

Chapter Twenty Six

As Elizabeth stood at the reception desk waiting to pay her bill, one of the young nurses stopped and admired Lawrence. "Hello, gorgeous!" she said. "Isn't he very well?"

"He's just been for his vaccinations, actually," said Elizabeth, basking in the attention her boy was getting.

"Aah, has he? Well, he may be a little quiet for twenty four hours after his jab, so just to keep an eye on him. But he will be back to his usual self in no time."

Elizabeth nodded and thanked her, but inside little alarm bells were ringing. She was due to go out! It was Sophie and Rob's barbecue tonight.

Driving home with Lawrence now asleep in his carrier recovering from the trauma, Elizabeth decided two things: one, that she really couldn't go out and leave him alone while she went to a party and two, that she should start putting a little money away each month for expenses like vet bills. It was this last decision that made her think about Pal and his master. What did Mick do when Pal was ill? To have an animal relying on you and not always being sure that you can afford treatment must be terrible. What if the worst happened? What did homeless people do? She knew she would do without anything to help Lawrence, but Mick had nothing to go without. It troubled her to think of Pal suffering. She knew she couldn't allow that.

She also found herself thinking about John Smullen. Despite his off putting manner, he did seem very genuine about helping and she might even consider ringing him if she was worried about Lawrence. How nice to have such a caring vet.

Once they arrived home, she found that she didn't actually mind too much about not going to the barbecue. She liked Rob and Sophie and she adored their little girls, Ellie and Ruby but she felt much more comfortable seeing them as a family and not with a crowd of people she hardly knew. She wasn't even very sure about the barbecue, if she was honest. She had never been one for outdoor events and the thought of cooking one's food over a little fire, didn't really appeal. She could just imagine herself standing alone, clutching a paper plate and looking forward to going home. It was thoughtful of them to include her but she was relieved to have an excuse to stay home. Just her and Lawrence and the TV.

But her invitation to Yew Tree Cottage was quite another matter. Leon and Rachael were so easy going, and she knew she would feel at ease with them and the lovely Gilmour. And so she settled Lawrence in his favourite bed, made herself a cup of tea, and prepared to ring Sophie.

On Bank Holiday Monday, Elizabeth was in her bedroom deciding what to wear. Her hosts were so casual and yet, it still didn't seem right to turn up without making any sort of effort at all. An old fashioned thought perhaps but one she couldn't dismiss.

On the bed now, lay various tops and skirts she had discarded and on one particularly silky beige blouse, Lawrence was stretched out and rubbing his face into the material.

"Are you trying to tell me something?" she said. "A little over the top for a local social evening, don't you think?"

In the end, she chose a pale blue blouse with a white Lily of the Valley motif over it. The sort of top that would have looked very nice with jeans, but she still hadn't quite managed to convince herself she could get away with wearing them. Aunty E had said you are never too old, but something about the roundness of her hips, told her otherwise.

All in all, it had been a pleasant Bank Holiday so far, if a little humid and the usual village events seemed to have gone ahead as planned, but that evening, as she was just about to leave, the sky grew gloomy and the village was submerged in the strange dark light that happens when a storm is fermenting.

Undeterred, she picked up the wine she had bought as a present, kissed Lawrence on his head, and with her mother's large umbrella in hand, she headed for Yew Tree Cottage.

As she walked across The Green, the people who had been enjoying the last of the late summer sunshine were now rapidly heading home and an eerie silence fell. It left Elizabeth feeling as though she was the only person still outside in the whole village, and in an odd way, in some sort of danger.

As she approached the cottage she was relieved to hear Leon shout a greeting, "Elizabeth, there you are! Come in, come in!"

He opened the front gate and led her in via the newly painted front door. "Come and have a look what we've done to the place," he said, obviously eager for her to see.

Inside, the cottage walls were now painted off-white, contrasting with the darkened original beams above their heads. The main sitting room was warm and homely, with solid furniture and rich red soft furnishings. Although it was late August, Elizabeth immediately found herself imagining the room in the depths of winter, with a roaring fire in the huge, blackened fire place.

"It's beautiful," she said.

"A bit different to your first visit? I haven't shown you the best bit yet. Come on through. Rach is in the kitchen." She followed him down two worn stone steps and then out into a huge light space.

"So, here it is: main kitchen, wet room through there, utility there and my favourite bit, our glass wall."

It was an apt name, for at the far end of the kitchen the wall seemed to be completely clear, giving a perfect view of the garden beyond. "Rach and I sit in here and enjoy the garden without worrying about the weather. We love it, don't we, Rach?"

Rachael was sitting facing the window on an elegant high stool.

"Elizabeth, it's lovely to see you. Forgive Leon, he is very pleased with himself. Come and sit down. Have a glass of wine."

Elizabeth went over to the island at the centre of the room and hoisted herself up onto a stool. "I can see why he is proud, Rachael. It looks wonderful."

Her hostess poured the wine.

"It does, doesn't it?" said Leon, making an expansive gesture. "I'm particularly pleased with how it flows, and then opens out. I like to think we've been sympathetic to the old part of the cottage and then adding this new space, they just seem to complement each other. Neither one fighting for supremacy."

Elizabeth had never seen Leon so animated. This had obviously been a project dear to his

280

heart. "It really is gorgeous. It's like a page from one of those ideal homes magazines," added Elizabeth.

"Listen, I know it looks like rain but let me open the doors for you, so you can get the idea."

"Your new toy!" laughed Rachael. "Go on!"

With just the lightest touch on a remote control, Leon folded the huge panes of glass back on each other in a concertina effect, revealing the garden beyond.

As Elizabeth got down from the stool and went towards the garden, the first heavy spots of rain landed.

"Leave it open, so we can smell the earth!" said Rachael. And so the three of them stood, looking out into the half-light as huge soaking drops fell onto the ground in front of them and the smell of growing things came to them from the garden and surrounding countryside.

They sipped their wine and said very little as the storm began to rumble across the fields towards them, until finally it enveloped the cottage in an oppressive darkness. Flashes lit up the evening sky and drop by drop, rain got heavier and heavier until they were forced to close up the glass wall and put on the kitchen lights. Once again Elizabeth got the feeling that she was sheltering from the unspecified doom she had felt on The Green earlier, and she shuddered.

A sudden rattling noise brought her back from her reverie as an animal dashed into the kitchen via a cat flap in the wall. It was Gilmour, soaked to the skin and looking several sizes smaller than he usually did. He stopped in the middle of the floor and began frantically licking at his fur. "Got caught in the rain, Gilmour?" said Leon. "Your cat isn't out, is he, Elizabeth?"

"No, I made sure he was safely indoors before I left. Poor Gilmour, he's soaked through."

Rachael grabbed a towel and began to gently rub the cat's fur until it stood out like a like a silver frizz all over his body.

"I really wish he wouldn't wander," said Rachael, wiping his paws. "He likes to go bin scavenging. Roger caught him by The Cock....oh dear, that isn't what I meant at all, is it?" The room fell uncomfortably silent and both Leon and Rachael looked worriedly at Elizabeth.

And there she was again, out of her depth, wondering how to deal with it. But this was the point of her socialising, like Edith had said, getting out there. So she smiled, drew in a deep breath and said, "Well, he probably deserved it, if he was in the dustbins."

Her hosts exploded with laughter, more with relief, she felt, than at the actual joke, but she had survived. The moment had passed and perhaps she wouldn't feel quite so like a nun at these gatherings in future.

"You know," said Leon, quickly, "my mother would have loved this, tonight. She is a bit of a storm chaser, you know? Jumps in her car and heads off into them. She loves a bit of excitement. We are hoping to have her here for Christmas, Elizabeth. We must all get together. We could go out to dinner."

The evening was a real success. As always the couple seemed to have just the knack of making her feel at ease. Dinner was a casual affair, a Chinese takeaway, delivered from a restaurant in Crayton and a dessert from Waitrose but Elizabeth couldn't remember when she had enjoyed a meal so much. Afterwards, sitting in the cozy lounge talking, she felt only one thing was missing and that was Lawrence.

Inevitably their conversation turned to Mick Latimer: "You've done nothing wrong, as far as I can see," said Leon. "You've just broken the Manners Manifesto. It doesn't bother Rach and I. We are outsiders and happy to be so. It means we don't have to abide by their rules. But you're part of the establishment; you have lived here all your life. Villages are like that. They don't like change. If I could, I'd have a big sign outside saying, NO NIMBYS IN MY BACK YARD!"

"He would too, Elizabeth. He isn't joking. He hates any sort of…"

At that point Elizabeth's phone pinged in her handbag.

"Is that you?" said Rachael.

"I think it is," said Elizabeth, rummaging in her bag. "It'll be a wrong number. Nobody messages me."

But the message was for her. It was from John Smullen, enquiring about Lawrence's health after his injection. "Oh, that's nice of him." she said "It's from my vet, Mr Smullen asking about Lawrence."

"That's VERY nice," said Rachael. "We go to John Smullen with Gilmour and we don't get that treatment, do we, Leon?"

"I think you have a fan there, Elizabeth," answered Leon. "You'd better send him an answer."

Chapter Twenty Seven

"Looks like its stopped raining. Don't forget, if you ever want me to come up and see what I can do with your place, let me know," Leon said, as they waved her off.

Elizabeth nodded and raised her hand but her mind was still very much on the text from John Smullen. Surely Rachael was reading more into it than there really was? He was a nice man and he obviously liked Lawrence, that's all there was to it. Even so, there was still a little bit of her that fluttered at the thought that someone might have noticed her. For so much of her life she had felt utterly invisible and even if the vet only remembered her because of her beautiful cat, she didn't mind.

As she approached home she was concerned to see the dark shape of a person standing next to her front door. Since the note incident, she had become a little more wary than she had been and was tempted to hang back and see what was going on, but when the shape moved she realised it was in fact Mick standing on her doorstep.

"Elizabeth," he called. "Sum-body's smashed one o't panes in your front window; I weren't quick enough to see who it were, sorry."

Her first thought was for Lawrence. Was he safe? Was he frightened? Without speaking to Mick she opened her front door and they both went inside.

For such a small window pane, the glass had spread a very long way. It was on the table, the floor, even in a plant pot that was near to the window, and lying on the rug was a decorative stone from her own garden.

She glanced at the chaos and then hurried upstairs, leaving Mick picking his way through the 'crystal' coated floor. She went straight to her bedroom and gently opened the door. At first she couldn't see Lawrence at all, but then she spotted his two huge blue eyes looking out over the rim of his bed. He was obviously frightened but it looked like he had flattened himself down and thankfully stayed put, rather than venturing down amongst the glass.

Elizabeth picked him up and held him close, carefully feeling his paws for injury or blood. Thank goodness, he seemed physically fine. "There, there sweet boy, it's all right. Mummy's

287

home, now," she murmured. "He's okay, Mick!" she called. "He's okay!"

When she finally went downstairs, leaving the now calmed Lawrence lying on her bed, she found Mick making a cup of tea in her kitchen. "I thought you might want one of these. I could help you clean up if you like. And you'll want to put summat o'er that 'ole for now. 'Ave you got any wood? I'll do it for you. Is he all right, then, Mr Lawrence?"

"Just a bit worried I think," she replied, smiling to herself at the use of the Mister.

"I wish I'd been a bit quicker, copped the buggers at it," said Mick, handing her the tea. "Pal knew there were summat up tonight. He wouldn't rest, he knew there were somebody about."

"It's horrible, Mick. I'd had such a nice evening and then I come home to this. I just don't know who could have done such a thing."

"Look, Elizabeth I know you say she's all right, but I worry about that Bunny lass. She don't seem the full shillin' to me and I'll tell you summat else, I saw her earlier just stood out in that rain! That's not right, is it? Have you ever upset her about owt, do you think? Could she have done it?"

"Bunny? No, we have been neighbours all our lives. She has never shown any sort of malice about anything. I can't believe it would be her."

"If you say so. To be 'onest though, I can't see why anybody would do it. I mean you…well, you know? You're a good person, kind an' all that."

"Well, somebody doesn't think so. I had a note pushed through my door too."

"What sort o' note? Poison pen?"

"Just saying I should make you leave, saying I was a do gooder."

"Oh now, Elizabeth! So, this is about you 'avin me 'ere. Look, we'll go, me and Pal…..it's."

"You will not!" said Elizabeth, suddenly feeling angry. "I've broken the 'manners manifesto' that's all. There is nothing wrong with you being here. The best thing we can do is ignore it. We can't let them get the better of us and that's all there is to it." Even as she spoke, she heard traces of her mother's sharp voice coming out in her own. That clipped way she would speak when riled, the very English phrasing. Somewhere inside, she was still Ruth Menier's daughter.

Looking a little taken aback by her sudden sharpness, Mick said, "Perhaps we'd best drink our tea and sort the mess out, eh?"

For the following two weeks after the broken window incident, things seemed to calm a little. Every time Elizabeth saw Bunny at Church she went out of her way to speak to her and Ellen, just in case she had unintentionally upset her. But she couldn't help thinking that the type written note would have been beyond Bunny, as would the term do gooder. It just didn't sit right at all. Her own suspicions led her to Dina Watkins. She had been very annoyed about Mick living in the garage and she hadn't really spoken to Elizabeth since her resignation from the committee. Of course, Elizabeth would never confront anyone and so she tried to carry on as normal, and it felt as though as time went on it was working. Whoever it was, seemed to have given up, maybe they didn't get the reaction they were looking for.

September started very pleasantly for Elizabeth. The weather held out and the days were gloriously warm and mellow. The chill of autumn had crept into the mornings and evenings, and the long shadows told how the year was waning, but in the daytime it was still possible to sit outside and feel the warmth of the sun on her skin before it disappeared for the winter.

Another pleasant development was Elizabeth's unexpected visitor. She tended to take her main holiday in September. People in the office with families preferred the summer months and as she didn't go away, it only seemed fair to delay hers. One afternoon, as she was pottering in the front garden, a car drew up and John Smullen got out. "I hope you don't mind this intrusion," he said stiffly, but I was called out to Beddow's Farm and I thought it would be nice to drop in and see Lawrence and yourself on the way back," he said.

Normally Elizabeth would have been a little disturbed by someone she didn't know very well just turning up unannounced, but Mr Smullen had found her Achilles heel - Lawrence. Anyone who liked her boy was welcome. "How nice of you. He's out and about at the moment, I'll call him. Come in, he's normally out in the fields at the back."

Elizabeth took off her gardening gloves and the two of them went into the cottage.

"What a lovely day, isn't it? So warm. Come through into the kitchen." John Smullen smiled and nodded. "Please take a seat, I'll call him. Not that he always comes of course."

"Well, he IS a cat," agreed the vet.

Elizabeth opened the back door and shouted. After a few minutes there was no sign of Lawrence and she and John Smullen sat awkwardly in the kitchen.

"Typical cat," said Elizabeth after a while, shrugging

"Mmmmm," he replied.

"He should turn up in a minute or two," she said. "Erm, would you like a tea or coffee while we wait?"

"That would be very nice," said John Smullen.

And so the two of them sat self-consciously drinking tea in Elizabeth's sunny kitchen, waiting for Lawrence.

"You didn't mind me dropping in?" said John.

"No, no not at all," she replied.

They fell into silence again.

"How long have you been a vet?"

"I qualified 28 years ago."

"It must be nice, working with animals, helping them."

"Yes, it is."

Feeling a little embarrassed, she got to her feet and called once more for Lawrence.

"It's a nice day. He will have gone wandering," she explained.

At length their tea was finished and John Smullen got to his feet.

"Well, it doesn't look as though Lawrence will be gracing us with his presence, so I had better get back to the surgery."

Ridiculously Elizabeth felt stricken with guilt and started to apologise but as she did so a dark brown face appeared at the back door and

Lawrence padded in like a cheetah, shoulders sliding, and head held high.

"Oh, here he is!" she said, relieved.

John Smullen scooped the cat up and held him to his chest, an action that would normally have caused Lawrence to struggle and wriggle for freedom, but he seemed quite happy with the situation and even rubbed his face along John's chin.

"Hello, Lawrence. How is my Siamese friend? Your fur is warm. Had you found a nice, warm spot, hmmm?"

He continued to stroke and talk to Lawrence and the cat appeared to enjoy every moment. When he was eventually placed on the floor, he chirped happily and went over to his bowl for some biscuits.

"Well," said Elizabeth, "you certainly have a friend there. He normally isn't that good with new people."

"A bit like myself, then," commented John. "Anyway, I'd best be off. It's been good to see you both. Hopefully I won't be seeing you at the practice anytime soon."

For a moment Elizabeth was taken aback, and then realising it was a joke, she said, "Oh yes, hopefully not."

As she saw John Smullen to the front gate, he commented, "You must come and visit me one day Miss Menier, you could meet my pigs, Crispin and Rupert."

"You have pigs!"

"I have quite a few animals. Occupational hazard. I can't resist a hard luck story."

Just as he was about to close the gate and get back into his car, Mick came out of the garage with Pal.

"Elizabeth, is it okay for me to teck Pal downt' field or is Lawrence out?" he shouted.

John Smullen's eyes registered surprise as he looked from one to the other. "Well, I'll see you at some point, then," he said, and hastily got into his car and pulled away.

"Who were that, then?" said Mick. "He looked like a doctor. You all right?"

"Yes, I'm fine," said Elizabeth, surprised to find herself just a little bit annoyed by Mick's appearance at that precise moment.

Chapter Twenty Eight

This year Elizabeth had decided that she would go with a purple theme. The beautiful dew covered array of Michaelmas daisies in her back garden had been the original inspiration and then by chance she had noticed some very pretty lilac wrapping paper at the newsagent's at Crayton, which had finalised her thoughts.

Since her school days she had always loved the Harvest Festival. There was something so joyous and golden about that time of year, and thanking God for his gifts from the earth seemed only natural.

We Plough the Fields and Scatter, *Glad That I live Am I,* and Keats *Ode To Autumn* were all welcome old friends, and she looked forward to hearing them each year. They gave her a feeling of continuity and reassurance. Living, as she did, in a farming area, it seemed a particularly appropriate festival to observe. She was actually able see the changes of the season and the crops in the field coming to fruition. Whatever the reason, she had always felt a strong connection to the harvest time. It was a time to be grateful.

This year St Martin's festival service was to be held on Sunday 25th September and she had already begun to make plans. The congregation traditionally 'brought forward symbols of the harvest' which were then distributed to various local causes, - food banks, old people's homes and the like. These were decorated boxes containing a selection of foods. It was a lovely tradition and one in which Elizabeth particularly liked to participate. She always contributed a box and though she did try not to be too proud about it, she did have a reputation for making hers especially decorative, and this time it was going to be purple.

Over the last few weeks, she had picked up a few extra things with her shopping and now having Lawrence and Pal in her life, she included pet food in her donation. There was something so magical and exciting about seeing people heading for church all carrying their brightly coloured boxes on Harvest Festival day.

On the Sunday before the service, she decided to see how all the various tins, boxes and packets fitted together. Her container this year was a seed tray she had acquired from the garden centre. Now covered in shimmering lilac and lined with purple tissue paper, it was hardly recognisable. Carefully she laid out the items. They all fitted nicely, and with fresh flowers filling the gaps, it was going to look spectacular. Feeling momentarily pleased with herself, she noticed the family sized tin of beef stew sitting on the dresser waiting to be added.

"Well, you'll just have to go," she said, picking it up and opening the kitchen door into the garage.

"Mick! "she called. "Mick! I thought you might be able to make use of this….."

Before she had finished her sentence Pal rushed up in a flurry of fur to welcome her. His enthusiasm and energy never ceased to surprise her. He was now touring the garage, head down, looking for a suitable gift to bring to her and he returned seconds later with an old peg bag minus the pegs, which he dropped at her slippered feet.

"All right, Elizabeth?" said Mick. "Pal, that's enough, now. Down!"

Obediently, Pal dropped to the ground and lay with just his tail twitching as he struggled to contain himself.

299

"I brought this for you," she said. "I can't fit it in my harvest festival box, so I thought you might like it."

"Won't you 'ave it your sen, then?"

"It wouldn't be right. I bought it to give away, if that makes sense."

"No, not really," he laughed. "But me and Pal won't complain. Ta very much, Elizabeth."

As she handed him the tin, Pal let out a low woof and sprang to his feet. He headed, straight to the garage door, and began sniffing and clawing at the bottom of it.

"What's up, big lad?" said his master. "What's mitherin' you"? He rose to his feet and followed the dog. By now, Pal was barking and growling at the door. Mick stopped and looked back at Elizabeth. "Can you smell burnin'?" he said. "I'd best get this door open and see what's what." Together, they hauled the garage door up and went out into the gathering gloom of the evening. There on Elizabeth's path, were three small bundles of newspaper which were all alight. Instinctively she ran to the first one and tried to stamp it out. As she did so two things happened simultaneously, Mick shouted a warning behind

300

her and her foot met a slimy ooze of excrement hidden inside the paper.

Oh, the filthy devils," she said, looking down at the splattered mess on her foot and trousers. "The filthy devils!"

****

Later that evening, a very sombre Elizabeth stood in her kitchen, and Lawrence watched as she very deliberately unpacked each item from the harvest festival box. The idea of attending the service had been sullied. It was irreversibly tainted. She could not sit amongst her neighbours, thanking God for all *Good Gifts Around Her*, knowing one of them might have done this. It was beyond any doubt. The headlight, the note, the window and now this. Someone in the village disliked what she was doing so much they were willing to persecute her until she changed her mind.

She remembered how she had hummed, *Dare To Be A Daniel* that first day as she had marched across The Green to Mick's tent. She didn't feel much like a Daniel now. As the bitterness of the acts against her began to sink in, her throat overflowed with emotion and she drew in a juddering breath. Tears welled up and slipped over the edges of her lower lids. But they were not tears of self-pity, these tears were angry and filled with disappointment. Silently they flowed down her face, one after another.

At nine-thirty, Elizabeth gathered Lawrence up and climbed the stairs to bed. In the past when it had been a particularly bad day, her mother had always said, "I think it best that we draw a veil over today and start again tomorrow." And that was what she was doing, drawing a veil, finishing the day early. She was sure it had nothing nice to offer her and so sleep seemed the best option. She was so worn out by the emotional turmoil she imagined that she would be asleep within minutes, but this was not the case. At 3.00 a.m. she was still awake staring into the darkness.

Lawrence, perhaps sensing her restlessness, came up the bed and curled into her neck, sighing a heavy whiskery huff, as he settled against her. His warm body and the pressure of his face next to hers was a balm and although she still couldn't let go and drift into sleep, she did at least feel comforted and safe having him there.

When it was finally time to get up, she felt as though she could have slept all day. Exhausted and reluctant to crawl into a new working week, she ignored the alarm clock and held Lawrence a little longer. By eight o'clock, however, she was up and despite having had so little sleep, she felt remarkably bright, a little like she was running on some sort of rather 'thin' energy. She had been extremely efficient, in fact. She had spent a little more time over her make-up and hair than normal and was now eating breakfast ahead of her usual time.

Having ten minutes to spare before she needed to leave the house, she found herself wandering around, fiddling with and straightening things, both restless and tired all at the same time. It was now eight-thirty and for some strange reason she decided she would call John Smullen.

It was something she couldn't have put easily into words, but she just felt the need to chat. Not with the intention of mentioning what had happened, just the opposite in fact. Perhaps it was just because he was an outsider and nothing to do with the village and its petty affairs. There was something about John Smullen that made her think he would be calm and measured, and that was exactly what she wanted at that moment.

She rang the surgery. Disappointingly, on asking to speak to him, she was told, "I'm sorry, it's Mr Smullen's day for Burford today. Could Mr Scott help at all?"

"Burford?"

"The Blue Cross. He likes to do his bit, you know?"

"Oh, I see well, it can wait, really. It isn't urgent. I just wanted a word. It was a personal call actually."

"He'll be in later. Who shall I say called?"

"Miss Menier, Lawrence's owner."

"Oh, Lawrence the big Siamese, isn't it? One of Mr Smullen's favourite patients. I'll be sure and tell him you rang. Bye."

Far from being calmed, Elizabeth was now on edge. She wondered if she should even have made the call at all. She was tired and it had seemed a good idea, but now it was just something else to worry about.

Was there a way she could undo it perhaps? What if the message wasn't passed on at all, he would never know? What if she had embarrassed him in front of his colleagues? She felt like a very silly woman at that moment.

There was a mobile number for him on his card. Maybe she should ring that and try and put it right. It was just so difficult. She had so little experience of these things, and try as she might, she hadn't entirely been able to embrace E's 'what the hell' attitude. She was just too English and now had a horror that she would be seen as throwing herself at a man!

There was nothing to be done now. She had to go to work. At least she could hide there and pretend it hadn't happened. With any luck the message wouldn't get through and nothing would happen. She kissed Lawrence goodbye, tucked his blanket around him a little more closely and went out.

Just as she reached her front gate, her phone beeped. It was a message from John. It said, *You rang?*

Unable to gauge anything at all from those two short words, Elizabeth ran out of courage and she quickly texted back.

Not urgent. Please don't worry.

A second later John rang. "Miss Menier?" he said. "Is Lawrence not well?"

"No, he's fine. I just felt, well…," her heart was beating so fast it was almost painful. "I thought, I might like to meet Crispin and Rupert," she said, and waited as the words plummeted into space never to return. There was a pause and then,

"Well, then you must. We will arrange something."

"Yes, that would be very nice indeed. I shall look forward to seeing you," she said.

"And Crispin and Rupert will look forward to seeing you," he said. The call ended.

Chapter Twenty Nine

October came and Elizabeth found her mood fading with the light. The afternoons became darker, the mornings colder, and the trees a little starker. As the month progressed she realised that her invitation to visit John was now looking doubtful. He hadn't been in touch for weeks and she wasn't altogether surprised when towards the end of the month she received a text from him saying that he was taking a two month placement at a specialist veterinary referral service in Birmingham. It was very state of the art and an opportunity not to be missed, apparently.

She understood, of course she did. John's career was his priority, not some middle aged woman and her cat. Even so, she couldn't help but wonder in her more paranoid moments if he had decided to take the placement to get away from her. She probably seemed a very sad case, an old maid with a homeless man living in her garage. She didn't really blame him for not wanting to get involved.

So, John Smullen was not to be her saviour and she chastised herself for being foolish enough to imagine that knights in shining armour really did exist. The truth was there were no easy answers. Nobody could come along and sort everything out for you. She had just got carried away because someone had shown an interest in her, and now she felt a little pathetic.

For a while, after the text, she hid away, finding the routine of work and home as much as she could cope with. After this latest disappointment and the nastiness she had been subjected to by an unknown hand, she wanted to insulate herself from the world. For all she cared it could carry on without her. She no longer felt part of it. Lawrence was now all she really cared about.

Then, one night as she was about to sit down and watch the drama she had been following, the doorbell rang. Her first instinct was to ignore it. After all, it was nearly eight o'clock at night. The bell went again. Lawrence tensed and prepared to hide. Sighing, she got up. Lawrence took his cue and streaked up the stairs while she went slowly to the door. In the past she would have just opened it but now instinct warned her to show caution and she called out, "Who is it?"

"It's Leon, Elizabeth. Just need a quick chat."

She unbolted the door and let him in. Still wearing his ancient jeans and a thin grey top, Leon appeared oblivious to the nippy autumn air.

"I have a directive from Mother," he said, smiling.

"Really? Well, you had better come in properly, then. Lawrence has just disappeared upstairs. Would you like a cup of tea?"

Leon remained standing in the hall with his hands clasped in front of him.

"No, no, no, I won't stay. I got an email from Mother tonight. She is worried about you. Says you've gone quiet, gone a bit into yourself. Anyway, she has sent me over to check on you and invite you to a bit of fun."

"Oh has she? Bless her kindness. Your mother is so special, Leon. But really, I am okay. I just need to be on my own for a bit. Things have got me down a little, but I'm fine."

"Well, E does not agree, and I have been commanded to bring you out of yourself. So, next weekend Roger is having a Halloween do at the Cock and you have to come with Rach and me. No arguments."

Elizabeth pulled a face. She always ignored Halloween; it wasn't a proper celebration at all in her mind. As far as she was concerned it was all very American and sinister and she had no time for it.

"That's kind of you, but it isn't really my cup of tea."

"Nonsense, it'll be marvellous fun and we really should support Roger, you know. Look, it's on Friday night. Rach and I will call for you about eight and we can walk over together. You don't have to stay all night, just pop in."

As usual she found herself taking the least line of resistance. She knew full well that when the event actually arrived, she would be beside herself and contemplating all sorts of excuses not to go, but for now it was easier to give in, and so she said, "Very well, but I'll only stay for a little bit."

"Great. We'll see you on Friday, then." As she opened the door to let him out, he added, "It's a costume do, by the way, so that should be even more fun. See you, Elizabeth."

As she closed the front door, that phrase sang in her mind, *"It's a costume do…. so that should be even more fun."*

Fun? That last detail made it even more unlikely that she would have fun. It was now an even worse prospect than before. Not only did she have to attend this thing, she was also required to dress up in silly clothes to do it.

Throughout the week, she found herself worrying incessantly about what to wear. Normally she was able to shove these things firmly to the back of her mind, but this one required forethought and it was not a comfortable feeling. Last thing at night before she slept and first thing in the morning when she woke, it was on her mind. What could she wear?

Her first thought was that she would go as a cat. But then thinking just how slinky and exposed she would need to be, she abandoned it almost instantly. Anything that might involve a leotard was out. What on earth did people go to these things as? She tried to remember what the children wore when they came trick or treating but nothing really stuck in her mind. It was all a jumble of capes, masks and hats. By Wednesday she was getting desperate. An old sheet with holes in it was by far her best idea, until she realised all her sheets were in fact patterned, and a Freesia sprigged ghost would simply not fit the bill.

Finally in the middle of her working day, when she wasn't even thinking about it, an idea came into her head. Upstairs, in the spare room was a black velvet evening gown that had belonged to her mother. She had never seen her wear it, or even attend anything that required wearing it but Ruth had kept it there, year after year, wrapped in tissue. Providing it fitted, she could wear that, buy a plastic hat from the supermarket and go as a witch. Relieved she wrote out a Post-it and stuck it on her handbag: GET HAT ON WAY HOME.

She did get a hat, her local supermarket had all but sold out of Halloween paraphernalia by the time she got there, so she was forced to take a slightly droopy witch's hat and a broom intended for a child, but it was done. Her costume dilemma was solved.

When Friday night arrived, her feeling of gloom all but enveloped her. There was something so unchristian about all this dressing up as ghosts, vampires and goodness knows what else. It didn't sit right with her at all to make light of such things. Her only consolation was that she had heard that Reverend Donavan and his wife would be attending and so perhaps she was taking it all just a little too seriously. Perhaps there really was no harm in it?

Her mother's dress fitted her after a fashion, as long as she left the zip at the back open part way and secured it with a safety pin. It did pull a little across her midriff, but for a few hours it was perfectly acceptable, or at least she thought so. Topped off with the slightly drunken hat and clutching her tiny broom, she knew she would not win any prizes, but at least nobody could say she hadn't tried.

With half an hour to go before Leon and Rachel were due to arrive, she went to call Lawrence in. He had gone out at dusk and now she wanted him safely home before she left for the evening. She went to the back door with his biscuit tin and rattled it loudly. "Lawrence! Lawrence! Come on now!"

The countryside around answered with rustles and creaks, but Lawrence didn't appear. "Lawrence!" she called again, and again nothing stirred.

She shook the tin. "Sweeties!" she called. "Come on!" She stood straining for the sound of him emerging through the hedge at the top of the garden, as he had done a hundred times before, but all she heard was the wind. A panic began to rise in her and she shook the tin again. Just lately she had noticed Lawrence had taken to sitting in the front garden of the cottage and so she quickly rushed through and out of the front door. Perhaps he simply hadn't heard her calling across the fields. She tried again.

"Lawrence! Lawrence! Come on now. Time to come in! Lawrence!"

Nothing, just the village and the lights of the pub twinkling across the green. "Lawrence!" she shouted even more loudly. "Lawrence!"

The garage door grated open and Mick and Pal came out together.

"What's up, Elizabeth? Mr Lawrence not come 'ome? I heard you calling him out t' back."

"He never does this, Mick. He always comes when I call. He's such a good boy normally. I'm getting worried, you don't think something..."

Mick didn't answer but he was looking toward a dark shape lying in the gutter just a few feet along from Elizabeth's front gate.

Elizabeth's hand went to her mouth and she felt her eyes sting with tears. "Pal, stop 'ere wi' Elizabeth, good lad. Now, stay. I've got to go and do summat." Reluctantly the dog sat but whimpered as he watched his master walk away. Mick opened the front gate and went slowly along the road towards the still shape in the gutter. She watched the bear like figure in silence while Pal fidgeted and whined at her side. This could not really be happening.

He bent down and Elizabeth could no longer see the shape as it disappeared behind the folds of Mick's coat. "It's alright, it's not 'im," he shouted. "Just a bin bag or summat."

Tears ran down her face and she closed her eyes to give thanks.

Mick came back to the cottage carrying the black material at arm's length. "I think it's a

315

kiddie's cloak, from trick or treat!" he said. "'Ad me goin' for a minute. Bloody 'ell!"

Elizabeth was still unable to speak, her throat was closed by emotion as her world righted itself. It could so easily have been a different outcome and it had shaken her to the core. Her legs felt weak under her and she wanted to get inside and sit down.

"Shall I call 'im again, little bugger?" asked Mick. She nodded.

"Lawrence! Come on lad!" Mick shouted but still nothing stirred.

Chapter Thirty

When Leon and Rachael arrived, Elizabeth and Mick were still standing outside the front door, staring out across The Green. Shakily she said, "Lawrence hasn't come in. I can't go out yet."

Leon appeared to be wrapped from head to toe in toilet paper whilst his wife sported a black chiffon wedding dress and veil.

"Come on, Elizabeth. I'm sure he's fine," said Rachael. "They love these dark nights. He'll have found something down in the fields. They all go a little deaf when they want to. You can pop back and check on him later if you like."

"Gilmour does this all the time, but he always turns up when he's ready," added Leon.

"I know you're right but I just wouldn't enjoy it not knowing he was safely home."

"Elizabeth, you look wonderful, you have to come! He's probably having his own Halloween party with Gilmour, come on!" pleaded Rachael.

"She's right, he'll be fine. I'll keep an eye out for 'im, Elizabeth. No need for you to miss your party. Go on. Would you like me to come over t'pub and tell yer when he comes 'ome?" offered Mick.

"See, that sounds like a great solution. Thank you, Mick," said Leon. "Now, Elizabeth let's go."

Gallantly Leon offered her his mummified arm and reluctantly the three of them went in the direction of the pub.

Already feeling gloomy, Elizabeth's spirits sank even further when she realised that although they were still a distance away she could clearly hear the music coming from the pub. It was going to be loud inside and Elizabeth didn't like loud anything. She steeled herself.

When they arrived at the pub, Elizabeth still hanging on to Leon's arm, it was immediately obvious that Roger had gone to town. The whole lounge area was a sea of orange and black, the overhead beams were covered in fake cobwebs, and plastic pumpkins were scattered across the bar and tables, while fake battery powered candles pretended to burn and drip in place of the usual electric lamps.

"Isn't this fabulous?" shouted Rachael over the thud of the muddy sound system.

Elizabeth was not at all sure it was 'fabulous' but she smiled and nodded anyway.

"Right, Elizabeth, you look like you need a stiff drink. Let me get you a brandy," said Leon, pushing them towards the bar.

While they waited Elizabeth looked around at the assembled Halloweeners: young men in dinner suits wearing plastic fangs, charmingly ragged young witches, beautifully made up zombies. It wasn't really what she was expecting and she found herself feeling very old and very out of place. Most people seemed to be from the New Houses, not even the vicar and his wife had put in their promised appearance. Her valiant effort at a witch didn't feel up to standard surrounded by all this glamour.

"Looking for someone?" remarked Rachael.

"No, not really. I can't see any of my neighbours."

"The villagers? Well, it's fun, isn't it? They don't do fun."

Standing at the bar, the music began to creep into Elizabeth's consciousness,

They did the Mash!

She now felt that she didn't belong in either camp.

It caught on in a flash.

She didn't belong here amongst these young people.

They did the Mash.

But she didn't belong with the villagers at home behind their closed curtains.

They did The Monster Mash…..

Why had she agreed to come? It was worse than she had expected and with Lawrence on her mind too, all she really wanted to do was rush out of the pub and go home. And then when Roger came through from the other side of the bar, it took all her self-control to stay put. He was dressed as the devil, just as he had been in her dream. A fiery red devil with a huge grinning mouth.

She let out a little involuntary squeak and instinctively backed away only to bump into the very solid figure of Bryan McConway. "Elizabet'! How are ya? I didn't know you were coming to this. Here look, I've Maeve with me. Come and say hello."

Gratefully she allowed herself to be steered away from the bar and towards a quieter area of the pub.

"Ah, you look great. I don't really do dressing up these days, did it too many times in the past I suppose. I've been everything in my time from Santa to a drag queen. Too long in the toot' for all that now. Here, this is Maeve."

Standing next to the fireplace was a middle aged red head with a voluptuous figure and a slightly ruffled air about her. Her green off the shoulder blouse and short skirt made her reminiscent of a buxom country barmaid.

"This is Elizabet'," said Bryan.

"Glad to know you, Elizabeth. Have you not got a drink?" Her accent was much softer than Bryan's and her manner much less extrovert but she was obviously well used to social situations and she quickly despatched Bryan to the bar for drinks.

"I hear you haven't been well?" ventured Elizabeth, politely.

"Indisposed, I like to say. But I'm much brighter now, thank God. This is a good turnout for one of these things, isn't it? Good to see people dressing up and having a good time. Life's too short to be miserable."

"There you go ladies, your drinks. Vodka and tonic for Maeve and a coke for you, Elizabeth," said Bryan, returning from the bar. "Are you sure you won't have something stronger?"

Elizabeth shook her head. "I'm fine, honestly."

"So then….." began Bryan but he was brought to a halt by an announcement from the bar.

"Ladies and gentleman! Can I just have your attention for a moment," said Roger. "Right, we are going to do a bit of a competition. Anybody know a good ghost story? There's a prize of a bottle of bubbly for the best one. When I say bubbly, I mean it's got bubbles in it all right. It might not be champagne but I can definitely promise bubbles. So let's hear 'em. Just step up

322

to the bar and tell us about things that go bump in the night and I don't mean Bryan fallin' out of bed."

There was a silence as the assembled ghouls, ghosts and grotesques looked at each other. Elizabeth looked at the floor, she wasn't keen on anything that might pray on her mind. She didn't even watch horror films, but it was too late to escape now, so she hoped nobody would come up with one. But she had forgotten that the biggest story teller in the pub was standing right next to her.

Bryan took the microphone from Roger and spoke into the silence. "You mean to tell me that not one of yous has a ghost story to tell?" He grinned. This was exactly what he enjoyed, having an audience. "Well, I can hardly believe that. Growing up in Ireland you get told tales from the moment you're born, it's a way of life. I could tell you any number of tall stories, but you know, I think, ladies and gentlemen, I will go for a true one. One known personally to me."

His audience relaxed, relieved to be off the hook and waiting to be taken on the journey.

"Well, this is going back now, maybe 82, 83, something like that. I knew this woman in County

Clare. Siobhan, a lovely woman, but a bit of a hippy, you know? Always into this fad and that fad. Crystals one week, spiritualism the next, you know the type? Sure, there was no harm in her but I always felt she was looking for something missing in her life.

Anyway, she'd a daughter, Roisin and a partner, Gerry. Now, Gerry, he was a character; they had never married and he'd come and go as he pleased. He always reminded me of a skinny stray cat, the way he'd turn up for a few months and then he'd be off again.

Siobhan, she said he was one of life's free spirits and it must have suited her to live that way. And you know, when Gerry he was home, their house was transformed. He'd invite everyone round and we'd be drinking and talking into the night. Aw they were grand times. Well, you might say, Bryan I don't care for the sound of this fella, he must have been a terrible partner and father, and I suppose he was, but you know he loved his daughter. He would hold her close and tell her she was the most beautiful, clever child in the world. And he would tell her, '*The day you were born, I came home from seeing you and your mammy at the hospital and what do you think I saw on my doorstep? One hundred pure white feathers, just sitting there. It was a sign from the angels that you were no ordinary child and I knew whatever happened they would be with you every step of the way. You remember that my Roisin, you are a very special child.'*

I did feel for her not having a father around but at least she knew he loved her. Anyway she grew up to be a very sensible young woman, despite her odd upbringing. I liked her a lot, she'd a wise head on her shoulders for a young girl. You could really have a good conversation with her, despite her age.

So, time goes on and this one year Gerry goes missing for longer than usual, but they carry on with their lives, knowing he will turn up when he's good and ready like always.

Then one night Siobhan is having one of her usual spiritual meetings at her home but this night it's going very badly. Messages keep coming through but nobody in the room knows who they are for. So they are just about to call it a night when the medium says, she has another message coming through. This time it is for a woman called Rose. Once again there's nobody in the room with the name Rose. Then says the medium, "No, I've made a mistake. He is saying it is for my little rose." Well, Roisin is Gaelic for Rose so laughingly the girl says

'Well that could be me then, I am sort of Rose. What does it say?

'It's a man and he says, the angels are with you every step of the way.'

And that ladies and gentlemen, is how they found out that Gerry was no more. He sent one final message to his daughter before he went. A few days later they had confirmation that he had in fact been killed on a building site in Dublin, two days before the séance. Now make of that what you will but that was the way it was told to me and I've no reason to doubt it. Gerry made one last effort to do the right thing."

The audience broke into a round of applause and looked from one to the other.

"And I swear every word is true," said Bryan, acknowledging their appreciation. When the clapping died down he asked, "Well, is there anybody else now I've started the ball rolling or will I claim my prize, for a tale well told?"

As the story had progressed, Elizabeth had been getting more and more anxious. With

Lawrence missing, the last thing she wanted to hear was a story about someone turning up dead.

Now feeling hot and stifled in her tight black dress, she turned and made her way to the door, determined to slip away and go home. But as she moved through the crowd, a hand reached out and grabbed her.

Chapter Thirty One

"Don't go, Elizabeth," said Maeve. "I was watching you just now. Was it the story that upset you?" Bryan's wife took her hand and smiled. "Come on, stay and have a drink with me. What'll it be? And I mean a proper drink, now. A wine? A sweet white. I'll bet that's your tipple, isn't it?"

Without waiting for a reply she shouted over to her husband, "Bryan, a sweet white over here please!"

"So," she said, turning back to Elizabeth, "what has upset you? The thought of the poor man dying and leaving his daughter like that? Well, let me tell you something, Bryan likes to spin a yarn, always has. It's as though he rewrites life as he'd like it to be, if you see what I mean. I don't think that counts as lying do you? More like having a good imagination."

Maeve finished her drink and said, "Excuse me a mo', I just need a top up." Having placed her order with her husband she returned with Elizabeth's wine. "There you are. Drink up now, there's no point being sad. It isn't true at all. He did know a lady who held séances, but as far as I know her man went off with another woman. He didn't die; it just makes for a better story."

A little confused, Elizabeth smiled. It all seemed slightly silly now. "Thank you, it's just my cat is missing and it made me think something terrible had happened to him."

"Ah God, so Bryan put his great big foot in it, there, didn't he? I'm sorry, I'm sure your cat will be just fine. He'll probably turn up right as rain."

"It's not Bryan's fault. I usually enjoy his stories."

"Oh, and he has a fair few of those, doesn't he? I'll bet he told you the one about the diabetic at the hotel, didn't he? How the fella died in his room because he had asked not to be disturbed?"

"Yes, he did. That was terrible, poor man."

"Poor man, indeed. Except he didn't die. We have a Christmas card from him every year. Bryan saved him. He fed him fruit juice and jelly babies until he felt better, then we took him to hospital. But that's a boring story, so Bryan embellishes it."

She smiled innocently as Bryan came over with her drink. "There you are my love," he said, before heading back to the bar.

She took a long drink and smiled. "You see, he's in his element here. He's a restless soul. That's why the hospitality work suited him so well. Always moving on, new gangs of friends to tell his tales to."

Elizabeth sensed a melancholy tone in Maeve's voice as she spoke about the old days, and she said, "Don't you miss it?"

"Me? No. All I really wanted was a home, sweetheart." She downed her drink. "A normal, settled home."

Elizabeth stayed and chatted with Maeve for quite some time, but all the while she was longing to go home and look for Lawrence. Mick had not arrived with good news and so she had to assume he still wasn't back. Maeve on the other hand, seemed content to stand in the corner of the pub talking the night away. It seemed rude to leave her there on her own, but eventually Elizabeth's anxiety got the better of her and she said, "Well, it's been lovely to meet you, but I really should be getting back. I only meant to pop in for a little while."

"Ah, that's a pity, but before you go, how about joining me for one last drink," she said, holding her glass up.

Elizabeth knew this could take quite a while if she agreed and so she said, "I'd better not, but thank you all the same. I really should go."

Maeve shrugged and tilted her head to one side. "Shame," she said. "I'll see you another time, then, eh? You take care now."

As Elizabeth made her way to the door she looked back and saw that Maeve seemed quite content to remain by herself, watching the other people having fun. She was a very self-contained sort of person and not at all what she imagined Bryan's better half would be like.

Outside The Cock, the coldness of the evening and the strange muffled cotton wool sound in her ears only reinforced her decision that it was time to go. She had wondered if she should have told Leon and Rachael that she was calling it a night, but she knew they would also have tried to encourage her to stay, and really she had had enough of the crowd and the music. It wasn't her sort of thing at all.

As she opened the door to her 'normal, settled home' the only thing on her mind was Lawrence. It was around nine-thirty now and far beyond the time he normally came in. She went straight to the kitchen, willing him to be there, curled up fast asleep in his bed. He wasn't there. With dread creeping in she went quickly upstairs, hoping to find him on her bed, snoring, but the room was empty.

Determined not to give way to the panic she was feeling, she went back downstairs and, taking a torch from the kitchen drawer, she unlocked the back door and went out into the garden, still in her witch's weeds and heels. She probably should have stopped and changed first but she needed to find Lawrence.

She called softly into the darkness and shone the torch along the bottom of the hedges, desperate to pick up the flash of his luminous eyes, but the garden felt empty and silent. Nothing moved and she knew her boy wasn't there.

Sadly she trouped back inside and flopped down on the sofa, not quite sure what to do. Her ridiculous outfit now felt like it was encasing and crushing her. Her hat and broom lay abandoned in the hall, and she decided the least she could do was get changed while she waited.

As eleven o'clock struck on the hall clock, Elizabeth was beginning her third cup of tea. She sat wrapped up in her dressing gown at the kitchen table. At intervals, she went to the window and peered out. She couldn't see very far down the garden, but she felt she had to try. It was pointless considering sleep without her bed mate.

At midnight, she made herself a strong coffee in an effort to keep herself awake but after a few minutes her head began to nod against her chest and she drifted off for a short time. When her head fell forward just a little bit more, the nod woke her. She realised her eyes didn't want to open and that she was exhausted. She knew she had to go to bed. With one last look out of the kitchen window, she made her way upstairs.

Her sleep was a light, restless one and as the October wind was now whipping round the cottage, it felt even worse that Lawrence should be outside in such a hostile place. Tiredness and emotion now got the better of her and she began to cry.

At 4 a.m. she was suddenly catapulted back to consciousness by the familiar clack of the cat flap. She was instantly alert and out of bed, tearing down the stairs and into the kitchen where she found Lawrence nonchalantly eating biscuits from his bowl.

The mixture of emotions that rushed through her was almost too confusing to bear. She was relieved, delighted, almost unbelieving and oddly furious!

"Lawrence!" she shouted, rushing to lock the cat flap. "Where have you been? I thought something had happened to you. Oh, Lawrence, I've been so scared."

She hauled him up from his snack and threw him over her shoulder like a baby.

Her anger boiled up and ridiculously she found herself shouting at him.

"Don't you ever do that again, Lawrence! Not ever! I have been so worried! Why did you do this? I don't understand why you went. Not ever, Lawrence, do you understand?"

Of course he didn't understand but she still felt the need to tell him, to express anger at being tortured like that. Then she cried. She cried standing in the kitchen, holding Lawrence in her arms. She cried into his fur like a child.

****

"Oh, you 'ave to let em wander. It's their way," said Lucy pulling Elizabeth's already painful head sharply back into the bowl. As the warm water ran its fingers through her hair, she felt soothed and almost as though she could have gone to sleep, but the girl persisted. "They might come in your 'ouse but they are still wild things. Garden tigers my mum calls them."

Elizabeth was so tired she really had felt like cancelling her hair appointment but she had made herself come and now she was regretting it. The constant whine of the hairdryers and the annoying chatter was singeing her already raw nerve ends.

"Now, my nan 'ad a cat. Big Eric they called 'im. He would take on anythin', 'e would. He even sorted the Alsatian next door out, got him right across the nose 'e did."

"Lawrence is a Siamese," said Elizabeth hoping that would end the conversation.

"Oh, now, see, aren't they spiteful an' a bit sly? I wouldn't have one of those. Conditioner?"

335

"Yes, please," answered Elizabeth, wishing the girl would just be quiet. And for a few moments, as she worked the cream into her hair she was and then,

"You come over from Newton Prideaux, don't you?"

"Yes," she said, wearily.

"Well, that must be a shocker for you then."

"Sorry?"

"Well, the pub going. At least that's what one of my clients told me. There is a sign outside this morning saying it'll be gone by Christmas. Nice old pub The Cock, shame really."

Chapter Thirty Two

Like a lot of village rumours, it turned out to be not entirely true. Something was about to happen at the pub but it wasn't closing. Roger and Lorna Hayden were giving up their tenancy, and moving to a pub in Oxford City Centre. The notice on the door was merely thanking customers for their support.

To read it, made Elizabeth a little sad, because she didn't feel Roger had received much support at all. Most of the villagers had disliked his energetic approach and the changes he had tried to bring. They talked about him in disapproving tones and called him 'The new man at the pub' long after he had ceased to be new. Now he was going and she would miss him and his lairy pirate's grin. She remembered being so afraid of him at first but now it was strange to think he wouldn't be there behind the bar any more.

There was to be one last party at the pub, a firework display and bonfire on the first weekend in November. Roger and Lorna would start at their new pub in the New Year and this was their farewell to Newton Prideaux. Elizabeth decided she had to go and wish them both well in their new venture but not before she had made sure Lawrence was safely tucked away inside the cottage. Of course, fireworks and cats were not a good mixture.

Lawrence's Halloween disappearance still haunted her and she found herself checking and re-checking that he was okay. She grudgingly let him out these days, but the cat flap was always locked to entry-only after dark. Once he came in, he was staying in. She liked to know where he was.

It looked like the weather would be kind for Roger's last hurrah. The mornings had turned frosty and sharp now, the days bright and the night skies gloriously clear. She would stand out in her garden some nights and look up at the millions of stars above her; she felt it was the nearest you could come to staring into infinity. She didn't know what the names of the stars were, and she didn't care, it was enough to stare up at them and feel that sense of wonderment and at the same time her own insignificance.

Just lately, Elizabeth had begun to experience a sensation of impatience and restlessness. Looking up into the enormity of the sky seemed attuned to what she was feeling. An indefinable urge to do something big! Something drastic, something life changing, before she disappeared from this tiny world without even leaving a ripple. It was just that she didn't know what exactly that could be.

She had started looking for signs, some sort of clue as to which direction she should be taking. She prayed constantly that God would point her towards the right path, but he didn't seem to be listening. This latest departure from the village had only served to rekindle ideas of being left behind.

As if to compound this growing feeling of unease, an incident occurred that would make her think even more deeply about how she was living her life.

On the afternoon of the pub party, she had set out to walk to the woodland just outside the village to look for teasel. All year she had tried to keep some sort of seasonal display in the cottage: daffodils in spring, Peonies in summer but as winter approached it was difficult to know what to choose. holly or ivy seemed too Christmassy and so she had gone in search of teasel.

Just outside the village on the Crayton Road was a small wooded area known locally as Pinches' Copse. In spring it was covered with drifts of snowdrops but at this time of year the teasel would be ready to bring in and dry. She had recently rediscovered an old copper vase that would do perfectly to display it in. And so with this in mind she set off, with a large shopping bag and a pair of gardening secateurs.

She had just passed the village hall and as she drew level with Heron House she noticed a woman bending to attend with something in the front garden. Surely it had to be the elusive owner Maggie. At that same moment the woman stood up, hands on hips and smiled at Elizabeth.

Dressed in a bright concoction comprising of a long vivid pink fringed skirt, a colourful Norwegian style jumper and a pair of startling purple Doc Marten boots, she looked every bit as eccentric as Elizabeth had heard.

"Afternoon," she said, convivially. "I'm glad I've seen you."

Elizabeth was amazed. Why on earth would Maggie be glad to see her? She didn't even think she was aware of her existence.

"My neighbour, Gordon, says you've been to my door a few times now. Was there something important you wanted, my lovely? He watches out for me while I'm away, does Gordon. He's better than a Rottweiler," she laughed.

Elizabeth cringed. She thought she had put all this nonsense behind her. It had never occurred to her that she was being observed each time she had knocked at the door. Now she was well and truly on the spot and she had no choice but to explain. "I was calling on behalf of the Residents' Committee but I'm not a member any more, so please don't worry."

"Oh, I'm not worried, lovely. Just curious. What have I done to upset that old committee?" said Maggie, mischievously.

Elizabeth considered for a moment. It was true that Heron House had looked dark and a little forlorn compared with the rest of the village and that this would be an issue again very shortly, and so she said, "Well, a few people have noticed that you didn't put any decorations up last year and as yours is the first house you see as you enter the village, they were wondering if…"

"Christmas decorations, you mean?" cut in Maggie.

"Yes. If it's a religious belief, I'd be happy to tell the committee on your behalf."

Maggie's face broke into a broad grin. "Look, my sweet, the temperature's really dropping now the sun's gone down. Come on in and we'll talk about these decorations, all right?"

Hesitantly Elizabeth opened the gate and stepped into the untidy front garden. "What's your name, sweetheart? I'm Maggie, but I expect you know that. Come on through, come on through. Let's get inside out the cold."

"Elizabeth," she answered. "Pleased to meet you, Maggie."

As she walked onto the porch, wind chimes hanging next to the front door sadly ding-dinged as if they were still hanging on to their memories of long lost summer. Their solemn sound made Elizabeth feel a little gloomy. All she had intended was to get some teasel and head home. Now she was about to become embroiled in something she would really rather not be involved in.

She was led through to a large high ceilinged living room, dominated by a huge fireplace and cluttered with objects. Every possible space seemed to be filled with ornaments and curios. On one wall hung a richly coloured rug and on the opposite wall, a strange tribal mask. This was a traveller's room without doubt.

"Sit down then, lovely. Take the weight off. Would you like a tea or anything?"

Hoping to keep the visit as short as possible Elizabeth declined the tea and sat down on the cushion filled sofa. Everywhere seemed to be filled with the scent of jasmine, adding to the odd, exotic feel of her surroundings, but also quite incongruous in the British wintertime. The whole place felt just a little out of kilter with Newton Prideaux in November.

Her neighbour planted her feet firmly, leant back against the fireplace and folded her broad arms across her stomach. "So, these decorations then, or lack of 'em have rattled a few cages, have they? Didn't think it would be that important what other people did or didn't do, but if it bothers them, I suppose I could sort a few lights out or something," she said, amiably.

"That would be lovely," said Elizabeth. "I think it's just because everyone else decorates and as you drive in from Crayton, your house is the first in the village, and..."

"I can see that, my love. But tell your committee, it won't be till Christmas Eve. None of this putting things up in September. Gotta be Christmas proper before I'll do anything."

"Oh," said Elizabeth. "Christmas Eve?

"It's Maggie's Law, I'm afraid."

With her shining, round face, Maggie reminded Elizabeth of a wholesome polished apple, but she could also see an edge of defiance in that jovial expression and so she decided to tread carefully.

"Well, yes it is a little irritating to see Christmas things in the shops so early but perhaps you would put them up on the first Sunday in Advent? That would only be a few weeks before Christmas."

"No, sorry I have lived by my law for a long time now and it seems to work for me. I won't be persuaded to get too far ahead of myself."

Knowing the committee would not be at all satisfied with such a late date, Elizabeth tried again. "How about Christmas week, then? Would that be better?"

"No, sweetheart, can't be done. Look, other people can buy their Christmas cards in January for the following year, have all their presents wrapped and put in the spare room by June if that's what they want to do, but I celebrate things in their proper time and that's it?"

"Maggie's Law?" said Elizabeth.

"Maggie's Law. Look."

She nodded to an old empty picture hook over the fireplace. "See that? The hook?"

"Yes," replied Elizabeth. "Are you having a picture cleaned?"

"No, it's always like that. I leave it empty. I take that hook with me every time I move. It's my Havisham Hook."

Elizabeth was now totally baffled. What on earth could a hook without a picture have to do with Christmas decorations? Maggie was clearly even more eccentric than she had been led to believe.

"You remember Miss Havisham in Great Expectations, don't you?" said Maggie. "Jilted on her wedding day, living in that big old house, keeping things exactly as they were on the day?" Elizabeth nodded. "Well, it happened to me, sort of. Well, in reverse I s'pose. I met a man, years ago. We got a house together, decided to get married and off we went. All sounds lovely, doesn't it?"

"Well, yes?" said Elizabeth already fearing the end of the story. This was not one of Bryan's tall tales, it was altogether more serious.

"It was lovely, for **me**. All I could see was the wedding. I didn't think about nothing else, not even my husband to be. I just went on and on, planning every tiny detail: flowers, favours, balloons, buttonholes. Everything had to be how I wanted. I planned the lot. Even where our wedding photograph should hang in our house. On that hook."

Maggie paused. "And so, he left, my other half. He just up and went. He got lost along the way, you see. Somewhere in all those arrangements he disappeared, and we never did have that wedding photograph taken."

346

"Oh," said Elizabeth. "I'm sorry to hear that." It seemed quite an inadequate thing to say but what else was there?

"Yes, it was very sad. But it taught me a lesson and I keep the hook to remind me of how stupid I was. I don't get caught up in planning any more. I live in the present, each day as it comes."

Elizabeth couldn't think of a single thing to say and so she just sat, hands in her lap looking at her neighbour.

"Aaah, you look really sad now, my lovely," said Maggie. "Don't be. Maggie's Law works both ways, you know? I'm not one for planning too far ahead, but I'm not one for worrying either. There's no point. Good or bad, not everything comes to pass, so what's the point of worrying about the future? Just enjoy today."

It seemed a very simple philosophy, but one to which Elizabeth knew she would never be able to subscribe. She couldn't help but think about her future and how she could influence it. Maggie was definitely a much more tranquil person than she would ever be, but Elizabeth now knew her future was entirely in her own hands. Decisively she got to her feet.

"Look, I'm sorry I've bothered you about this. I'll leave you in peace now," she said.

"You haven't bothered me, my lovely. You haven't bothered me at all, and rest assured, those decorations will be up on Christmas Eve as promised. So you can tell that to your committee."

"I will do," said Elizabeth gathering her bag. The teasel could wait, she decided, what she needed now was her home and some time to think before the party. She was running out of patience.

Chapter Thirty Three

Elizabeth returned from her visit to Heron House full of resolve. She knew it was no good, just waiting for things to change; she needed to change them. She realised she had retreated into herself, the bullies had forced her to hide and she had forgotten what E had taught her about getting out into the world. Talking to Maggie had brought it into sharp focus for her. Maggie was happy to go along from day to day and see where life took her, but Elizabeth could not trust to luck, or fate, she had drifted for the last forty years and life had taken her no further than Bicester.

She needed a different outlook and she would start straight away. Instead of going along to the pub to see something come to an end, she would embrace it, not as a farewell to Roger but as a new beginning, a catalyst. Buoyed up by her new plan, she went upstairs to pick out the brightest outfit she could find. As though he sensed her excitement, Lawrence bounded up with her.

But Elizabeth would have very little time to consolidate her plans and begin her new way of living because there was about to be several events in the village, the reverberations of which, would occupy her mind for a long time to come.

The first of these incidents had been building to a climax for many years. It had started miles away but was about to reach its conclusion there in the village. Sometimes it had faltered in its progress but ultimately there was only ever going to be one outcome. It was now so close to that outcome that the final course of actions had already began to unfold.

The Cock was busy for once. It seemed such a shame that people had taken the time to come out now that Roger was leaving, Elizabeth thought, but wasn't that human nature? It took a lot to shake people out of their complacency. She had fallen into that trap herself but now she was determined to break out. She hadn't even decided how yet, a trip to see Edith, perhaps? A change of job? She was determined to do something and with God's help she would find her way.

Trying her hardest to feign confidence she pushed her way to the crowded bar, where Roger was talking to Leon. "Hello, both," she said.

"Elizabeth! said Leon. "How lovely to see you. I was just telling Roger, Gilmour is going to miss his fish pie. He was always hanging around the bins on Friday night!"

"Well, I shall miss you too, and not because of the fish pie," said Elizabeth boldly. "I'm sorry to see you go."

"Aah, that's nice of you. Hear that, Leon? Somebody is gonna miss me. What can I get you to drink, love?"

Her first thought was a wine, but she played safe and ordered a coke. She wasn't quite ready to throw caution to the wind.

"I shall miss this place a bit, I suppose," Roger said, handing her the glass. "Beautiful countryside round 'ere, but it's a bit quiet for me. I came into this pub thinking I would liven things up, but sometimes people just don't want to be livened up, do they? I've realised I'm flogging a dead horse. That's fine, if that's the way you want to be, but I always think you're only here once, you have to enjoy it. I'm 52 next birthday. I want some fun before I go." He gave her a typically roguish grin. "No, a city pub will do me. Students, tourists, a bit of life. Bound to be a challenge at first, but that's what I want. I don't want to stop trying. The day I feel content is the day I snuff it. When I was a kid we had a Welsh English teacher, if that makes sense? He was always quoting a poem that said, 'Do not go gentle into that good night,' and I don't intend to. I wanna go down fighting."

"Good for you, Roger," said Leon. "Carpe Diem and all that!"

"Back to fish again, then?" quipped Roger. "So, you both sticking around for the fireworks? I've got some big 'uns lined up. They'll shake a few people out of bed, I can tell you. Going out with a bang!"

"I'm coming!" said Elizabeth, raising her glass. "There hasn't been a display in the village for years."

"Good, good! I'll be starting about nine, out in the courtyard. Anyway best get on... Yes, sir what can I get you?

Elizabeth exchanged glances with Leon. Both knew just how much they would miss Roger's lively presence.

"How have you been, Elizabeth?" began Leon, but the conversation was cut short by a sudden stir near the pub's entrance. Bryan came in looking what could only be described as stricken. Usually such a neat man, he now looked dishevelled and distraught.

Instinctively Leon and Elizabeth went towards him. "Bryan, are you all right?" said Leon, reaching out to steady him.

Bryan's eyes looked wild and full of anguish, and for a moment it was difficult to tell if he had even heard Leon's question.

"Bryan!" he said again.

"Yes, yes, I'm fine. I just don't know what to do. I just don't know! Oh God, I just …"

"Bryan," said Leon, firmly, "tell us, what's happened? We'll help you, but tell us. Have you had an accident?"

They were joined by Rachael. Elizabeth was relieved to see she was as serene as ever and without hesitation she put her arms around Bryan and steered him to a bar stool.

"Now then," she said quietly. "What's happened, Bryan?"

"It's Maeve," he said, as though even now he still couldn't believe it. "They've taken her to hospital."

"Was there an accident?" said Leon.

"They've taken her to the John Radcliffe," said Bryan, appearing not to hear. "Ah God, just seeing her taken away like that. What will I do now?"

"What's wrong with her?" tried Leon. "Roger! Can we get a brandy over here?"

Bryan continued to stare into space, as though he was still picturing his wife being taken away from him.

"He's in shock," said Rachael. "Do you want to go and see her, Bryan? Do you know where they've taken her? Which ward?"

Roger put a glass into his hand and patted his shoulder. "There you go son," he said.

Bryan took a sip and finally seemed to engage with the little group of people standing around him.

"She's in intensive care. They didn't call it that, but that's what it is. She was so ill, ya know? I'd to call for the ambulance. It was like her whole body just gave up. I couldn't help her."

"Look," said Leon, "one of us should take him over there. He needs to be with her."

"You can't," pointed out Rachael. "You've had a drink? And so have I?"

Bryan silently sipped his brandy, like a man freshly pulled from the sea.

"I could take him," said Elizabeth. She really didn't want to. She found the idea terrifying, but she also knew it was the right thing to do. There could be no running away.

"No, no, you're fine," said Bryan. "I'll get a cab or something. Don't you worry."

Something about this pathetic show of bravado on Bryan's part helped her find her courage and she said, "Of course you won't. I'll be happy to take you. Let me go and get the car and we'll be off."

Elizabeth would never forget that drive through the countryside, with a silent Bryan McConway next to her, lost in his own shattered world, and bursts of light flashing overhead as distant fireworks exploded inaudibly around them. The pretty sparkling waterfalls of light seemed at odds with the grim task in front of them.

Eventually the John Radcliffe came into sight, a big white liner with rows of brightly lit cabins along its sides. Neither of them acknowledged it, they just continued to their destination.

Intensely lit and stifling, the hospital took them both in and processed them accordingly. Bryan answered all their questions in a dazed, slightly vacant way and, as hospitals do, they made the extraordinary and the tragic seem commonplace and normal, even though they never can be to the people concerned.

Maeve McConway was in Intensive Care as Bryan had said and at the heavy security doors, they rang a bell to be admitted.

"Do you want me to come in with you, or shall I wait out here?" said Elizabeth.

"God, no. Come on in. She'll be pleased to see you."

Its subdued lighting, overly warm atmosphere and the mixture of plastic and rubber smell, made the ICU feel totally synthetic and devoid of life. An odd pocket of silence in the hectic hospital.

The patients were in separate curtained bays and instinctively she looked for Maeve, but with all the tubes and machines, it was hard to tell one shape from another.

Bryan asked at the nurses' station and they were directed to a bay in the far corner. Relieved, Bryan rushed over and sat down next to the bed.

Not wanting to intrude, Elizabeth hung back. It didn't seem right to rush in on their reunion. After a moment, Bryan beckoned her over.

"Come on and say hello, Elizabet'. She's in a bit of a state, but she says she doesn't mind you seeing."

Not knowing quite what to expect Elizabeth went to stand next to Bryan. The person lying half concealed on the bed was not the woman she had been talking to in the pub, the robust, voluptuous, twinkling woman with red hair and an easy charm. This was a stranger.

What she saw on the bed in front of her jolted her to her very core. Maeve's skin was orange, not yellow and jaundiced but a deep burnt orange, like she had been smeared in ochre.

The shape of the body was now barely discernible and appeared to be one huge bloated stomach with distended limbs attached to it. Elizabeth was so shocked she looked away. It couldn't be Maeve, there must be a mistake. She had stood next to her in the pub just a few nights ago, alive and bright and full of charm.

At that moment Maeve pulled herself up a little in the bed and turned to look at them. To Elizabeth's absolute horror the whites of Maeve's eyes were as orange as her skin, giving her a ghastly alien appearance that took Elizabeth's breath away and made her knees buckle beneath her. Almost as bad as the lurid colour was the desperate look in them, a look that Elizabeth would never forget.

Steeling herself, Elizabeth reached out for her hand and Maeve pulled her closer. With the bizarre tube taped to her nose and the musty sweet smell emanating from her, Elizabeth found herself wanting to wretch.

"Elizabeth, thank you for coming," she said.

Chapter Thirty Four

It's was so good of you to bring Bryan," continued Maeve, sitting up a little further and attempting to brush a straggle of auburn hair back from her face. "I know I look terrible. They won't let me get a look at myself. I wish I could've at least combed my hair for ya."

Instinctively Elizabeth recoiled, repulsed at the sight of what had become of Maeve. Feeling both pity and shock it took her a moment to reply, "Don't worry about that," she said finally, in the most upbeat voice she could manage. "Just get yourself better again and home to Bryan. That's all we care about, isn't it, Bryan?"

"Elizabeth, would you do me a favour?" asked Maeve, leaning closer. "Would you scratch my arms for me, they are itching like billy-o. Just rub them, will you? They are driving me crazy!"

Reluctantly and shamefully Elizabeth rubbed each arm as quickly as she could, not wanting to touch the yellowed skin for longer than necessary.

"Thanks a million, sweetheart. I'd ask those others to do it, but they aren't really nurses, you know?"

"Aren't they?"

Again the yellowed eyes took on a look of distress, "God, no. They are all actors, every one of 'em. I've seen them in the soap operas on the television."

Elizabeth glanced nervously towards Bryan, not really sure how to respond. A moment ago she had seemed quite rational but now she wasn't making any sense at all.

"No, darlin'," said Bryan, "You're fine. They are nurses, I swear to you. You have to let them look after you."

"Yes, I'm sure they are, too," added Elizabeth.

"Well, I know what I know. Bryan and I know I've seen them on the television. They're just acting."

"Ah, well, you're probably right," said Bryan, changing tack. "You know, you're looking a wee bit tired now. Would you not like a sleep? I tell you what, you have a sleep and we'll go and see

360

about getting you some proper nurses, how's that?"

"Yes, that's a good idea," said Elizabeth, seeing her chance to escape. "I'll go and wait outside for you, Bryan, and you have a good sleep, Maeve and get yourself better."

She knew the words sounded pathetic and merely a way of excusing herself from a situation she couldn't deal with, but she had to leave. The room, Maeve, and Bryan's parental tone were all suffocating her.

Outside in the corridor she sat gratefully down on a plastic chair and drew in a deep breath. She had never experienced anything like this in her life. What had happened to Maeve? What disease had ravaged her? Was this what cancer looked like? All she really wanted was to get as far away as possible from it, but for Bryan's sake she knew she had to stay.

Sometime later when he joined her outside in the relative freshness of the corridor, Bryan looked exhausted and overwhelmed. "I don't know about you, Elizabet,'" he said, "but I'm in need of caffeine."

The hospital cafeteria had a desperate feel to it, now only inhabited by other late night refugees of personal disaster. They sat in small huddles, some of them clutching impersonal hospital carrier bags, trying to make sense of what was happening to them.

Bryan and Elizabeth chose a table at the far end of the room, away from other people and their adversities. Theirs was quite big enough to deal with on its own. The catering staff had gone home and so the glowing, solid vending machine provided them with coffees in cardboard cups.

For a while they drank in silence, and then Bryan very carefully put down his coffee and said, "All this is my fault, Elizabet'. Maeve always liked a drink, maybe a little too much, ya know? But she was a shy girl when I met her and it seemed to help, gave her a little bit of confidence. I loved her, how could I say no to her? She was always so happy when she was drinking, I liked to see her happy, but I let it go too far."

"Don't blame yourself," mumbled Elizabeth, feeling much too shocked to offer anything more sensible or meaningful.

"It wasn't too much of a problem when we ran the hotels together, she was always so busy, but when we went into the pub business it got worse. I always made excuses for her but deep down I knew it wasn't right. She was surrounded by it all day, every day and bored out of her mind, while I was having the time of my life. All she ever wanted was a proper home and I finally gave her one here in the village. I thought I could save her. We worked on cutting it down, kept a diary of how much she drank, all that, you know? But it was too late. She's needed it just to feel normal these last few years and now….."

He didn't finish the sentence, he didn't really need to. Now, Elizabeth understood, this was all about drinking. She had no idea this sort of thing could happen, not to middle aged respectable people like Bryan and Maeve.

She hadn't really come face to face with drunkenness. She had seen pictures of intoxicated young people wandering around Banbury on Saturday night and old men with long beards sleeping it off on park benches, but it hadn't really impinged on her world. Her world was a Christian world, where nobody really over indulged or took to strong drink.

The bible preached moderation and that is what she had lived by. To be brutally forced to come face to face with this other world was

363

shocking. All sorts of judgmental thoughts raced into her mind, but somehow she could not bring herself to apply them to Bryan and Maeve. They weren't wicked people who lived debauched lives. They were just normal people, and Bryan in particular, was a person she had become very fond of.

"I'm so sorry, Bryan," she said, and she was sincere. This felt just as much a tragedy as if Maeve had been in an accident. She even felt that it was an accident in a way; it had just been going on for a very long time.

Bryan nodded. "Her body is packing up now, you see. That's the problem, even her brain."

"What can they do?"

For the first time, she saw tears gather in Bryan's eyes. "The damage is done now…," he said, burying his face in his hands.

Elizabeth reached out and touched his shoulder. She was not equipped to deal with this at all and she sent up a silent prayer to give her the courage she needed to help him.

Bryan cried in silence whilst Elizabeth sat opposite, willing him to find strength.

Finally he said, "Ah well, this won't do, now will it? I can't sit here when my Maeve needs me." He ran his big hands over his face and forced himself to sit upright. "I need to be getting back to her. But look, you go. You've done so much. I don't know how long I'll be here but I'll get a cab back. Please don't worry. You've been kindness itself, Elizabet'. I can't thank you enough but don't be waiting here for me. You go home now. We'll be fine."

For a split second she was tempted to offer to stay for as long as it took, but she knew that it wasn't really practical. There was so little she could do. So little anyone could do, it seemed.

"Is there anybody I can call for you, Bryan?" she offered.

"Ah no, we've no real family now, and I'm not sure Maeve would want people to see her in this state. Look, Elizabeth will you do something for me? Will you keep this quiet? I don't want people talking about her. Will you just say she's ill? Say she's pneumonia or something?"

Elizabeth nodded. It went against all her principles, but her compassion overruled her head and she agreed. She couldn't have the whole of Newton Prideaux condemning and demeaning them. This was their private sadness and not entertainment for the village.

"Will you let me know how she is?" she said, scrawling her number on a cafeteria napkin. "Just a quick call, if you can."

"Of course, of course, I will. Now you go. Get on home to that cat of yours. He'll be wondering where you are. I'll get back to Maeve now."

****

When she arrived home, feeling stiff and cold, she found Lawrence hiding behind the magazine rack in the living room. His whole demeanour suggested that he had been terrified by something. His tail was fluffed and his eyes wide. Gathering him up she spoke softly to him saying, "Oh, Lawrence what's the matter? What's happened? Sweet boy, what is it?"

She held him close to her and stroked him gently. Together they sat down in the armchair and she tucked him inside her coat. Instinctively he hid his head against her, pressing it into her side.

"Fireworks!" she said aloud. "Roger's fireworks! Aah, poor Lawrence." She pulled her coat further over him and held him close.

She was awoken by the phone at just after 3 a.m. It was Bryan with the news that Maeve had passed just a little while ago.

As she listened to his calm voice explaining what the doctors had told him and how peaceful it had been, she felt at a loss. Bryan let her go without having a conversation. It seemed as much as he could do to deliver the message. He had a lot to sort out, he said, and excused himself.

Elizabeth of course had never lost a partner. Her mother's death had left her feeling guilty and indifferent but the grief in Bryan's voice told her, that this was a pain she could not imagine.

It seemed strange that she had become part of this tragedy when she wasn't even a close friend, but it occurred to her that despite Bryan's big personality, they had had no real friends. Was that because of their secret? Were they afraid to let people in? The price was that when their world collapsed, there was no one there to help. As a Christian she was glad God had sent her to be their friend that night, and she had no doubt in her mind that it was God's doing.

It was ironic, she thought, as she and Lawrence made their way to bed for what was left of the night, that Bryan's saddest story of all had turned out to be his own.

Chapter Thirty Five

The dark and secret nature of Maeve McConway's death left Elizabeth feeling isolated and introspective. She was one of the very few people in Newton Prideaux who knew what really happened to Bryan's auburn haired wife that night, and it was a difficult burden to bear.

The whole story had been a tragedy and it brought home to her how much she had accepted things at face value. At forty she was still as naïve as a teenager. Bryan's life had been steadily falling apart for years and nobody, including her, had had a clue. Looking back she felt she should have noticed something was wrong: Maeve's unspecified illness, Bryan buying whisky early in the morning and the pace of Maeve's drinking at the pub. It all seemed significant now but at the time, it passed by as simply normal and explainable. A lot of people liked to drink, it was innocent enough.

There was another problem troubling her, too. Elizabeth, by nature a truthful person, she was also a Christian and so when Bryan spread the word that his wife had died of pneumonia, she wasn't sure what she would say if someone were to ask her a direct question about it. Of course she understood why Bryan wanted to keep it a secret. He didn't want his wife remembered as an alcoholic, but it did put her in an invidious position, and one that she couldn't share with anybody. She prayed to God for guidance and as always, she already knew the answer. It was one of the Ten Commandments. She didn't need to ask. She must not lie.

She also decided that it was somewhat of a warning to her. Over the last few months she had started to have the occasional tipple to be sociable. It had seemed quite daring and sophisticated to drink wine with the likes of Leon and Rachael but now it felt like a dangerous road to take. The thin end of the wedge. Since that night at the hospital, she had been haunted by the picture of Maeve lying bloated on the bed. The yellow skin and orange eyes flashed into her mind, sometimes quite unexpectedly and jolted her. She had been shocked to be brought face to face with something so out of her experience. The world seemed a much more frightening place than it had this time last year.

The weight of her knowledge bore down on her and she found herself engaged in a game of cat and mouse with the other villagers. She was desperate not to get into conversations that might stray into dangerous territory. She had already decided that she would attend the funeral service for Maeve but not the wake. That would be too much to cope with. An unguarded word on her part and it could all go horribly wrong.

She hid herself away as much as she could, and hoped that with Christmas approaching, people would quickly move on to other topics. It usually was that way with village life, *nine day wonders*, as her mother would have said. Lately she had begun to feel that even Mick was no longer a talking point. She had received no further hate mail or attacks on her property and everyone seemed to be treating her normally again. She had to be grateful for small mercies, she supposed.

One misty, dreary Sunday at the end of November, the first real cold of the winter was beginning to bite and Elizabeth remembered an ancient oil heater that was kept in the pantry. Dragging it out and dusting it off, she felt sure it would be well received by Mr Latimer and Pal. The garage was pleasantly cool in the summer but with the coldest months ahead, she wanted them to be warm.

She plugged it in and waited to hear the tell-tale clicks and clonks that told her it was warming up. It was quite dusty and smelled so, but she could soon remedy that. She went to the cupboard under the sink and looked for a suitable cloth. While she was bending there, a soft, leathery paw tapped her face. Two large blue Siamese eyes were looking imploringly into hers.

"Oh, Lawrence!" she said. "You can't possibly want to go out! It's horrible and murky today. Stay in by the fire with me."

But the cat was determined and went pointedly over to the cat flap and nudged it. "Really?" she said, standing, duster in hand. "You really want to go out in that? Oh. Very well, but I think you'll soon be back."

She unlatched the cat flap and waited for him to go. He stuck his nose out and sniffed the air tentatively before the rest of his body followed like a graceful diver aiming for a pool. "Bye, Lawrence," she said. "Be careful."

She was about to return to her cleaning when blue flashing lights racing past the front of her cottage stopped her in her tracks. This was something so rare in the village that she couldn't help but go to the window and unashamedly look out.

The police car and ambulance went quickly down the hill and around the corner before vanishing from view. Clearly something was taking place on the other side of the village. Perhaps someone had been taken ill, but it was quite alarming.

She went back to the kitchen and continued to clean the oil heater. She was sure to hear all about it at some point.

In the garage Mick was nowhere to be seen. This wasn't unusual. He often took himself and Pal off for long walks, and she didn't pry. He was a free spirit and asked very little of her, so for the most part she was happy to leave him alone. She dragged the heater in and set it down near to his few belongings.

She was about to go back into the cottage when the garage door creaked up and Mick ducked in with Pal.

"Mick, hello. I brought this out for you," she said. "I thought you might be glad of it in the

373

cold. There's a socket over there. And by the way, I was wondering if you would like to have Christmas dinner with me? There won't be too much God... what was it? bothering?"

"There's summat goin' off in't village," he said, worriedly. "Police and ambulance. Its ova by t' mad girls 'ouse. It looked bad. The coppers were runnin'."

"Oh," said Elizabeth. "At Ellen's house?"

"Looked like it were. I just saw 'em all runnin' up path."

"I'd better go and see if I can help. Perhaps Bunny isn't well. I'll see you later," she said, suddenly serious.

"Elizabeth," he called after her. "Thanks for t'eater."

By the time Elizabeth arrived at Ellen Kitteridge's cottage there was quite a crowd gathered outside.

As usual Dina Watkins, the sharp nosed receptionist was to the fore, standing as close as she could to the cottage gate.

"What on earth has happened, Dina? Is it Bunny?" asked Elizabeth.

"Ellen, apparently. Christopher's inside, seeing if he can be of any assistance."

"Do we know what's wrong with her?"

"Well, between you and me, Elizabeth," she said, lowering her voice, "We overheard the police radioing about an overdose."

"No, really? That's so sad. Poor Ellen, to be in such a state. I had no idea, had you?"

"Well, I'm not surprised, if I'm honest. She just hasn't been herself since Kim died, has she? And it's coming up for the anniversary soon. It's so often the way, you know? Something triggers it and ….."

As the crowd stood whispering and murmuring, the ambulance crew came out of the front door carrying Ellen Kitteridge on a stretcher. To Elizabeth's relief she could see she was moving, and she appeared to be talking and trying to gesture.

"They must have caught her in time. Silly girl," said Dina. "That's not the answer, is it? And who would look after poor Bunny? It's so selfish."

The doors thudded shut and the ambulance pulled away, no doubt destined for The John Radcliffe just like Maeve. For a moment Elizabeth winced, remembering the night she had driven there with Bryan at her side. Now it was Ellen making the journey.

A few moments later the two police officers came out, and to the absolute and audible astonishment of the assembled villagers, so did Bunny Kitteridge - but in handcuffs. As she was led to the waiting police car she smiled at her neighbours and tried to wave. For all the world she looked like a celebrity acknowledging the paparazzi on her doorstep. No hint of concern or worry showed in her beaming round face as the policeman pressed her head down and loaded her into the car.

Speechless, Elizabeth watched them drive away. What on earth had happened in that cottage?

Christopher Watkins emerged with more police officers and walked swiftly over to his wife. "I'm going to the Radcliffe to see Ellen. I can't say much."

"I know, I know, but was it an overdose? What's happening to Bunny? Why have they taken her away?" begged his wife.

"Dina, I really can't say. But what I can say is, thank God it was SSRIs not TCAs."

He left them and went back to talking with the police officers.

"Antidepressants," said Dina. "She's taken antidepressants."

Chapter Thirty Six

Elizabeth felt dazed and shaken to the core over the latest incident with Bunny. It was as though her world had suddenly gone mad, as though she was in an alarming dream that would suddenly end. She told herself that God would not send her anything she couldn't cope with, but this seemed close to her limit. From years of an almost cloistered existence she had been plunged into this maelstrom and it was beginning to make her feel ill.

When she got back to the cottage and told Mick what had happened, she felt overwhelmingly tired. She made herself a cup of tea but it went cold on the kitchen table, as she stood and stared out into the garden with unfocused eyes.

What had happened at Ellen's house? What could Bunny have done that warranted her being taken away in handcuffs? It didn't make any sense. Bunny had always been like her silent twin but now their ways had parted. Bunny was on her way to the police station in handcuffs, and she couldn't begin to understand why.

She had no idea how long she had stood looking out with unseeing eyes at the misty garden and fields beyond. It was as though her brain had switched off for a while, shut down under the stress of all that had happened. She had longed for freedom, to experience life without her mother's interference, but she had found herself pushed to the very edge of her strength over this last year. On the other side of it all, would she emerge as a strong woman, or would it all be too much for her? Would she fail at living on her own? Would she be the useless creature her mother always thought her to be?

At a little after 1. 00 pm the phone rang. It was Dina Watkins. As always she was to the point. "Well, It wasn't suicide!" she announced. "No, apparently Bunny tried to poison Ellen."

"What?" said Elizabeth, unable to take in the matter of fact sentence she had just heard.

"Yes, I don't think she meant it, you know?"

Not mean it? Elizabeth was still struggling.

"It was just attention seeking, apparently. She wanted a party, like they had for Kim, you know. His wake? There was no malice in it. She wouldn't think of the consequences, you see. Anyway, I just thought you'd like to know."

"What will happen to her?" said Elizabeth.

"I don't know. Christopher seems to think she'll have to go to court, but I don't suppose she'll go to prison or anything. Well, it wouldn't be right, would it? Like locking a five year old up. She doesn't know she's done anything wrong. No, she'll probably get some sort of psychiatric treatment or something. Now, Elizabeth, I know we haven't seen eye to eye on your erm, guest but you will always be welcome back on the committee. Just have a think about it. We all need to stick together at the moment, what with Bunny and poor Mr McConway's wife. Now you take care, and let me know if you want to join us again. Bye, Elizabeth."

Elizabeth sat down and brought both hands up to her face as she tried to process the conversation. She had to respect Dina, despite her sharp ways. She was such a resilient woman who seemed able to protect herself by compartmentalising everything in her life. Nothing really touched Dina, she dealt with things and moved on. Elizabeth, on the other hand, felt every last jolt and shaft of pain.

To Dina, Bunny was now sorted out, resolved. Ellen hadn't died, Bunny would be treated, and life would go on. But to Elizabeth the darkness in the situation was overpowering. Perhaps because she had always seen Bunny as a shadow of herself. She, of all people, knew what it was like to be buried alive in Newton Prideaux, prevented from ever having a normal life. Had that suffocation led to Bunny's action? Was it desperation to be noticed? Perhaps, if the village hadn't treated her like a dirty secret and instead encouraged Ellen to have her assessed long ago, things would have been different. Now it all just seemed rather grotesque. She wasn't sure she could brush it off as easily as Dina had seemed to.

It was well after lunchtime now and yet she didn't feel hungry. She felt full up with emotions and worry. She re-made her cup of tea but this time she made an effort to sit and drink it. This last year had been baptism by fire. She had longed to experience life as an adult but now, just a small part of her wished she could return to her days of uneventful boredom.

She spent the rest of the afternoon ineffectually starting various tasks before lapsing into thought and abandoning them. At that time of the year, what little light there was, disappeared by half past three and the night closed people into their houses. She briefly wondered if she should get ready and attend the evening service at St Martin's but the lethargy of shock prevented her from doing anything more than just thinking about it.

As she went to draw the living room curtains, she saw a streak of tabby grey shoot across the road and disappear toward The Cock. Taking it to be Gilmour on a bin hunt, it suddenly occurred to her that she hadn't seen Lawrence for a while. He usually popped back for a snack or simply to warm his chilly brown feet before going out again, but today he hadn't been home. It was dark now and time he was in.

She grabbed his box of biscuits and went out on to the back garden. It was still misty and the cold, damp air made her shudder.

She shook the biscuits: "Lawrence!"

Nothing.

"Lawrence! Come on now. Time to come in, Lawrence!"

Nothing.

On summer nights it sometimes took a few attempts to get him in, but in the winter, he almost seemed glad to return to the warmth of the cottage. A little trickle of fear entered Elizabeth's mind. She pushed it away.

"Lawrence, come on!" she said again.

He had done this before, hadn't he? And then just strolled in as though nothing had happened. She calmed herself and rattled the biscuits once more.

Nothing happened, just an awful heavy silence. She knew she should calmly go inside and wait but in her heightened state of anxiety she found herself running down the garden to the hedge and calling loudly over into the field.

"Lawrence! Lawrence!" She was conscious now that it sounded more like a plea and her eyes scanned the foggy horizon desperately for him, but nothing moved.

Seized by a sudden panic she rushed back inside and went in search of Mick in the garage.

She found him and Pal sitting, wrapped in blankets with their backs to the oil heater, looking relaxed and set for the evening.

"Elizabeth, yer all right?" he said, alarmed by her frantic appearance.

"Lawrence won't come in! I've been calling him and he just won't come."

"Aye but he's done this before, an't 'e? Don't get worrying, 'e's probably found a lady friend."

"No, Mick I'm scared. He's just not out there."

"Okay, well, where does 'e go, when you let 'im out? Over t'fields, is it? Perhaps 'e's gone further than usual and 'e just can't 'ear yer."

"I don't think that's it. I don't know why, but I just don't. I'm really worried about him."

"Right, I'll tell you what then. 'Ave you got a torch? A good un? If you 'ave I'll teck it and 'ave a walk over in t'fields. Ow's that?"

Pal looked up balefully as though he knew he was about to be disturbed in his warm spot.

"Would you, Mick? I would be so grateful. I don't think I could cope if he didn't come home tonight."

Having been given the torch, Mick Latimer climbed awkwardly over the fence at the end of the garden and dropped down into the field on the other side. "Right then, I'll scan from side to side and you keep callin' 'im," he said.

He waded out into the darkened fields like a man up to his waist in a swamp. She watched as the flashing torch swept across the fields, pausing occasionally in the hedgerows, but no moon diamond eyes were caught in its beam.

By eight o'clock Mick had walked the field and the ones beyond it several times but to no avail. If Lawrence was out there he didn't want to be found and no amount of calling and biscuit shaking was going to change that.

He trudged back toward the cottage and climbed back into the garden.

"I don't think 'e's comin', Elizabeth. I'll 'ave another look in't mornin' if 'e's not back, but I don't think we're gonna do any good tonight. It's cold, let's go in. I still think 'e'll turn up when he's ready."

Slowly they walked back along the path together, Elizabeth close to tears now. She knew Mick was right and there was nothing more to be done. But she couldn't help wishing this wasn't happening, not now, not after all that had taken place. She willed Lawrence to appear at the last moment as she closed the back door and wished Mick good night, but once inside, she was quite alone.

For a while she stood in her kitchen staring out into the garden and praying. She didn't think she had the strength to withstand this and she needed help. If only Lawrence would come running down the path and clatter through the cat flap, she could cope with everything else.

As midnight approached she knew she needed to go to bed. She had work in the morning and she was already feeling washed out and exhausted. Mechanically she turned out the lights, unplugged things and slowly climbed the narrow stair to bed.

As she finally lay down and stared at the white cracked ceiling over her bed, she couldn't prevent a tear slipping out of the side of her eye and running slyly onto the pillow.

Something was telling her this wasn't right. Lawrence hadn't just wandered off. It wasn't like last time, she could sense it.

Chapter Thirty Seven

Elizabeth had finally fallen into an exhausted sleep just as the birds had begun to sing in the dawn, only to wake an hour later feeling as though she has been knocked down and trampled on. Her face still bore the wrinkles from the pillow and her left arm felt dead beneath her. Her sleep had been heavy and strangely disorientating.

Once she pulled herself back to full consciousness, the horror of the day before rushed into her head and she shot out of bed and downstairs, desperate to see if Lawrence had returned. Somehow before she even reached the kitchen door, she knew that she wouldn't find him there. She was right. The kitchen was empty and still, just as she had left it. Lawrence's food lay untouched and his bed unused. Even though she had expected it, it still came as a body blow.

She sat down wearily at the kitchen table, feeling as though she had been in some sort of terrible accident, weak and shocked. She had gone over and over the day before in her mind. If only she had called Lawrence earlier, if only she'd kept him in with her, he would have been safe. How could she have not noticed he had gone? It felt like she had been punished for not appreciating him enough.

At nine o'clock she rang work and feigned flu. She sounded so ill that it wasn't questioned. Gemma, the office manager was very sympathetic in fact, telling her to take care and not rush back until she was "fighting fit". Usually this kind of unwarranted sympathy would have made Elizabeth feel extremely guilty but not today. Elizabeth had lied and she didn't even care. She knew she was simply unable to face the office today, unable to pretend that everything was fine, and unable to share her unhappiness with any of them. They would never understand how much she loved Lawrence.

For the next two days Elizabeth didn't leave the house. It was as though she really was ill. She constantly stared out of the window, hoping to see Lawrence running into the garden. She could barely bring herself to eat, and sleep, when it came, was thin and ragged, full of dreams of being lost and walking and shouting. She didn't speak to Mick or even answer the phone - she didn't trust herself not to cry the minute somebody asked how she was.

She was constantly haunted by one train of thought, Lawrence, and his whereabouts. If only she knew that he was just lost or that he'd been taken in by someone thinking he was a stray. A million ideas came to her, and the worst one of all…..What if Lawrence was dead, run over and lying in a gutter somewhere?

Occasionally, she would nod off in her armchair from sheer exhaustion and wake, thinking she had heard a cat meowing outside, thinking Lawrence had returned and needed to be let in, her heart pounding as she held her breath and listened, only to find silence.

It was a torture like she could never have imagined. Every single thing made her think of Lawrence. Even catching sight of her handbag out of the corner of her eye made her think for an instant, that he was back, sitting in his usual place. She automatically left doors open for him to follow her and at night she slept in the same position, leaving room for Lawrence to curl up next to her.

On the fourth morning, she crept downstairs and forced herself to have breakfast. She had decided she really needed to go back to work. As much as she hated the idea of Lawrence returning and finding her gone, she knew she couldn't carry on like this for much longer. She would leave a note for Mick and ask him to keep a lookout. There was nothing more she could do. She didn't want to admit it to herself, but other than putting posters up around the village, she was absolutely powerless to change things.

When she was finally ready for work, her clothes felt odd and stiff, like putting a school uniform on at the end of the long summer holidays. She was sure her face looked swollen from crying, but she would just have to put on a good act, think of Auntie E and paint on a smile.

Feeling fragile, tiny and weak she pulled all her strength together and stepped outside the door. The daylight made her light-headed for a moment and she seemed to be taking huge steps when she walked. Everything felt disconnected and distant. Even sitting in her own car, a thing she had done so many times before, now felt cold and alien to her.

Before she turned the key in the ignition, she took a moment to try and move her mind away from home, away from Lawrence and into normal mundane thoughts. Wondering if the house sale at Chesterton had gone through, wondering if anyone had bought tea and coffee while she had been away. All the usual day to day things, that normally would have concerned her. None of them seemed important now, but she had to try.

Christmas was now only three weeks away and she would need to start thinking about that. She would have to ask Mick if he was joining her for lunch, and there would be presents of course......, but no present for Lawrence. That dark little thought darted into her brain and within seconds, the treacherous tears were running down her face.

****

It was now two weeks since Lawrence had gone out and not returned, and Elizabeth had carried on as best she could. It was true she was only partly engaged with the world. A large part of her had left with the little brown figure that had disappeared through the cat flap and hadn't come back. To the outside world she seemed normal, perhaps a little subdued, but none would have sensed the true depth of her grief.

She now felt that Lawrence wasn't coming back. She would never see that little worried, brown face or look into those big blue eyes again and it was almost unbearable. She went through the motions of preparing for Christmas but she had decided that this year she would spend as much of it as she could at Church. She would find solace in her faith and the special nature of advent.

One evening, as she sat at the kitchen table writing Christmas cards, Mick knocked on the back door. "Eh up, Elizabeth," he said. "Ow yer doin'?"

"Just writing a few cards, Mick. It has to be done," she said, flatly.

"Oh right. It were just, I wanted to check if I were still invited to Christmas dinner?"

Elizabeth smiled. "Of course you are, and Pal too. I shall be going to church throughout the day, but we will have lunch together. I'm looking forward to it."

"I'm glad to 'ear it. It's just I've not liked to mention it since….," he paused, "since Mr Lawrence went."

It was the first time anyone had said it out loud and somehow hearing it spoken made it feel worse.

Elizabeth looked away and swallowed hard.

"I were so sorry about that, yer know?" said Mick. "I wish I could 'ave found 'im for yer, you know, that night?"

"I know, Mick. I think about him all the time. I would just like to know what happened. It's the uncertainty I can't bear. I miss him so much."

"Aye well, that's the thing wi' animals in't it? They become like your family. I don't know what I'd do if owt 'appened to the lad. I don't even want to think about it. Right then, I'll leave yer to your cards."

Mick shambled towards the door and not for the first time Elizabeth thought that, for all his gruff ways he was a very gentle man at heart. As he turned to pull the door to behind him, he stopped.

"Elizabeth, I've not liked to say this, but it's bin on me mind. Yer don't think somebody 'ad 'im, do yer?"

"Had him?" said Elizabeth, frowning. "How do you mean, had him?"

"Well, you know, took 'im. Knowing 'e were your cat."

"Why would anyone do that?"

Mick didn't answer but even as she asked the question, Elizabeth's mind quickly turned to the poison pen letter, the brick and all the other nasty little occurrences since she had taken Mick in.

"You don't think that really, do you?" she said, suddenly alarmed.

"Look, Elizabeth, it's probably just me. Cats go missing. You see signs up about 'em all the time. I'm probably puttin' two and two together and meckin' five. Forget it, it's daft. I'll see you in the mornin'."

He hurriedly closed the back door and went, leaving Elizabeth staring after him.

What if he was right? It had never even occurred to her that someone would have taken him to teach her a lesson, or as a protest for her association with Mick. She thought that had all died down, but now it seemed an awful possibility. Had her bloody mindedness dragged that innocent creature into this?

And then the most awful realisation of all.....what if someone had taken their revenge on her by murdering him? Her beloved Lawrence.

Rage welled up inside her as she pictured someone inflicting suffering on her beautiful, trusting boy, Lawrence. And madness crept into the tiredness and sorrow. She began to think that Mick was absolutely right, someone had taken Lawrence.

Chapter Thirty Eight

In the cold light of day Elizabeth felt calmer and more rational. No one would really abduct her cat. It was tiredness and her raw emotions that had made her think such a silly thing. Mick meant well but he didn't understand villages; nobody did things like that in Newton Prideaux. In cities maybe, in Oxford even, but not here. For whatever reason, Lawrence had wandered away and she could only hope he was safe and sound somewhere with people who cared about him.

In the kitchen she made herself a coffee and reflected on the day ahead. It was Saturday. Mick would be dropping in for lunch and she had to find her decorations out for the front of the cottage and finish her gift shopping. She had to get on with Christmas whether she felt like it or not, and at the moment she was simply going through the motions.

As she pottered about the kitchen, automatically putting odds and ends away, she noticed Lawrence's bed still lying in its usual place and she knew if she really did want to feel better she would have to tidy it away. She could never part with it, but for now maybe she would just put it out of sight, just so that her heart didn't lurch quite so badly each time she spotted it.

As she bent to pick it up, she saw it still contained some of Lawrence's downy brown fur, clinging to the edge were he liked to rest his chin. That little scrap of fur was all it took to fling her emotions back into chaos once again. She began to weep, deep sobs from her very core and it was all she could do to stand upright as she was racked by wave after wave of sadness. How could she have loved him so very much and lost him like that?

Very gradually the sobs became less and less until all that remained of them was a strange breathless, sniffing hiccup. She turned away from the bed and went to the sink to splash water onto her hot painful, salty face. Feeling ill and old, the cold water was a shock and she caught her breath. At that moment she couldn't imagine being happy or even normal again.

As she raised her head from the bowl and looked out of the kitchen window, a movement caught her eye. Quickly, she grabbed some kitchen towel and dabbed her eyes clear, rubbed at her nose and swallowed. There he was, crawling along the path, half closed eyes fixed desperately on the back door, grimly determined to finish his journey. Lawrence.

Shock and joy rushed into her and she ran to the kitchen door, calling his name. As she reached him, he tried to lift his head and look at her. It was then that she noticed there was something stuck to him. A white sheet of something on his back. What on earth had he crawled through to get home?

On hearing her shouts, Mick ran round from the front of the cottage to find Elizabeth sitting on the path talking to Lawrence and crying.

"Look, Mick! Look what they've done!" she said.

Carefully Mick bent and gently picked the cat up.

"Come on owd lad, let's 'ave you inside," he said, before letting out a whistling breath. "Oh, bloody 'ell!"

On Lawrence's back was a piece of white card and written across it in black ink was, 'Get Rid Of Him!' The card had been stapled to his skin.

At Smullen and Scott, John Smullen was back from Birmingham and the hectic pace of the referral centre. He had been looking forward to seeing his old patients again but on his first morning back on duty, an emergency admission had taken him by surprise. Even after all these years as a vet, you never quite knew what was coming through the door.

He now stood in his consulting room with a solemn Elizabeth by his side, gently stoking Lawrence and resisting the rather unprofessional urge to put his arm round her.

"He's still a bit subdued from the anaesthetic," he explained. "We probably could have removed the staple without it, as it had only punctured the scruff, but we didn't want to distress him further."

"Thank you," she said.

"Not at all. He's a model patient, aren't you my friend? He may not feel like eating for a while but you can try him with a light meal later tonight if you wish; something like a little fish or chicken. Make sure he gets plenty of water to drink. He has been quite dehydrated, which of course fits

399

with my theory that he's been locked up somewhere."

Elizabeth looked sadly at the emaciated shape of Lawrence lying quietly in front of her on the consulting table. At least she had him back, she told herself, and she would make him better. He would be more precious than ever now.

"You seem very sure, that he's been locked up," she said.

"Look at his front paws," John said, lifting one up for Elizabeth to see. "Can you see that scuffing there? He's been trying to scratch his way out of somewhere. Now, he might have just got stuck in someone's shed or something like that, but I don't think so, - not with...that attachment."

"You've been so kind," she said. "I'm so grateful to you, for helping him."

Uncomfortable with being thanked, the vet resumed his professional tone, "Well, you are very lucky to have him back. I've given him a long lasting analgesic, so he should be comfortable tonight, but any problems, just call us. And, I really think you should tell the RSPCA about this, you know."

Elizabeth gathered Lawrence gently to her and lowered him into his carrying basket where he folded down without so much as a murmur of protest.

"Come on then, shall we get you home?" she said, and began to make her way to the door. As she was about to turn the handle, John said,

"Elizabeth, I had been looking forward to seeing you again, but not in these circumstances, of course. I'm so sorry about Lawrence. Would you mind if I popped in to see the patient over Christmas?"

"Thank you, it would make me feel easier if you would check on him. And you're always welcome to visit, of course."

They both stood awkwardly for a moment and then he said, "Right then, I must get on, but remember what I said, you really should call the RSPCA about this matter. I'll be happy to provide any assistance if they contact me."

Elizabeth carried Lawrence carefully to the car. She had a lot to think about but for now she was happy to be taking her boy home. She had promised herself she would never let him out of her sight again, and between them, she was sure that she and the prickly but gentle, John Smullen would get him well again.

It was a happy homecoming. As she opened her front door a wave of relief washed over her. Lawrence was home. So many times she had forced herself to think that he had gone forever and yet against the odds he was here with her. She knew John was right that she should report the incident but she couldn't help thinking that nothing could be done now. They probably wouldn't find out who did it and it would just keep the horror of it alive in her mind. She would think about it, but there was no rush. Christmas was nearly here and she had her boy back.

She took Lawrence into the kitchen and laid him gently in his bed. Her heart sang to see him there in his accustomed spot. He instantly settled down and snuggled gratefully into the softness and resting his chin, as ever, on the rim.

Smiling she went back into the hall to pick up the bundle of Christmas cards that were lying on the floor. But half buried amongst the cards she spotted a folded piece of paper. Immediately her heart faltered. What was it now? Another threat? Evil words from evil people? Wasn't it enough that they had hurt Lawrence?

402

Shaking both inwardly and outwardly, she opened the note. It was a grubby bit of paper with dark handwriting dashed across it, but it was no threat.

It was from Mick:

Dear Elizabeth,

I've decided it's time me and Pal moved on. You have been so kind to us both and we want to thank you for all you have done for us. But we have caused enough trouble and now after what has happened to Mr Lawrence we think we should go.

We don't want to cause any more problems for you, so please take care of yourself and have a nice Christmas.

Mick and Pal (PS don't forget to smile and laugh more often.)

She read the note three times, and each time she felt more and more indignation rising inside her. Her relief at having Lawrence home disappeared and it was replaced by pure anger.

Someone had taken her beautiful boy away! Kept him prisoner and then inflicted pain on him and all because she had chosen to help Mick

Latimer! All because she had done the right thing. And now Mick had gone! All alone on the streets at Christmas because of someone's wicked intolerance!

Her anger boiled and exploded as loud angry sobs.

This was not right! This place was not right! The malicious notes, the judgmental attitudes. All the things she had dismissed as accidents she now saw them for what they really were. Threats, hatred and intolerance.

She slammed the note down on the hall table and marched towards the phone.

Newton Prideaux was her home!

Newton Prideaux had driven Mick away!

Newton Prideaux had harmed her beloved Lawrence!

And Newton Prideaux had just gone too far!

Chapter Thirty Nine

In the week leading up to Christmas the weather mimicked Elizabeth's mood exactly: grey mornings made of mist and cast iron, with muffled sounds and an undercurrent of expectancy. Things were about to change.

After work one evening, Elizabeth was getting ready to go and visit Leon and Rachael, partly to make Christmas arrangements and partly to ask their advice on a few matters that were troubling her. Edith would be coming soon and she wanted to see them before she arrived and 'started the party' officially.

Her doorbell rang and she automatically gathered up the bowl of sweets she kept on the hall table for carol singers. When she opened the door she was surprised to find Bryan there, who obligingly sang her a song.

"God rest ye merry, gentlemen! Let nothing you dismay! ......do I get my sweet now?" he asked jovially, obviously enjoying her surprise.

"Bryan, this is lovely, come in, come in. It's a horrible night."

He stepped inside, bringing the damp air with him. Tiny silvered pearls of moisture clung dewily to his dark overcoat and hair as he stood in the hallway. He seemed to have shrunk a little since Maeve had died and now of course Elizabeth knew that the face Bryan presented to the world was far from being a true representation of how he was feeling.

"Are you well, Elizabet'?" he asked.

"I am, thank you, Bryan. It's been a horrible few weeks but I've survived."

"As we all must, Elizabet'. As we all must."

"Come through, Bryan. I'll pop the kettle on."

"No, no. I won't keep you long. I'm on my way to The Cock, but I wanted to tell you my news." He paused. "I'm leaving. Roger has offered me a job at his new pub, The Red Cow, in Oxford."

"Oh, Bryan. I will be so sad to see you go, but you must do what's right for you."

Twelve months ago she would have been devastated at the thought of anyone leaving the village but now it hardly disturbed her at all. People had to move on when the time was right.

"Well, yer know how it is? Since Maeve, I've just been totally lost. This'll keep me out of trouble, and I like to think it'll give Lorna and Roger a bit more of a life. Assistant Manager, it'll be. I can run the place if they want to go out or maybe have a little holiday. Some things are more important than your job, you know? And Elizabet', thank you for not saying about Maeve, God rest her soul. She would love yer for it."

"It's no one's business, except yours. People are too quick to judge. Well, I'm pleased for you. I hope you will be happy and who knows I might just pop in and see you all one day, you never know."

"That'd be grand, you'd always be welcome. Anyway, I'll be off. If I don't see you before, have a good Christmas, now won't you?"

As she showed him to the door, a thought occurred to her. "Bryan, I'm taking the lesson at Church on Christmas Eve. I don't suppose you'd care to come, would you?"

"Ah, I'm not one for the old God stuff, really. Had too much of it back in Ireland."

"Please, Bryan, it would mean a lot to me."

"Well, as it's you, and I suppose I do owe you one, I'll try and look in, all right?"

"Thank you so much. It would be good to see you there."

"God bless yer, Elizabet'. You take care now and I'll see you around."

As she let him back out into the dank evening, she wondered if she really would go and find the pub in Oxford. He turned and waved at the gate and it felt final.

Another goodbye. It was strange how everything seemed to have stayed the same for so long but now things were beginning to change, all at once. People were dispersing, going their separate ways. She supposed it must be what people called the end of an era. A natural end to the status quo she had known for so long.

She had found herself becoming more and more introspective since Lawrence had returned. It had occurred to her that until that point she had been like a fledgling struggling to find her wings, but in these last months the adult had begun to form. The village had moulded and bent her almost to breaking point, but despite all the sadness she was finally beginning to feel worth something. She was beginning to feel like a whole person instead of just Ruth Menier's mousey old maid of a daughter.

She had also found that she was much more like her mother than she cared to admit. She had fallen foul of Ruth's obdurate nature on many occasions and lately she had found that some of that unyielding resolve had surfaced in her too. She was much stronger now, stronger than she ever imagined she could be.

She kissed Lawrence on his head and ran her fingers over the angry raised wound on the back of his neck.

"Mummy loves you very much," she said.

Out in the village, the fog obscured the shapes of the buildings, and sounds reached her through a deadening wall of vapour. She paused for a moment and looked across at The Green, now hidden behind a wall of swirling grey. The place she had made the very big decision to get involved with Mick Latimer all those months ago. So much had happened since then, but she was

409

sure she had done the right thing that morning when she had marched over and invited him home.

Beyond The Green the lights twinkled from the pub. The 'terrible' pub that she had always been so afraid to go into. She knew now it wasn't a dreadful place, full of dangerous people. It was a place she had found companionship and where she had seen the sad story behind Bryan's bravado unfold, and it was also where she had learned to take a joke.

On the other side of the village Ellen Kitteridge's cottage lay temporarily empty. Ellen was staying with her sister in Milton Keynes and Bunny was being assessed. Bunny, her dark twin, no longer a shadow in her life. Their paths had diverged. They were not so very alike after all. Bunny had craved attention; it was as simple as that. She on the other hand, had craved a life.

In the distance Heron House also lay in darkness. Would there be lights on Christmas Eve, as Maggie had promised? It really didn't matter any more. She felt sorry for its occupant, she had never recovered from her mistake and it had informed her every choice since.

With a final look at the now ghostly St Martin's with its tower disappearing up into the gloom, she set off for Yew Tree Cottage.

****

Christmas Eve dawned crisp and blue. The cold seared into Elizabeth as she stood amidst the hoar frost in her back garden, staring up at the huge multicoloured hot air balloons making their way silently over the fields, so high that even the orange flames that lifted them appeared to be noiseless. Seeing them made her feel calm. They were there every year, weather permitting, beautiful, glowing and tranquil.

When they had finally disappeared into the distance she went inside to change. Today was a big day; she knew she must take care and get things right. Her new dark green suit was laid out on her bed, next to it a crisp white blouse and a red scarf to finish the Christmassy look. Slowly she put it on piece by piece, like a knight preparing for battle. She gazed into the mirror and smiled. It was just right.

It was still early, so calmly she made herself coffee and tried to focus on the task ahead. Somewhere deep inside she felt God's pleasure. She had heard him at last, not like she had

411

expected, not like talking on a telephone, but through her whole being and with total clarity. Elizabeth finally knew his will.

At ten minutes to ten she drained her coffee cup and with a final smile at Lawrence sleeping soundly beside his radiator, she left for Church. Despite the cold, she was gloveless, hatless and coatless. She was determined to look smart today

At St Martin's people had already begun to arrive. As she passed through the lych gate and into the frost covered churchyard, she nodded to a few familiar faces: Dina and Christopher, Ron and Marie, the vicar's wife, all standing huddled around the entrance. Without pausing to speak she went inside.

The church was icy. Above the alter, Jesus hung on his cross but today, to Elizabeth, he didn't look sorrowful. He looked strong, undaunted by all his suffering and her heart rejoiced. She took a seat right at the front of the church and sighed contentedly.

When everyone was seated, Alan creaked up to the pulpit and held out his hands in a blessing, beaming at his assembled flock like a benevolent Humpty Dumpty. The softly played organ music ended and he said,

"Good morning, everyone. It's wonderful to see you all here on this beautiful day. Now, normally on Christmas Eve, I would implore you all to remember the real meaning of this holy season but today one of my parishioners has come to me and said she would dearly love to speak to you all for a very special reason. As you can imagine, I am more than happy to have a little holiday and sit back and listen for a change. So, to that end, I would ask Elizabeth, whom I sure you all know, to step up and read the lesson. Elizabeth? Please." Alan beamed in her direction and descended the pulpit steps to make way for her.

Her heart racing, and her new shoes clacking across the cold church floor, Elizabeth took up her position. She looked out over the congregation and smiled. Looking down, her eyes rested on the large black Bible before her, open at the lesson she and Alan had prepared. Without a word, she closed it gently to, and breathed a heavy sigh.

"I wonder," she began. "I wonder, when any of you last looked inside this book." Still smiling, she went on, "Because it seems to me that Newton Prideaux has its very own peculiar version of Christianity." People shifted

413

uncomfortably in their seats but she pressed on. "Let me explain. In your version, you have all been mysteriously elected as God's own residents' association and it's your sacred duty to decide who is allowed to live in the village and who is not. People in 'the new houses'? Not allowed! The homeless with nowhere to shelter? A man who did no harm to any of you, a carpenter like someone else you may like to think of! Not allowed! The people of Bethlehem could have learned a thing or two from you - pregnant women with nowhere to stay? Not allowed!"

Alan started up from his seat but Elizabeth looked defiantly at him. She had rehearsed this speech over and over in her mind and she wasn't going to be stopped. Her voice rang out clear and sharp into the cold air.

"Pull up the drawbridge! Don't let them in! In fact, if someone dies, seal up the house. Don't let outsiders have it, whatever you do! We mustn't spoil our image." By now people were starting to shuffle and whisper in shocked tones amongst themselves, but Elizabeth went on. "When people pass through Newton Prideaux we want them to say, 'What a pretty village, what a lovely place to live.' They would never guess the truth, would they?..... Oh, and if any of you do

414

decide to have a look in your Bibles, I can recommend the passage about the whited sepulchers. I'm sure Alan can tell you where to find it!"

"Elizabeth!" protested the vicar, growing pink in the face, "I really think you should…." She ignored him. "I've lived amongst you all my life and that was fine as long as I behaved, and I always did, but then of course I sinned, didn't I? I tried to help another human being and so I had to be punished, and not only me, of course but one of God's innocent creatures too. That was the turning point. When Lawrence came back with that note cruelly pinned to him, I knew Newton Prideaux needed to change. Ironic really that that act of callousness should have given me the idea." She paused just long enough to see the looks of horror spreading amongst the parishioners. "A few months ago, ladies and gentlemen, a housing association contacted me. They were interested in buying up all the land at the back of the cottage, for social housing they said. At the time of course, I wasn't interested. Happily living here amongst my dear friends, why would I even consider it? But now, well, that's a different story……. I rang them yesterday and accepted their very generous offer. They are sure they will get planning permission. So, you will be getting lots of new neighbours very soon. They tell me they are hoping to build at least two hundred houses and flats on my plot.

Oh and finally, my cottage will be up for sale in the New Year and I won't be consulting you on who should be allowed to buy it, but I'm sure you'll understand. Thank you, ladies and gentlemen and a very merry Christmas to us all."

Elizabeth smiled and left the pulpit on slightly shaky legs. The church was utterly silent. As she made her way smartly down the aisle, a lonely round of applause broke the air. Bryan McConway was on his feet clapping heartily. She looked across at him and beamed with pride. Now she understood. All this time, it wasn't God who wasn't listening….it was her.

Also by the same author:

FRED THE RED'S DOTTIR

Birmingham 1981 and the recession is biting hard. The summer of riots, a Royal wedding and the summer that Julie Reynolds was forced home, to live with her father in the "Little Kremlin" and the people she grew up with on "The Kingsbury", the people she had tried to leave behind.

But sometimes it is impossible to leave things behind….. like secrets for instance…

Also by the same author:

Moon Diamonds

A Siamese Cat Story

When actress Monica Pinto finds her memory is beginning to fail, she is forced to go in search of a new way of life. After years of being on stage, her world suddenly becomes a lot smaller. What Monica doesn't expect is just how much her life is about to change because of her love for Siamese cats.

24675898R10231

Printed in Great Britain
by Amazon